SPARK

TEMPEST BEACH BOOK ONE

TRACY BRENTON

Cover Design: Tracy Brenton
Cover Images: www.Bigstock.com

For all the romantics who believe in
love at first sight

NOTE FROM THE AUTHOR

This book is set in Australia and Australian terminology and spelling has been used. If you have questions or need further explanation about anything in the story please contact me via my website.

love, Tracy x

www.authortracybrenton.com

1 WHO'S THERE?

It's a beautiful day and normally I'd take the time to appreciate that the sun is shining and the sky is a brilliant shade of blue. There's a touch of heat despite the early hour, hinting at the sweltering temperatures to come later in the day. Yep, another beautiful day in Tempest Beach. Paradise to some, hell to me.

I ran as far from here as I could when I finished high school four years ago. Distance wise, I could've gone further, but five hours drive is far enough.

Yet here I am, back. *Running away again.*

Funny how my big brother is the only person I trust when the shit hits the fan.

I pull up in the concrete parking area at the front of his motor workshop and frown as I take note of the open roller door. It's seven on a Friday morning.

I've driven all night, planning on waiting here until Dan opens up around eight-thirty. I didn't tell him I was coming home and I'd decided to just rock up. I could knock on his door, but he told me you can only access his new upstairs flat from inside.

I get out of my trusty Corolla and flick my hair impatiently out of my face and over my shoulder. I smooth my skirt, attempting to remove the deep creases from five hours sitting.

Lost cause.

I sling my handbag over my shoulder and walk to the open doorway, heels clicking on the concrete.

A strange sound comes from inside. Stomping, grunting and weird shuffling sounds.

What the hell?

Sweat trickles down between my shoulder blades as I slow my pace and pause at the entrance. My eyes take a moment to adjust and for a second I think there's no-one there; I was imagining things.

Movement at the back catches my eye.

A dark-haired man is in there and he's shirtless. He's definitely not my brother. His upper body is glistening and I don't think I've ever seen that many muscles in my life. Those surfer type models in the Home and Away ads on TV or in music videos, sure. But right in front of my eyes? Nuh-uh. And oh boy, have I been missing out.

He's moving through a series of movements, martial arts of some sort, his body flowing as he kicks, blocks and punches, twists and turns, forward and back, now jumping, now darting ahead or side-stepping. It's beautiful to watch.

The sun is streaming through the back window highlighting the curve of his shoulders and biceps and the dips of his six-pack stomach. I'm mesmerised. I might even be drooling.

Abruptly he swings and shoots towards me in a flying side kick move, straight out of the movies. I squeal and take two steps back as he lands mere millimetres from where I had been standing. Even from two paces away I have to look up to see his face clearly.

Up close he is even more impressive with messy, wavy hair falling across his eyes until he flicks his head sideways in a practised move. I take another small step backwards before I can catch myself, and then quickly reclaim it.

"Coming or going?" He smirks, his eyes travelling from my face to my hair. "What can I do for you, Blondie?"

I close my mouth with a snap. Heaven forbid he realise I was drooling.

"Who are you? And what are you doing here?" I blurt out.

"Uh-uh, I asked first." He lifts an eyebrow at me and grins. "Well?"

"Listen here, Mister." I take a step forward and poke my finger at his chest. There's a spark. I'd never believed in love at first sight until this moment. Belatedly, I remember he's shirtless and snatch my finger back.

It tingles from touching his smooth skin and I want nothing more than to rub myself all over him like a giant cat. What is wrong with me? I shake my head to clear it and try to remember what I was saying.

"You're not helping, you know. Go and put a shirt on."

His grin grows wider and he flexes his biceps skywards in the traditional bodybuilder muscle pose. "Does this bother you?"

He does a slow turn, straightening his arms out behind his back and showcasing those shoulders and triceps. I can't stand show-offs but I can't take my eyes off the man and the urge to touch him grows stronger by the second.

He comes back to face me and I might have thought he was grinning before but now he is straight out laughing at me. "Your face!"

His stomach ripples as he laughs and I can't help myself. I reach out and put my palm on his stomach, the draw to touch him too powerful to ignore. His stomach muscles tighten beneath my fingers.

I rip my hand away so I don't totally embarrass myself and start rubbing the hard ridges of his abs. I grip both his shoulders instead, trying to turn him around. He doesn't budge.

"Far out, I can't believe this! Turn around! Get a shirt on! Please, I need to talk to you and seriously I can't concentrate with you standing there all hot and shirtless."

I realise what I've said and cover my face with my hands, leaning forward so my hair creates an extra barrier between me and this gorgeous man. Oh boy. I need to figure out who he is and what he's doing in my brother's workshop.

"So." I have to take control. I straighten and tuck my hair behind my ears. "I'm guessing you work here. Otherwise you wouldn't be able to get in and you seem to be quite at home. What's your name?"

He's still grinning. At least he's not laughing any more.

He shakes his head, then turns and strides to the back of the workshop. He picks up a worn T-shirt from the workbench. I want to touch it too. Stupid hormones.

"Is this better?" He strides back over and holds out his hand. "Let's start over. Hi, I'm Jake."

I frown at his hand and then reach out gingerly to shake it.

"This is where you say, 'Hi, I'm Blondie' and tell me what I can do for you." He tilts his head to the side but doesn't let go of my hand. His touch is warm and rough, just like Dan's, calloused from working with engines and tools all day.

"Hi, Jake. Nice to meet you officially." I smile up at him and he grins back. He's got at least five inches on me meaning he's over six foot. Okay, so maybe a tad more than five inches, I'm only five four in bare feet but my heels give me a bit more. Not much more, but every bit counts.

"And you are?" His eyes, a brilliant sky blue, twinkle as if he knows exactly what I'm thinking. That thing about touching him some more.

"I'm Alex. Dan's sister. Do you work here?" I ignore those stomach flips and extract my hand from his grip.

His grin slips. "*You're* Alexandria?"

"It's Alex." I scowl.

"Somehow I pictured you much...bigger." He makes a vague hourglass figure with his hands.

"I lost weight, okay." What the hell? Who is this guy to judge? And how the hell does he know I used to be...bigger?

He nods. "How's Dan doing? I heard about the accident but they wouldn't tell me anything when I went up there. I might be his right-hand man but I'm not family."

"What accident?" I laugh. "Another soccer injury? He's got to realise his high school glory days are behind him."

Jake frowns. "You haven't heard? I thought that was why you were here." He gestures behind him. "Why don't you come in and have a cuppa. You might need to sit down."

I follow him into the main workshop towards the back. My stomach is jumping but it doesn't have anything to do with his abs now.

Workbenches and tools fill one corner and a doorway leads to the staff-room, but he takes me the other way, past the office to a flight of metal stairs that wind up to a mezzanine balcony.

Jake strides straight up the stairs and pauses at the top, waiting for me to catch up.

"Where are we going?" I'm not sure about going any further with this man. Sure, he's nice to look at and I'm getting a good vibe from him. Real good. But I don't know him. Dan's right-hand man or not, it goes against every instinct to follow him any further.

"Upstairs, to the flat." He points over his shoulder. "Come on. I don't bite."

By the time I catch up he's at the door of the flat at the end of the mezzanine. The mezzanine is flooded with light from a high window which runs along the back of the building. Another three steps go up to the door and Jake stands on the bottom one, easily reaching the lock.

The roof of the workshop is actually the floor of the flat, but you wouldn't know it was there from downstairs.

"Why do you have a key?" I ask.

"I live here." Jake frowns. "How long have you been away? I thought you said you were Dan's sister?"

I shrug. "Long story. I've been gone a while. Dan was still at home when I left, but he moved into the new flat above the workshop after it was built. This flat." It's my turn to frown. "He didn't mention a flatmate. But we don't talk much."

"I guessed that already." He turns, taking his cute backside up the steps and into the flat.

Get a grip, girl. Don't ogle. He can probably feel my eyes on him.

I walk up the stairs and stop in the doorway. It opens into a small, galley-style kitchen. The laundry is off to the right and the sink is to my left under a window, looking out onto the mezzanine.

I walk in, past the breakfast bar into the dining area, while Jake puts the kettle on. I'm feeling a lot less nervous now that I'm up here. My eyes wander around the rest of apartment and I don't hide my curiosity.

Lots of big windows along the north wall give the space an open and airy feel.

"Can you open the door to let some air in?" Jake asks.

I walk through the living room to the double sliding glass doors at the front of the flat. Floor-length windows are covered by timber blinds. I open the doors and step out onto the huge, Queenslander style veranda. The veranda runs the width of the flat, with another sliding glass door into the bedroom. I know this because I have no shame, I looked in.

Curiosity satisfied, I wander back to Jake. A small balcony opens off the dining area, a clothesline folded down against the wall. It's an efficient use of space.

"Take a seat," Jake says. He sounds amused. "Is tea okay? I'm out of coffee."

I look from the four-seater dining table to the stools at the break-fast bar and decide on a stool.

"Sure, I've had way too much coffee in the last five hours." I scan the benches for the teapot. He's obviously not a connoisseur. "Teabags, huh?"

"Yep." Jake opens the fridge and grabs a two litre bottle of full cream milk. "Milk? Sugar?"

"Black and one, thanks." I repress a shudder when I see the supermarket brand of tea. Not everyone likes Earl Grey, I guess.

I sit on my stool and watch as he busies himself getting cups out of the overhead cupboard.

"So what did my boofhead brother do?" I ask, waiting as he pours the water into the cups. Still no teapot in sight. I sigh. I guess that would've been too much to ask for.

"Your parents didn't tell you?" Jake asks. His blue eyes are steady on mine.

"Ah, no. I'm not on speaking terms with them. That's why I'm here instead of their place." I look away for a minute to gather my thoughts. "I was going to crash with Dan while I get myself sorted."

Jake whistles. "You really are out of touch." He scrubs his hands over his face and a nugget of worry unfurls in my stomach. "I've got a lot to tell you."

2 PLEASE EXPLAIN

MY STOMACH LETS OUT A LOUD RUMBLE AND I DROP MY HANDS quickly to cover it.

The corner of Jake's mouth turns upwards but he doesn't say anything. Instead, he turns to the fridge and takes out eggs and bacon. He gets a battered stainless steel fry pan from a drawer under the hot plate and an egg flip from another.

He splashes olive oil into the pan and adds the bacon. As it starts to sizzle he pulls two plates from the high cupboard.

"Toast?" he asks, putting bread into the toaster without waiting for an answer.

He's feeding me, I realise. I'm about to protest but my stomach lets out another loud grumble. I haven't eaten since I started my shift last night.

"Yes, please." I frown. "But stop stalling. I want to know what's going on with Dan." The way he's putting off telling me, I'm getting worried.

He won't meet my eyes and I tell myself it's because he's focused on cracking the eggs into the frypan.

"You do the toast while I finish up here. We'll talk while we eat."

My chest tightens and I take a shaky breath. It's been so long since someone looked after me and after what happened last night it's almost too much. But I'm not thinking about that yet. I'm not ready.

I focus on the toast and five minutes later we're sitting opposite each other at the round table. I dig in, unable to contain my hunger now that I can smell the food. Yum.

I finish my bacon and eggs and use the last of my toast to mop up the gooey egg juice. "This is so good," I tell Jake. "Thank you."

His grin lights up his face. "I like cooking. And you look like you need a good meal." He frowns and looks away before meeting my eyes. "You look like you need a good hug too, and I'm sorry, but you're going to need it even more in a minute."

My gut clenches. Not hungry now, just worried.

"What is it? Just spit it out." I'm going to ignore the hug comment for the moment.

"First things first, I'm not Dan's flatmate."

"What? It's Dan's flat, isn't it?"

"Yes, but he doesn't live here. I rent it off him."

"But..." I break off as I think back to what Dan told me. "You know, he didn't say he was moving in. I just assumed."

"I've been here since it was finished. Dan still lives at home with your parents."

"That doesn't make sense." I shake my head.

"I think he'd planned to live in it, then changed his mind." Jake won't quite meet my eyes and I sense there's more to it.

"Because?" I prod.

"Not my story to tell."

"All right. But that doesn't explain why I'm going to need a hug. I mean, except for the fact that I'm going to have to beg a bed off my parents while I'm in town." I frown. I really don't want to have that conversation with them. I'm not ready. I might not ever be ready.

"Oh boy." Jake shakes his head. "I'm so sorry."

"You're really worrying me now. Just tell me what's wrong."

"It's Dan." His eyes are gentle, the playful look he had when he was showcasing his muscles long gone.

"There was a fire." Jake reaches one hand out like he'd like to touch me. His face is serious. "From what I've pieced together, Dan's a hero. He saved your parents from the burning house. But something happened and he's in a coma. The hospital won't tell me anything else. I'm not family."

My head starts spinning and I drag in a deep breath.

"Are you sure? How did it happen? When?" My brain is swirling with questions. "Are Mum and Dad okay?"

"I think so. But the house is gone, Alex. It's a miracle any of them got out."

I push back from the table and stand, glaring, my hands on my hips. "You should have told me straight away. I've got to get to the hospital."

"Whoa, steady on." Jake holds up his hands. "You were almost dead on your feet."

I deflate quickly as I realise he's right. Five hours driving will do that. My eyes fill as I think about Dan in the hospital and the fact that Mum and Dad haven't even bothered to phone me. If I hadn't come home would they have let me know? Probably not.

Jake stands and opens his arms. "Do you need that hug now?"

I take a step closer but pull up when I realise what I've done. No hugs from this gorgeous guy. This guy who's taken better care of me than anyone I can ever remember. And who I'm incredibly attracted to. I don't deserve to have anyone looking after me. No, no hugs for me.

I shake my head. "No, I just need to see Dan."

"I'll drive you." Jake gathers our plates and puts them into the sink on his way to the door. "And no protests. I want to see him too."

"Why are you being so nice? You've made me smile, fed me, given me tea, and offered me hugs. Now you want to play taxi driver. Why?" I'm slightly suspicious of his motives.

He rolls his eyes. "Maybe I'm just a nice guy."

I shake my head. "Sure you are."

"You're my ticket to see my best mate. I've got to look out for you. Bro code and all that." He sounds like he means it so I nod. Maybe he *is* just a nice guy.

I brush past him, heading to the door.

"And Alex," Jake calls. "I'm here with that hug whenever you need it."

Gorgeous man. Good-looking and a self-declared nice guy. I might not deserve it, but maybe I'll take him up on his offer.

WE TAKE my car to the hospital. Jake jumped in the passenger seat before I started the car.

"You look after your car?" He's sitting twisted sideways in the seat so that he can watch me drive. I'm a little self-conscious.

"Stop looking at me. You're distracting me."

He huffs out a laugh and faces the front. "Better?"

I love my car. I'd saved up, working part-time at a restaurant through high school. Dan helped me pick it out, putting it through its paces and checking all that engine stuff guys think is so important.

"Dan does the enginey stuff when I visit," I say.

"So that's a no, then." Jake taps the front dash. "I'll take a look at it for you while you're here."

"What do you mean 'that's a no'?" I sneak a quick glance at him.

"This is the first time I've seen you and I've been working with Dan for three years."

"Oh." I grip the steering wheel tighter. "It's a good car and doesn't need much looking after."

"Every car needs an oil change a couple of times a year, Blondie. Even if you don't drive it much." He taps the dash again. "You're way overdue."

We drive in silence after that. I'm too worried about Dan to make small talk and Jake is lost in his thoughts.

We pull into the hospital car park and I drive around looking for a park. And then I see it. The familiar white station wagon that belongs to my parents. My gut twists tight and I swallow. I'm not sure I'm ready to see them yet.

3 HOSPITAL VISIT

We enter the hospital and ask for Dan at the front desk. The lady on duty directs us to the high care ward.

As we turn to go an older woman about Mum's age, walks in. Her eyes light up when she sees Jake.

"Mabel," Jake says. "Has Lilly had her baby yet?"

"Early this morning. A little girl. Mum and bub are both doing well." Mabel's eyes flick to me and she looks back at Jake, a question in her eyes.

"This is Alex, Dan's little sister," Jake tells her. "Alex, Mabel."

"Nice to meet you." I hold out my hand but Mabel draws me in for a hug, surprising me. I try not to flinch. Hugs from strangers are really not my cup of tea.

"Sorry to hear about your brother, dear," she says, pulling back. "He's quite the hero."

I nod. "We're just going to see him. Nice to meet you." I take a step back and turn to walk away. I know it's rude, but I just want to see my brother.

"Say hi to Lilly for me," says Jake. We leave her, walking briskly to the high care ward. At the nurses' station I stop to ask for Dan.

"Sorry, it's family only," says the nurse. She's got her hair pulled back in a tight ponytail and looks like she could use a couple of days' sleep. I know the feeling.

"I'm his sister, Alex. I only just found out what happened."

Jake is a solid presence at my shoulder.

The nurse asks for I.D. and I hand her my driver's licence.

"All right." She hands my licence back. "I'll take you to his room. Your boyfriend can come too but you can't stay long. He's still in a coma."

I let the boyfriend comment slide. I know Jake wants to see Dan as much as I do and I'm his ticket in.

We follow the nurse along the corridor to a room with a bed surrounded by medical equipment. Flowers crowd the small night-stand and oddly, a soccer ball.

The man in the bed looks so foreign, hooked up to the monitors and tubes, that for a second I'm not even sure it's Dan. My brother is a big, tough guy. But with the bandaged head, plaster on his right arm and leg and pallor he looks so small. Fragile even. The tribal tattoo snaking down his left shoulder is the only familiar thing about him.

I stifle a sob as it hits me how serious his condition is.

"What's wrong with him?" I turn back to the nurse.

"He took a blow to the head," she says. "They're keeping him in an induced coma until the swelling on his brain goes down."

Tears well in my eyes. "How long will he be like this?"

"That's up to the doctors. Five minutes," she says looking at her watch, and walks out. She pauses at the door and looks back. "He's a hero, you know. He pulled your parents out of the fire. The firies said he saved their lives."

I nod mutely as she turns and walks away.

I'm not sure I'm going to be able to stay for five minutes. That's not my brother. His personality is loud; he fills a room. He's got a booming laugh and is the life of the party. More so after a couple of beers.

He's a drinker, loves a bet and plays soccer with his mates on the weekends. In fact, he and Jake seem to be an odd fit. Jake doesn't strike me as the type who'd play a team sport.

I walk around the bed to get closer and crouch awkwardly beside Dan's head.

"Hey there, big brother," I say. "Looks like you've got yourself in a bit of a mess."

I focus on his tattoo, the intricate swirls of blue and green winding up his arm and disappearing under the sleeve of the hospital gown.

He'd hate lying here in a hospital gown.

If he was awake he'd be doing a walking dead impression. That first scene when Rick wakes up in the hospital and realises he's the only one there. Then he'd come at me with his arms outstretched all zombie-like and when he got to me he'd catch me up in one of his huge hugs, the ones that make you feel safe and loved and so damn happy to be his sister.

My cheeks are wet and realise I'm crying. Far out. I don't cry. I take a deep breath, my chest hitching, and swipe at my eyes with the back of my hand.

Wordlessly, Jake hands me a handkerchief. It's clean, folded neatly, and smells like fresh washing detergent. I take it without looking at him and dab at my eyes.

"Love you, Dan." I lean forward to kiss his forehead and then think better of it. There's no gap in the bandages and I don't want to put any pressure on his head for fear of hurting him more. "You get better. We need you back here with us."

I stand to leave before I break down completely. My legs almost give out, numb from the weird half-crouch I was doing.

Jake grabs my arm to steady me and I turn to him gratefully.

"I think I need that hug now."

Jake gives good hug.

Hell, he gives Dan a run for his money.

Strong arms tighten as I burrow my head into his firm chest. I feel sheltered from all the bad things of the last twenty-four hours.

Has it only been that long? He smells good too. Spicy with a hint of ocean.

I could stay in his arms forever.

Reluctantly I pull back.

"Thanks. I needed that."

Jake smiles and there's warmth in his eyes. "I did too."

His eyes flick to Dan and he loses the smile. A frown creases his forehead. He looks just as worried as I am. "Come on, let's get out of here."

We walk out and I thank the nurse on our way past. She takes my mobile number, saying the hospital will phone me if there's any change.

We're nearly free of the hospital when I see them. Walking down the long corridor towards us, from the direction of the cafe.

Mum and Dad.

I FREEZE. Jake walks a couple more steps before he stops. My eyes are fixed on my parents and in my peripheral vision I see Jake pivot to face me. He turns back, tracking my line of sight to where Mum and Dad are closing in.

"Problem?" Jake asks. He moves back to my side and raises his hand to my arm. "You're shaking."

"Nope, all good." I push off my back foot and power forward, arms swinging. If I act confident and keep moving they won't even notice me, will they? It's worked in the past. Act as if you belong and people don't give you a second glance.

It hasn't worked with Mum and Dad. They halt a few metres away, looking right at me. No avoiding them today.

I'm pretty pissed with them for not letting me know about Dan, actually. I know we didn't part on good terms and they thought that Nanna did the wrong thing leaving me her investment property, but it was her choice. She passed away about two weeks after I finished my HSC and I was devastated. We all were.

Even if I wanted to give it back I couldn't because it was her final wish for me to have somewhere to live in the city. She wanted me to follow my dream and go to uni. If Mum and Dad had their way I'd still be living at home and doing their bidding.

Nanna knew how hard it was for me, living up to all their expectations and facing the prospect of being trapped here forever. She always told me to fly away, and then she gave me the means to do it.

I let the tenants stay on in the main house and lived in the granny flat, which meant the rates and insurance on the place were covered. It also led me to my part-time job.

I got chatting with the property manager when I went to sign the new paperwork, back when I started uni. Her husband needed staff for his bar. I was looking for a job and had experience. A perfect match. In hindsight, it might have been my extra twenty kilos that made her put in a good word for me.

Although it didn't work out. But I'm not thinking about that.

"Alexandria." Mum's voice is cold, like I'm in trouble. I think she's still holding a grudge. Nanna was her mother and she didn't take it well when the will was read.

Or maybe she's just in pain from getting hurt in the fire. Her face is kind of grey but I can't see any injuries. She's aged about ten years since I last saw her, three years ago, and her knuckles are white as she clings to Dad

Dad smiles at me. "Hi, honey. You look good. There's something different about you." I haven't seen them since I reached my goal weight. My dad never cared that I was overweight though. I was always just his little girl.

I move towards him for a hug and it's an awkward, almost arms-length, pat-on-the-back affair. Dad is having none of it and pulls me closer for what he calls a 'proper' hug. "I've missed you, sweetie." His voice is low in my ear.

I don't even bother with Mum, intending to ignore her but she clears her throat. This hug is even more awkward, if that's possible, and I step back as quickly as I can. Mum doesn't pull me in closer or say nice things just for me to hear. Definitely still holding a grudge.

"David." Jake shakes Dad's hand. "Shirley." He nods at Mum. "How are you two holding up?"

Jake is doing a lot better than me when it comes to social graces during this trip to the hospital. So mature. I stifle an inappropriate giggle.

"A bit of smoke inhalation, but they only kept us in overnight," says Dad.

"What happened?" And why didn't you tell me, I add silently.

"There was a fire, a couple of nights ago, wasn't it, Shirl?" Dad seems confused. "I'm losing track of the days."

Mum nods and Dad continues.

"Dan heard the smoke alarm and woke us up. He got Mum and I out and then went back in for that stupid soccer ball. I went after him. I was yelling, telling him not to be an idiot, to get out of there." Dad stops talking and Mum takes over.

"One of the rafters came down. Dad was standing right under it but your brother tackled him and pushed him out of the way." Mum's grip on Dad's arm tightens.

Dad picks up again. "Dan pushed me and I landed on my back. I saw what happened, seemed like slow motion. The rafter came down. It hit Dan on the head but he had momentum. If he hadn't been moving forward already he probably would have been killed. As it was the beam caught the back of his head. It knocked him out cold. He kept his grip on that damn ball though. Death grip, the ambos said."

"Bob turned up with the fire-fighters and made sure we all got to hospital," Mum says. "He gave the ambulance an escort."

Uncle Bob is a policeman. He's married to Mum's sister, Aunty Joy, who's ten years younger than Mum.

An orderly pushing a trolley of covered meals trundles up behind us, and we shuffle to one side of the corridor to make way.

"I'm glad you're all right." I mean it. We might not always get on but they're my mum and dad and I love them.

"Is there anything left of the house?" Jake asks.

Dad shakes his head. "No. It's gone. Everything's gone."

I take a moment to let this sink in. The house I grew up in, no more. It's sad, but it's just a house. There was nothing left for me there anyway. Mum and Dad must be feeling lost though. They've lived there since they got married.

"Where are you staying?" I ask.

"With your Aunty Joy and Uncle Bob," says Mum. Aunty Joy and Uncle Bob have four kids, including a set of twins. The three boys are at school already. Aunty Joy has been a stay at home mum ever since their youngest surprise package was born. A little girl I haven't even met yet. I can't imagine how they would squeeze my parents into their tiny house.

Mum isn't finished. "Family's important at a time like this.".

Unbelievable. I give up being polite and ask the question I really want an answer to. "Why didn't you tell me about Dan?"

Mum pretends she doesn't hear. She won't even meet my eye. Then she turns it back on me. "Why are you here, Alexandria? What are you running away from now?"

I gasp. She didn't just say that. I know we parted on bad terms, but really? I ignore the little voice that tells me she's right. I did run away from here four years ago and now I'm running again. Except I'm running back home this time.

She sees straight through me.

"Come on, Alex, we're going." Jake takes my hand in a firm grip and pulls me close to his side. Our hug was like a green light and now he thinks he can manhandle me.

Not that I'm complaining. I feel a bit numb and have definitely had enough of my mother. I wasn't sure how to extract myself from the situation so I'm grateful to Jake for taking charge.

"David." Jake nods at Dad. "Shirley." He's polite to Mum too.

I give Dad another hug, one-armed, and let myself be towed away by Jake.

I hear Dad talking to Mum as we walk away. "Now, Shirl, don't be too hard on her. She's here now."

I don't hear what Mum says in reply. I don't want to hear either. She can go get... I shake my head to clear it.

No need to swear at Mum, even in the privacy of my own head. I've got to stay positive. I've also got to find someplace else to stay.

4 SOMEWHERE TO CRASH

"So Dan was still living at home. That's why he was there when the fire broke out?" We're back in my car and I'm trying to figure out what to do next so I'm stalling.

"And I'm renting his flat. We've been over this."

"I just don't get it. Why did he need rent money?"

Jake sighs. "I'm sure he has his reasons. I know part of the story but like I said before, it's not mine to tell. You'll have to ask him yourself when he wakes up."

An image of Dan lying in that bed wrapped in bandages and tubes springs into my mind and I have to use Jake's handkerchief again to rub my stinging eyes. Dan's going to wake up. He has to.

Jake reaches over and awkwardly pats my back. "I'd give you another hug if we weren't in the car. Sure you don't want me to drive?"

"You're a really nice guy, Jake." I shake my head. I don't deserve his help, but I'll take it. "Thanks for being here for me."

"Don't tell anyone, it'll mess with my rep." He grins and flexes his arms in another body builder pose. "Besides, I know you want my body."

I chuckle. "It's actually your bed I want." The words slip out before I can stop them and I slap a hand over my mouth. Jake's eyes crinkle in a smile and he looks like he's trying not to laugh out loud.

"That came out wrong. What I meant to say was, do you know somewhere I can crash?"

"I guess you can't stay with your parents. There's no house left."

"I wouldn't stay with them anyway. You saw how Mum was. I went straight to Dan's place for a reason."

"Yeah, I get that. You don't have anyone else?"

I let out a huff of air and put the car into gear. "Forget about it. I'll find somewhere. I can sleep in my car if I have to."

"You're seriously telling me that after growing up here you've got no-one you can ask for help?" Jake shakes his head.

"My friends all left town for greener pastures. Uncle Bob and Aunty Joy live in a postage stamp house and Mum and Dad are there. God knows how they're fitting them in. My nan passed away four years ago and there's no-one else." There really isn't. "But it's not your problem. I'll be fine."

"Alex, that's not what I meant. You can stay with me. I don't have a lot of room, but I don't mind sharing. I'd want someone to look out for my sister if she was in this situation."

"You have a sister?" I ask. I'm relieved he's not turning his back on me and need a change of subject. Trying to camouflage my bitch moment just now. My only excuse is that I'm tired. This thought triggers a bone deep, gut wrenching yawn, and I fight it back down.

"Yeah. She lives back home with her husband and baby boy. I don't get to see them as often as I'd like."

"Where's home?" I'd never run into Jake while growing up in Tempest Beach but I didn't realise he wasn't a local. Not that it matters. I'm not one of the oldies who think you've got to live here ten generations and have all your relatives within arm's reach to be classed as a local.

"I'm from Sydney. My family is still there. I escaped the big smoke and moved up here three years ago and I'm never going back. I love it here." I can hear the smile in his voice. "It's big enough to have a cinema and decent restaurants but small enough that you can get to know people. And the beach is only, like, a five minute drive."

"It doesn't seem so good when you grow up here. I always felt trapped and couldn't wait to get away."

"And now you're back?"

"Jury's out on that one. I'm not sure what's next." I pull to a stop in front of Dan's workshop and look across at Jake. "You're sure I can stay? I don't want to be any trouble."

"Already said you could, didn't I? Come on, let's get you settled, then I've got to get to work."

I pop the boot but Jake beats me to it, grabbing my bag. "Is this all you've got?"

Not too much thought went into my packing. I was in a hurry, and basically emptied the clean washing basket straight into my overnight suitcase. I grabbed my toiletries, my black leather boots and my joggers, and I was done. I was more focused on getting out of there and, quite frankly, finding it hard to see through my tears. Jake doesn't need to know all that.

"Yep, I travel light."

The long night is catching up with me and I stifle another yawn. Jake is already through the roller door and halfway to the stairs and I hurry to catch up. Mission impossible. I don't reach him until he's at his door, unlocking it.

I follow him inside and through the living room to the door on the far side.

He points left and right. "Bedroom, spare room." Then nods straight ahead to the bathroom. "Self-explanatory."

He turns left to the bedroom. I detour to the spare room and peek in. It's an office. A desk with a laptop sits under the window and a bookshelf is along the wall. A three drawer filing cabinet sits beside the desk. An old weight bench is flush against another wall with some dumbbells stacked on the floor beside it.

What I don't see is a spare bed.

"Alex," Jake calls and I follow his voice into what is obviously his bedroom. A sliding glass door opens onto the veranda. Smudge marks blur the glass where my nose was pressed to the glass earlier.

The bed is neatly made, dark timber with matching bedside tables featuring a lamp and a clock on the side closest to the veranda. A mirrored sliding door to the wardrobe makes the room look bigger and there's a chest at the foot of the bed but otherwise it's open space. Very Zen.

"You don't have much room." I nod back towards the office. "I'll find somewhere else to stay. It's fine."

"You can have my bed and I'll sleep on the couch." Jake hoists my suitcase onto the chest. "I'll clear you some space in the bathroom."

"No, Jake. I'm not going to turn you out of your own bed."

"Too late, it's done. The couch folds out and it's only going to be for a couple of days, a week tops. I'll be fine."

I nod reluctantly, deciding I'll find somewhere else to go before the week is up. "If you're sure."

"The sheets are clean. I changed them this morning." He grins. "Must have known I'd be having a gate crasher. Towels are in the hall cupboard. Make yourself at home and if there's anything you need, just ask. I've got to get downstairs and open up."

The bed looks absolutely divine and another yawn strangles me. I'm about to fall over I'm so tired. It's hit me all at once now I've slowed down. I'm ultra-aware of the dirt and grime of the road and suddenly I can't wait to be clean and tucked up in bed.

"Is it okay if I have a quick shower and catch some sleep?"

"Whatever you need. Come downstairs and find me when you wake up."

"Thanks, Jake." I step in and place a quick peck on his cheek, my hand balancing on his hard chest as I go up on tiptoes. "You're the best."

His face goes red, the colour building from his neck and travelling up to his hairline and ears.

"Don't mention it." He ducks his head and then leaves the room. Moments later I hear the front door click shut.

I'm going to have to find a way to repay his kindness. And I will. Just as soon as I wake up.

5 WHAT ARE YOU, FIVE?

WHEN I WAKE UP IT'S THREE IN THE AFTERNOON. I STRETCH
and then rub my eyes, refreshed. It's a wonder what a good sleep can
do for you and Jake's bed is particularly comfy.

I'm still not ready to think about why I'm here. Yes, I admit that I
ran, but it was with good reason. It will keep. For now I've got to
help Dan.

And I've thought of the perfect way.

I pull on my jeans, seeking comfort over style.

My work clothes, the miniskirt and shell top, lie in a pile at the
end of the bed where I dumped them after my shower. I probably
won't need them ever again.

I was naughty and raided Jakes drawer for one of his T-shirts to
sleep in. I think I'm going to keep it. Soft and faded, it hits me mid-
thigh. I fold it neatly and put it under the pillow and put on my own
top. It's a silky camisole style with a shelf bra, and black looks great
with my hair and skin. My brain wasn't in total shutdown when I
packed. Or maybe I just got lucky with the contents of my washing
basket. Either way, I'll take it. Thank goodness I grabbed my boots. I

can't face the thought of my work shoes and their three inch heels right now.

I head into the bathroom to brush my teeth and put on some light makeup, just a mineral powder, mascara and lip gloss. I'm a self-confessed 'girly' girl and I feel naked without something on my face. Yes, I'm shallow, but I like to look good. Sue me.

When I'm done I head downstairs to find Jake and tell him my big idea.

Uneasiness ripples through me when the door clicks shut as I leave. I can't get back in. I pat my pocket. Yep, I've got my phone and my car keys. Jake's just downstairs. It's all good.

He's bent over an engine, a tool in his hand. My breath catches in my throat. He looks rugged and capable, his shirt moulded to well-defined arms and shoulders. He looks up when he hears my heels tapping on the concrete and he does a quick, full body scan before meeting my eyes. I can't hold it against him for checking me out, seeing as I just did the same thing.

"Hey, have a good sleep?" he asks.

"I did." I nod. "And I've worked out how I can help Dan."

"That's great." Jake straightens from under the bonnet, still holding the tool. It's some kind of spanner I've never seen before.

"What's your idea?" he asks.

"So." I rock back on my heels, suddenly nervous to tell him. Breathe, Alex. "I'm going to run the business for Dan until he's back on his feet."

"Whoa, wait a minute." Jake swings around to face me with a hand on his hips, the other hand clenched tight around the spanner thing. He doesn't look happy. "What do you mean you're going to run the business?"

Not the reaction I was expecting.

No problem, I'll explain.

"It's obvious. It's got to be me. Dad can't do it, he's got his council job, and Mum doesn't know the first thing about cars. Or business."

"And you do?" An eyebrow goes up. "Why not leave it to the staff to run things for Dan? That would be me, in case you didn't realise."

"I'm sure you're good at all that engine stuff but someone's got to look after the paperwork," I explain.

"And you don't think I can do that?" Jake's scowling, a storm cloud on his face.

"Well..."

"Or don't you trust me?"

"I don't know you." The words come out before I can think about them. "Hell, I didn't even know you existed until this morning."

"I could say the same about you. I've been here three years and this is the first time I've laid eyes on you, and now you want to take over? I don't think so."

"It's not your business," I say through gritted teeth. How dare he? He's not telling me what to do.

"And it's not yours." Jake glares at me.

All signs of the easy-going nice guy are gone. I can't believe I wanted to hug him. That guy is nowhere to be seen.

"Look. This isn't about you. It's not about me either. It's about looking out for Dan so he's still got a business to come back to."

Jake spins away from me and slams the spanner onto the nearby workbench. It makes a sound like thunder, matching his face, and scaring the crap out of me. I jump, my heart in my mouth.

I instantly realise my mistake. A man like Jake doesn't take kindly to being called incompetent.

"I didn't mean to offend you," I say in a small voice.

"Which part wasn't I meant to take offence at? The bit where you think you can come in here and take over? Or the bit where I'm not good enough to keep the business running, you know." He glares. "So that Dan has something to come back to?"

"Look, can we talk about this like mature adults?" I try to sound reasonable, to calm the situation down.

"Can we talk about this like mature adults?" Jake mimics me, his voice high-pitched.

My mouth drops open. I cannot believe he just did that. "What are you, five?"

"What are you, five?" He does it again.

"Oh. My. God. Are you serious right now? We need to have a conversation." I put my hands on my hips and glare.

"There is nothing to have a conversation about. You're not needed. That's all there is to it."

Jake spins on his heel and walks away. He moves fast, heading straight to the workbench. He grabs a set of keys off a hook and goes to a big, white, Ford F100 ute. He hops in, revs the engine and reverses savagely out of the workshop. When he drives off he spins the tyres, and they squeal on the driveway. Definitely not happy.

My heart is hammering and I feel like I've been punched in the gut.

I was being reasonable and offering to help and he's just thrown it back in my face. He doesn't need me, and by extension Dan doesn't need me. In fact, nobody needs me. The old nursery rhyme about eating worms echoes through my head. Nobody wants me, nobody loves me. I'm all alone. Worms are sounding mighty tasty right about now.

I look around the workshop to see if there is anyone else here. Nope, it's just me. I vaguely recall Jake saying it was a flex day for the workers. It's a little bit spooky if I'm honest.

My stomach roils after the confrontation with Jake. He went from Mr Nice Guy to Mr Seriously Pissed Off in zero point five seconds. I need to get out of here. In fact, even if I wanted to go back upstairs to lick my wounds I can't, I'm locked out.

I pat my pockets and fish out my car keys. Decision made.

I'm going for a drive.

I might not come back.

I look around for a way to lock up and spy a button beside the roller door. Little Miss 'Do the right thing' to the last. Taking one last look around, I hit the button and step outside, ducking under the door as it comes down.

My car decides to be a bitch and takes a few attempts to get going. This isn't unusual; it often stalls before it warms up, but I really don't need it today. Finally it starts and I drive off. I know exactly where I need to go.

6 BEACH WALK

I DRIVE EAST UNTIL I HIT THE COAST. THIS TAKES ALL OF FIVE minutes. The conversation with Jake replays itself over and over. By the time I get to the Bay I'm all worked up again. I need to walk off the bad energy.

The Bay is my favourite beach and near the centre of town. I find a parking spot and grab a hair tie off the gear stick, then rummage around in the back until I come up with a baseball cap. My joggers are rattling around back there too, so I change my shoes before I get out.

There's nothing like a beach walk to clear your head. A path goes in both directions along the Bay. It goes south around the headland and along the river and the break wall all the way into the city centre to the north.

I hook my cap over my pinkie finger and use both hands to bundle my hair into a ponytail. Then I poke the ponytail through the hole in the back of the cap and tug it securely onto my head. Sunnies on, and I'm off.

I used to do this walk all the time when I lived here and I've missed it. I head south to the headland. The track winds around the base of the hill with the beach to my left. It's a pretty walk and there's quite a few people around.

A brisk ten minutes of pissed-off walking calms me down and brings me to the base of the lookout at Flagpole Hill. I decide to take a quick detour up the stairs to the top to check out the view. It's always been my favourite place in this town.

It's short but I forgot how steep. I thought I was pretty fit. I run to keep in shape, it's how I lost the weight. But it's flat up home where I usually run. I am so out of shape when it comes to hills. I'm out of breath by the time I get to the top but oh, the view.

It's majestic. No other word for it. I take in a deep cleansing breath, the crisp salt air filling my lungs.

Bliss.

Three hundred and sixty degrees as far as the eye can see. The town is all laid out below, to the south and the west. Fading away in the distance are the mountains, the sun already beginning its downward descent. To the east is the ocean and Tempest Island off the mouth of the river just to the north.

The path continues south around the headland and disappears onto the next beach, Lazybones. Further south is the nudie beach which is tucked away, small and sheltered, and then the dog beach.

The final bow in the string of beaches flowing down our coastline is Lighthouse Beach. Apart from Lazybones they've all got pretty unimaginative names. They probably have other official names but that's what the locals call them.

A man appears at the top of the stairs, startling me. He's a bit creepy. Straggly hair, about my height, with dirty jeans and something odd about his eyes. I notice, because he's staring at me. It takes long seconds but I finally realise they're different colours, one blue and one brown. His jeans stand out amongst all the other people I've seen in their active wear. But then again, I'm wearing jeans. I nod at him and turn back to the view, keeping watch out of the corner of my eye. I'm going to head back down the stairs as soon as he's out of the way. The lookout is pretty isolated, something I never took notice of before.

The thump of footsteps on the stairs gets closer and I breathe out a sigh of relief. A fellow jogger. I'm itching to get my running gear on and revisit these tracks properly. Although I'll probably skip the lookout next time, favourite spot or not. It's a bit too isolated.

The creepy guy has moved away and is leaning over the railing as far away as he can. Maybe I was imagining things.

The girl who appears around the final corner looks familiar and I stare.

"Bri?" I take a step towards her, unsure if it's my old high school friend Brianna.

She stops and squints at me.

I take off my hat and sunnies so she can see me better and her face lights up in recognition. "Alex? Wow, what are you doing here?"

She comes closer and we hug, upper bodies only so as not to exchange too much sweat.

"It's so good to see you. You're looking good. I almost didn't recognise you." Bri beams at me, obviously impressed with my twenty kilo weight loss. "Why didn't you let me know you were coming? When did you get here? It's been way too long!"

"It was a last minute thing and to be honest, I forgot you were still in town." Bri and I were in the same friendship group in school but we've lost touch. We're still see each other online, obviously, but we don't talk. That's true of all my old high school friends, actually. I got out of this town and reinvented myself.

"What are you doing with yourself nowadays?" I ask.

"I work at Wilsons Real Estate as a property manager," says Bri. "And I've just moved in with my Gran. She's not doing so well and can use the company."

"That's good of you." I rack my brain trying to think of her boyfriend's name. "Are you still with..." I pause, hoping she'll fill in the gap.

"Corey?" she supplies. "Sort of. We broke up but he's finding it hard to let go and I keep caving and letting him back in. What's going on with you?"

She takes a step closer. "Actually, are you all right? You look kind of, I don't know, stressed?"

"I don't want to keep you from your run," I say, not ready to talk about it. "I'm a runner too, when I'm dressed for it." I gesture at my jeans in a 'you know what I mean' type of way. "I know what it's like to get interrupted halfway through."

"I'm just getting into this running thing and I could use a break." Bri's eyes flick over to the creepy guy. "Let's walk and talk."

Bri had always been perceptive. And easy to talk to. We start walking, back down the stairs and along the headland path to the south. We get into an easy rhythm and I find myself telling her all about Dan and the fight with Jake.

"Oh boy," Bri says when I'm done. "I heard about the fire. I didn't realise it was your parents' house. Let me know if I can do anything to help."

I nod. It's nice to know I'm not totally alone in this town after all. "Thanks. I appreciate it."

Bri looks over at me as if there's something she wants to say. We walk in silence for several minutes before she finally spits it out.

"I know you don't want to hear this, but do you think you might have overreacted with Jake?" She shakes her head. "I know him through work. He's got a property with us, and he's usually pretty easy going. He's one of the good ones. I mean, I can see your point, but I can see his side of things too."

"Look, Bri," I say. "Dan has always been there for me. Always. Now he's lying in that hospital bed in an induced coma and I can't just leave without trying to help him. I don't know if I can run his business. I've only just finished my degree."

Jake's got me doubting myself. And he's right. I don't have any practical experience. I've never been naturally good at anything. I'm one of those people who's had to work my arse off for everything I've ever achieved in my life. But it doesn't matter. I'm still going to try.

"I know I'm not the first choice to look after things for Dan, or even the second or third. My parents, my mother anyway, would prefer to see the back of me. But I've got to try. He's my brother. He's all I've got. Darned if I'm going to stand by and do nothing."

I've been walking faster and faster as I talk, arms pumping.

"Whoa, all right." Bri stops and I don't realise for another four steps, I'm so swept up in my rant. "We've got to turn back here or we'll never get home before the rain," she says.

"Oh." I spin and start back towards her.

She's standing in my way, blocking the path. "What?"

"Come here, girl. I think you need a hug," She holds her arms wide and steps forward to hug me. Bri doesn't give as good a hug as Jake. But it's nice to know my friend is there for me.

We break off and start heading back the way we came. I think back over my conversation with Jake, again, and then think about everything he's done for me since I turned up on his doorstep this morning. Was it really only this morning? I look at my watch. It's nearly six and it will be dark in half an hour.

"So what are you going to do?" Bri asks after a couple of minutes of silent walking.

"You're right about Jake," I say. "He's a good guy. And I think I might have insulted him."

"That's what I think too," Bri agrees. "He's a guy, and no matter how nice he is guys like to be in charge. They like to fix stuff. You've basically told him he's not good enough to do either of those things."

I groan. "I'm going to have to apologise. And not just because I need a place to stay tonight."

"You're staying with Jake?"

"I don't have anywhere else. I thought Dan lived above the workshop and I was planning on staying with him. Then I found out that, not only does Dan still live at home, but the house burnt down."

"If you get stuck you can crash at my place. It will be a bit awkward with my gran; she has her good days and her bad days. But we can make it work. I'm more interested in why you came back if it wasn't because of your brother."

"It's a long story. And I'm not ready to talk about it yet." I'm too worn out to be diplomatic.

"I'm here when you are. Have you got my phone number? We should do this again or at least catch up for a coffee."

I pull my phone out of my pocket and we exchange numbers. "I'd like that," I say. "Let's do a morning run together next week. We can get a coffee afterwards."

"Sounds good. Wednesday?"

I don't have any plans so any day is good for me. "Sounds good," I say.

We've arrived back at the Bay in much less time than it took to get to the turnaround point. I guess there wasn't a detour up to the lookout on the way back.

"This is me," I say. "Have you got far to go to get home?"

Bri shakes her head. "I'm on the river a bit further along. I should beat the rain if I run. Don't be a stranger."

We hug again and I watch her jog away before turning to look out at the ocean. It's beautiful this time of day. The clouds are rolling in and the rain's not far off. I take a deep breath of the crisp salt air.

Lights flick on over town but it's almost dark out to sea. Behind me the mountains are showcasing a spectacular sunset, courtesy of the pink and gold clouds.

There are still a few people about but they're getting thin on the ground. I spot the creepy dude from earlier sitting on a bench further along the beach. He's not looking at me but I decide to get moving anyway.

I walk to my car, fish the keys out of my pocket, and get in just as the first drops of rain start. I lock the doors straight away, still a bit spooked by the creepy guy.

I turn the key and my car does its usual thing of not starting first go. It doesn't start second go either, or third, or fourth, or fifth. With a sinking feeling I realise that it's not going to start at all.

It's nearly full dark now. No-one else is visible. It's like the people disappeared while I wasn't looking.

My gut clenches as I realise how isolated I am.

The rain is pelting down now and there's thunder in the air, the storm's getting closer.

What am I going to do?

7 BREAKDOWN

I DO THE ONLY THING A SENSIBLE GIRL CAN DO. I CALL ROADSIDE assistance.

The nice lady on the phone tells me it might be a while. Her voice is familiar but I can't place it. When I ask her how long 'a while' is she says there have been a few call-outs so it could be up to an hour. But she'll see what she can do.

I release the bonnet catch and wait for a lull in the rain so I can hop out and open it like she told me to. The rain shows no sign of easing. I grit my teeth and pocket my keys so the car doesn't do the auto-lock thing and lock me out. Then I take a deep breath, open my door and brave the rain.

I'm soaked within seconds. I hurry to the front of the car and fumble under the bonnet for the lever to unhook it. It takes forever to find but finally it snaps free. I heave the bonnet open and jam the little stick into place to prop it up. Then I rush back to the driver's side and get in. Not sure why I hurry; it's not as if I could get any wetter. I lock the doors and settle in to wait.

My cap shielded my face from the worst of the rain but now it's dripping onto my front so I take it off and toss it into the passenger side foot well. I'm cold, my clothes are drenched, I'm covered in goose bumps and I'm shivering.

I twist and lean into the back seat, head low, butt in the air, foraging around in hopes of finding a towel when a tap on the driver's side window scares the crap out of me. I scream, then haul myself upright and back into the front hoping to God that whatever, or whoever, isn't a serial killer.

It's worse. It's Jake.

What he is doing here I'll never know. He's the absolute last person I expect, or want, to see. I unlock the door and scoot over the centre console to the passenger seat so he can hop in behind the wheel. It takes him a minute to work out what I'm doing but he finally gets it and opens the door. He gets in, bringing a fresh flood of water with him. His hand gropes under the seat until he finds the handle and he slides the seat all the way back.

I sit sideways so I can face him, still shaking from cold.

"What are you doing here?"

"Mabel rang me when she figured out who you were." Jake grins. It's like he was never angry. "You look like a drowned rat."

"Mabel?" Then it clicks. The nice lady from the hospital visiting her new granddaughter. Small town grapevine working overtime, just one of the reasons I ran from this place.

I give my head a violent shake, splashing water all over him. Juvenile, I know. He brings out my inner prankster.

He just grins bigger. Guess he likes the prankster. Then the grin slips and his expression goes serious. "Why didn't you just call me?"

Well. We didn't exactly part on good terms this afternoon. In fact, I didn't think I ever wanted to see him again until he knocked on the window. Now that he's here I'm feeling a little relieved. The creepy guy is in the back of my mind and I really don't like storms. I don't want to think too hard about this rollercoaster of feelings.

"I was trying to avoid you," I admit. "For one, I didn't think you'd want to come near me after our argument. And two, I'm still a little bit mad at you. Also, I don't have your phone number."

"Ah, well. I'm still a little bit mad at you too. But I've calmed down and I can see your point." He shrugs and I decide to interpret it as an apology. Although words would be better. "I might have overreacted. I've never even looked at the paperwork side of things. I'm more of an engine guy. I've decided I'll let you help."

'You'll *let* me help?" My voice is shrill. This is not an apology. "I don't need your permission."

"Maybe not. But you do need my keys to get into the office. Not to mention my bed." He smirks and eyes my wet clothes and hair. "You're going to have to dry off before I let you near my bed again."

"Right. Fine. Whatever," I huff. He's right, I do need his keys. And his bed is very nice. I'll take a win any way I can get it. I think about what he said about the paperwork. It looks like he needs me, after all, even if he won't admit it. Or apologise properly. Stubborn man.

"Now." Jake's voice is deep. "About your car."

He frowns, holding my gaze, his fingers tapping on the wheel. I fold my arms tight across my chest.

"This is what happens when you don't look after it properly. I bet you haven't even looked under the bonnet since you left town."

That's true, but I'm not going to admit it to Jake. "The rego check guys do all that stuff. It's not like I totally neglect my car."

I do, but he doesn't need to know that.

He snorts. "Right. So what exactly are you doing to look after it?"

"I check...." Shit, what do I check? I should know this, my brother's a mechanic. "...stuff." Phew. That will cover it. "I check stuff."

Jake laughs. "And that's why I don't even need to see under the bonnet to tell you're going to need a tow."

"What?" My voice chokes on the word as my throat goes tight. This is the last straw in my recent string of shitty life events. The accusations at my job, Dan getting hurt, Mum's nastiness. My eyes well up, although with all the water Jake hopefully won't notice. He's more observant than I hoped.

"Don't cry, Blondie." He reaches out and cups my cheek in his hand, his thumb brushing a tear away. "I can fix your car, just not tonight. And I'll even teach you what stuff you need to check to look after it yourself, so this doesn't happen again."

I scrub at my eyes with the back of my hand trying to stem the flow of tears, but it's no use. I cry harder, still shivering. This doesn't go unnoticed either.

"Come here." Jake leans over, grabs me around the waist and pulls me up and over the centre console and into his lap.

"Hmmph." I gasp, taken by surprise.

"You definitely need a hug right now," he says, tucking my head into his neck and holding me close. Way close. "Bit hard to do from way over there."

I try to push away but his arms tighten and he strokes my hair. I give in. Warmth and calm sweep over me and my tears slow. The gaps between bouts of shivers grow bigger and then they stop altogether. It's like he's got some super power. Scrumptious man power. I melt into him, comforted by his nearness, my brain switching off.

"This is better," he whispers in my ear. "I don't like fighting with you."

I nod in agreement. Fighting bad. Jake good.

"And now we've had our first fight we get to kiss and make up."

Say what? This is moving way too fast.

And then he dips his head and kisses me.

8 FIRST KISS

FOR A MOMENT I'M TOO SURPRISED TO DO ANYTHING. THEN instinct takes over and I try to push him away.

His hands wrap in my hair, he touches his tongue to my lips and I melt. My hands reverse action, latch onto his T-shirt and pull him closer.

My lips part slightly and that's all it takes. His tongue is there, wrapping around mine. His mouth consumes me, lips moving in slow circles as our tongues dance.

My hands move from his shirt to wrap around his neck, winding up into the hair at the nape of his neck. His hands are moving too, one staying in my hair and the other moving to my hip and pulling me closer.

I'm twisted, legs sideways over the centre console, and I can't get close enough. I feel heat on my side as his hand finds skin and our chests connect. My breasts push into him and I feel his hardness against my outer thigh.

I want more. More kisses. More hands. I want to touch and be touched. My happy place tightens, wanting more too. And still he kisses me.

I start pulling his shirt from his jeans, frantic to get it over his head so I can reach skin. I've almost got it off when there's a tap on the driver's side window. It scares the crap out of me. I scream and pull back from Jake.

The windows are fogged up and whoever is out there can't see in. I can't see out either and it could be the serial killer.

"Seriously?" Jakes voice is low and rumbly. He leans his forehead on mine, his hands straightening my shirt. He kisses my hairline and then deposits me effortlessly back in the passenger seat and shifts himself in his jeans.

The knock sounds again, followed by a muffled voice. "Everything all right in there?"

A torch shines in but I don't think there's much chance of the light penetrating. The windows are seriously fogged up. The rain stopped sometime during our make out session.

"Hold your horses," Jake says in a voice loud enough to be heard by our mystery interrupter. He opens the door and gets out, shutting it quickly behind him.

I hear a rumble of conversation but I can't make out the words. Then the door re-opens and Jake climbs back in.

"That's our friendly local policeman, come to see if you need help. I told him I've got you," Jake says. He won't meet my eyes. "We should lock her up and get home. There's nothing more to be done here until daylight."

I'm embarrassed to have been caught making out like teenagers. Maybe Jake feels the same way.

"Right," I say. I reach for my door to hop out but before I do he reaches out to grab my arm.

"Alex," he says. He's looking at me, something moving behind his eyes that I can't interpret. "About the kiss."

"It's okay," I say, panicking. "I know you didn't mean it. Heat of the moment and all that."

"That's not what I was going to say." Jake says. His face has tightened.

"It doesn't matter," I tell him. "It can't happen again. Not if we're going to be working together."

Jakes doesn't look happy about my statement but I open the door and jump out before he can say any more. Running yet again.

The stars are out now. It's turned into a beautiful, clear night, the summer storm over as fast as it began.

Jake is at the front, shutting the bonnet before I can get there. I lock my car with a beep and look up at his monster ute, parked right beside me. The fact that I didn't hear him pull up tells me just how torrential the rain was.

He helps me climb up into the passenger seat, his hands lingering on my waist, but I shake him off and give him my best defensive glare.

"I meant what I said," I say. It doesn't matter how sweet he is. "If we're going to be working together then we have to keep our relationship strictly business."

"That's going to be difficult, Blondie. Even if you are my best mate's little sister." Jake runs his hand through his hair, making it even messier. "Now that I know what you taste like I want more."

He shuts the door and walks around to the driver's side.

"So do I," I whisper. But we can't get involved. I just wish I'd thought of that before I started kissing him back. It's going to be so much harder to keep things all business now I know what I'm missing.

9 CLEAN UP

I wake up to the alarm blaring right beside my head.

I reach over and wave my arm blindly, sending something crashing to the ground. That wakes me right up. And the blaring hasn't stopped. I sit up in time to see Jake run in, all silky skin and grace, coming to a stop at the end of the bed.

He takes in the damage. His boxers ride low on his hips and he's shirtless. Mmm.

I tear my eyes from the ridges of his six-pack stomach and look at the floor. The alarm is still blaring, sitting intact amidst the pieces of shattered lamp.

"Far out, I'm so sorry," I whisper. "I'll buy you a new one. But please, for the love of God, can you make that awful noise stop."

I put my hands over my ears and close my eyes tight. It's the alarm clock from hell. Indestructible, loud, and ugly with its black chromey chromeness. Who even has alarm clocks anymore? Everyone I know just uses their phone. Jake's doing it old school.

"I like doing it old school." My eyes fly open. Jake's grinning as he looks over at me. I guess I said that bit out loud.

Whoops.

His gaze flicks over my body and the grin widens. The sheet is pooled in my lap, seeing as my hands are up over my ears. I'm wearing his T-Shirt again with my own heart-covered boxers, just visible at the edge of the sheet.

"Like seeing you in my shirt, Blondie," Jake says, his voice low. "Makes up for the lamp explosion."

He bends over and presses a button on the alarm clock. The blaring noise stops, thank goodness. He shakes the clock free of lamp pieces and sits it back on the bedside table.

I lower my hands. "Thank you. I can think again."

"Stay put while I get the vacuum cleaner," Jake says.

Not likely. I crawl to the end of the bed as soon as he leaves the room and grab a pair of jeans, a bra and shirt from my bag. I'm going to have to do laundry soon, or buy new clothes.

I hurry into the bathroom to get dressed before he can see any more of me in his shirt. Then I head into the kitchen to get started on the toast.

HALF AN HOUR later I'm sitting in the same place as yesterday morning while Jake cooks me breakfast. The lamp has been dispatched to the bin, alongside the pizza box from the night before.

We'd arrived back from the beach and ordered a pizza, watching the Friday night football on the television in an uncomfortable silence.

I'd made excuses and gone to bed as soon as we'd eaten after a half-hearted attempt to get Jake to let me take the couch. He insisted I stay in his bed and I can't say I was too disappointed. It's a great bed.

"What's your plan for today?" Jake asks. "I'll organise Harry, the tow truck guy, to bring your car back here so you don't have to worry about that."

He hands me a plate stacked high with bacon and eggs. Seems like last night's awkwardness is forgotten.

"Thank you. For the food and for organising the tow truck." I dig into a bite of gooey, eggy goodness while I decide on my priorities for the day.

"I think I'll get stuck into Dan's office and see what needs doing. You do have the key, don't you?" I raise an eyebrow.

Jake grins. "Yep. I'm heading downstairs to work on my car so I'll let you in."

His car turns out to be a vintage 1960 Chevrolet El Camino that he's in the final stages of restoring.

It's left-hand drive and Jake's grandfather imported it from the U.S. Jake inherited it when, at eighty-five years of age, his grandfather moved into a retirement home. He was unable to look after himself anymore, let alone finish the restoration.

This place is like the Tardis, so much bigger on the inside.

The staffroom opens onto a hallway lined with storage shelves. Doors open off the hallway, one leading to Jake's garage which is set up with his workbench and tools.

"I don't like to use Dan's equipment unless I have to," Jake says. "I pay him to use the panel beating and spray painting gear. Mate's rates, but I pay."

"Dan does panel beating now?" I ask.

Jake grins big. "Come check it out, it's this way."

He takes me through another door. We enter a huge room, big enough to fit at least four cars, with a double roller door and a smaller normal-sized door opening onto the back laneway.

"This will be our paint and panel workshop," Jake says. "It's not fully operational yet, but it's got everything we need for a rebuild."

Various unidentifiable car parts of different colours, hang on racks and sit on trestle frames.

"Those parts have had their final coat and are ready to be attached." Jake points to some lovely pale blue pieces of metal. "They're for my Chev."

A wheelless car body rests by the wall, covered in plastic, duct tape, and brown paper.

"That's Dan's Mustang," says Jake. "The body work is finished. We're getting started on the painting while we wait for engine parts to arrive."

"I didn't know Dan was into restoring cars." I walk over to inspect the brown paper more closely. It's not actually paper at all, not any kind of paper that I've seen.

"That's my fault." Jake frowns. "He saw my Chev and when he found out how much it will sell for once it's fully restored he decided he wanted to do one."

Jake gestures around the space. "He got a loan from the bank to buy this gear. He's planning on expanding from straight mechanical repairs to doing the work. Panel beating, bodywork and paint shop all in one. This is as far as we've got."

A tall stand in the corner on the far side of the room is draped in large panels, car doors perhaps. Jake leads me that way.

"Come on." He disappears behind the stand and there's yet another door. You wouldn't know all this was back here from the front. Tardis.

We walk through into another huge space. It's like a secret room. This one has two old cars which look like they should be at the dump and yet more equipment I can't identify.

"These are Dan's latest project," Jake says. "He had them shipped in from the States. I tried to talk him out of it but he thought he was getting a bargain."

"A bargain? They should be paying him to take them." I shake my head. "I don't know much about cars but I don't think he's going to be able to do anything with these."

"He's about fifty in the hole so far, so he's going to have to restore at least one of them to get his money back."

"I'd cut my losses if I was him. It's going to cost a lot more than fifty dollars to fix these up. Even I can see that."

Jake's grin slips. "It's fifty thousand dollars, actually."

"Say what?" I spin around to face Jake, my hands on my hips.

"You're not serious? Fifty thousand dollars on those two rust buckets? They don't even look like real cars."

"To be fair, they're classic Fords. And they're rare. That one," Jake points to the black one with torn red seats, "is a 1930 Model B Ford. And the other one is a Hi Boy roadster. It's the original hot-rod."

I roll my eyes. Boys and their cars. "That's a lot of money for cars. How did he pay for it?"

Jake shakes his head. "I'm not sure. He must have got a loan."

I take another look around the space and notice something odd. I turn to Jake.

"How did you get the cars in here?" The only door is the one we used to walk into the room.

"Noticed that, did you?" Jake's eyes gleam, as if he's proud of me for noticing. "The paint and panel room's fairly new. We only finished it six months ago. Before that this was one big open space."

"So the cars were here first?"

Jake nods.

"How are you going to get them out when they're done?"

Jake grins. "The plan is to put another roller door in at the back. We just haven't got around to it yet."

HE LEADS the way back out front to the main workshop and the little office.

"I'll leave you to it." He unlocks the door and flips on the light switch. "Good luck."

I walk slowly into the room. It's a cave, no natural light although there's an internal window which faces out to the main workshop. It's covered in dusty venetian blinds. The desk has a horror story antique computer monitor, the type they had before flat screens. A desktop computer is tucked away under the desk, smothered in a layer of dust.

I can't actually see the desk. It's covered in unopened mail, docket books and bills. Cables, car parts and tools litter the desk and every available piece of floor space. A photo of my family, taken at my Year Twelve graduation before I lost my weight, sits in a dusty frame near the wall. That explains how Jake knows I used to be bigger.

A rusty four-drawer filing cabinet sits in the corner, piled high with more crap. The two chairs in front of the desk are barely visible under car bits and dusty boxes of stuff. Who knows what stuff? Not me.

Another chair behind the desk is free of clutter and is the only thing in the place that looks like it might actually get some use. It's old, battered, and missing an arm. The filthy upholstery is ripped and torn.

I sigh. This is going to take some work.

The first thing I do is pull on the cord to raise the blind so I can open the window and let in some fresh air. It won't budge.

"Jake," I call. "Can you come and help me?"

There's no answer so I go off in search. He's in his garage with the radio playing, bent over the bonnet of his Chevy. He's got a paintbrush in his hand and a tin of red paint beside him. His back is to me and he's focused intently on what he's doing.

I don't want to interrupt him so slip quietly back the way I came.

I'll start on the desk instead.

My heart sinks as the enormity of the task hits me. I really need some fresh air in here so I can think. Those blinds are coming down.

An old milk crate sits in the corner, upside down, with a dead pot plant on top of it. I take the plant and put it just outside the office door, bringing the crate back and jumping up on it. Not high enough.

I start moving things off one of the chairs so I can stand on it instead. Then I stop. I'm going about this all wrong. There's no point in double handling; it will take forever. Fresh air or not, the window will have to wait.

I go into the workshop and forage until I find some empty boxes.

Then I start sorting. Tools go into one box, cables into another, unidentified bits of metal and car parts into a third and everything else into the milk crate. I place the boxes outside the office door next to the plant and have to go scavenge a second one for car parts when I fill the first one almost straight away.

It takes me two hours, but I get it done. I'm not even sure what most of the stuff is, but it doesn't belong in an office.

I pause and stretch my back, looking around the room with a satisfied smile. I'm hot and dusty but the floor and chairs are clear. The only thing on the desk is paperwork, which I'll think about later. It's mostly unopened mail.

Finally I can get to the window. I drag one of the chairs over and stand on it so I can see what I'm dealing with. The blind is held on by screws.

I jump down and dig through the tool box until I come up with a Philips head screwdriver. Brandishing it like a sword I climb back up onto my chair and stretch up to start unscrewing the blind.

My arms are about ready to give out, but I stick with it. Stubborn is my middle name. It's nearly done when I'm grabbed around the waist and hauled off the chair. I shriek.

"Jesus, Alex," Jake says in my ear. "What the hell are you doing?"

"Put me down, you big oaf." I wriggle, trying to free myself.

Jake sets me onto my feet and I take a step away from him, my heart racing.

"I'm taking the blind down so I can open the window."

"Why didn't you ask for help?" he asks. "It's not safe standing up on a chair like that."

Wordlessly I hold out the screwdriver. He shakes his head, then takes it from my hand. In less than five minutes the blind is down and the window open.

"Thank you," I say. And I mean it. I'd still be standing up on my chair with no feeling in my arms if Jake hadn't come along when he did.

"No more chair standing." Jake's voice is serious. "I don't want you to hurt yourself trying to prove a point."

"I didn't want to interrupt you," I say. "It's your day off, and you've got your own things to do."

Jake shakes his head and frowns. "Doesn't matter. You need help, you ask."

"All right, I get it. Next time I'll come and get you." I put my hands on my hips, then realise how aggressive that is and fold them over my chest instead.

Jake smirks.

"Now that you're here I want to know what the go is with that monitor." I nod my head towards the outdated tech. "Does it even work?"

"Dan's computer guy didn't want him to get a flat screen monitor in case the pixels broke or some shit." Jake looks amused. "He's been putting up with that piece of crap so that he doesn't offend the guy."

"Right. Well, seeing as I don't know the computer guy I think I'll be upgrading it. Assuming the computer actually works."

Jake looks dubious. "It's a bit of a dinosaur. I think Dan does most of his paperwork old school, on paper."

I shake my head. "I've got my laptop with me, maybe I should just use that instead?"

"Might be an idea." He smiles. "Are you ready for lunch? I'm going to head down to the bakery and grab something. Then we should go and see Dan."

"Sounds good."

10   HANG OUT

W HEN THE ALARM GOES OFF THE NEXT MORNING I'M READY FOR it. Sort of. Seriously, who has an alarm on a Sunday?

I swat at it blindly, safe in the knowledge there will be no exploding lamps today because there is no more lamp.

Jake appears beside the bed and plonks himself down at the side, close to my hip.

"Morning, Blondie," he says as he switches the alarm off.

Thank goodness.

I ignore him as I roll over and burrow further under his doona.

His hand settles on my shoulder and then he tucks the doona in around my neck.

"Do you want pancakes for breakfast?" he asks. "I'm making them after my workout."

I groan but don't reply and he chuckles. I burrow deeper under the doona, my muscles aching from the previous days exertions. Surely if I ignore him long enough he'll let me go back to sleep.

The next time I wake it's to the smell of something delicious. I roll over and look at the clock. Seven. Still early for a Sunday but much better than the ungodly hour when the alarm went off.

I dress then follow the mouth watering smell all the way to the kitchen where Jake has created a huge stack of pancakes.

"Morning sleepyhead." He smiles at me. He's wearing the same workout pants he was wearing the first day I saw him. Guess he was downstairs doing his martial arts moves.

"Pancakes, yum." I smile. "I'm surprised you eat pancakes. I thought you'd be all healthy, looking like you do."

Jake chuckles. "I think you just gave me a compliment." His eyes are warm. "Sunday is treat day. Pancakes for breakfast and lunch with the guys at the pub. Burgers and beers."

"Sounds good," I say. "Everyone needs a treat day. Was Friday night pizza a treat day too?"

"Friday night was an exception to the rule," he says. "What's your plan for the day? Do you want to come to the pub?"

"I'LL PASS, thanks anyway. I want to finish getting the office sorted and I need to get to the laundromat." I take a bite of pancake. Yum.

"You can use my washing machine and there's a clothesline on the balcony. I'll have a look at your car this afternoon."

"You don't have to do that on your day off," I say. "Just schedule it in for during the week. As long as you don't mind playing taxi so I can see Dan."

THERE'S BEEN no change in Dan. I tell him what I'm doing to his office. If that doesn't make him wake up, then nothing will.

It doesn't work.

Jake drops me back at the workshop while he heads to the pub. I feel a bit sad and alone so I dig out my headphones to play some tunes on my phone while I work.

An hour later I throw my hands up in frustration. It's never-ending and I've had enough. I should have gone with Jake.

It's too late now, so I'll go for a run to the beach instead. Maybe I'll think of the best way to tackle this mess while I'm there.

11 SOCCER MUMS

Jake appears at the doorway, scaring the crap out of me, as I roll back from turning off the stupid freaking alarm. I'm sooo over this alarm.

"I think we might be able to replace that lamp now that you've figured out where the off switch is." His eyes sparkle with good humour.

I ignore him and shoo him away so I can get up and get ready for my day.

I didn't hear Jake get home last night. I made toast for dinner after my run while feeling sorry for myself, envisioning him with his mates at the pub stretching the lazy Sunday session from lunch to dinner. I took myself to bed early and tossed and turned, eventually falling asleep.

When I get out of the bathroom he's in the kitchen cooking me breakfast once more. Now this is a routine I could get used to.

"What's your plan for today?" Jake asks.

"I'm ready to start sorting out the paperwork," I say. I'd come up with a plan of attack on my run yesterday. "I want to get a handle on where Dan's up to with it. You?"

"I've got a couple of rego checks booked in as well as a service for Mrs Winchester and hopefully we'll get a delivery of some parts I've been waiting on."

"Will you take me to see Dan again this afternoon?"

Jake nods. "Of course."

TWO HOURS later I've worked out that, actually, there is no system.

The unopened mail consists of bills, reminder notices, a demand notice and a letter from the bank. More than one. I stack them up and can see a disturbing trend. The first one is a reminder that a review of the loan is due. Then a series of letters about missed loan payments, each more serious than the last, with the final one threatening default action if Dan doesn't make contact. This last one is dated from two weeks ago. It was unopened like all the rest so it's unlikely Dan did anything about it. Not good. I'm hoping it's just a mix-up and I'll be able to sort it out.

I answer the phone and take bookings using the huge appointment book Jake showed me. They are booked out several weeks in advance so it's not lack of customers causing the apparent cash shortage.

When the first service is finished Jake gives me the paperwork so I can write up the invoice. Several grimy invoice books float around, and the most recent invoice date is almost six months ago.

"Jake?" I wander out to the workshop to where Jake has his head under a bonnet. "There must be another invoice book. The ones in the office are really old."

Jake stands up and looks over at me. "All the paperwork is in the office. If it's not there I'm not sure where it is."

"Well, maybe Dan hasn't been doing the invoices?"

Jake frowns. "I'm not sure. You're going to have to earn your money, Blondie, and figure it out."

"Yoo hoo." A lady is standing at the open roller door peering in. "Helloooo."

Jake and I both turn.

"Bloody Cindy Turner," he mutters.

I glance at him, surprised at his curse, then look back at the lady.

She's blonde. Bleached blonde, not natural blonde like me. Small, tight denim shorts, and a scrappy singlet top cover her short frame. She's curvy. Nothing wrong with that, but she's clearly not dressed for her figure.

Way too much figure and not enough fabric. Oh well, it takes all sorts.

"You deal with her," Jake says. "I'm not in the mood."

I look between the woman and Jake, puzzled. Surely she can't be that bad.

"Hello, can I help you?" I approach the woman cautiously.

"I'm looking for Dan," she says. She's checking me out like I'm her competition. "I haven't seen you around here. Dan didn't tell me he was hiring."

"You know Dan?" I ask, surprised. She's talking like they're best buddies and I don't want to be the one to break it to her about the accident.

"Oh, we go way back." She tilts her head to the side. "Where is he?"

"There's been an accident and he's in the hospital," I share. "Can I help you with something?"

"I hope he's all right," she says. "When you see him, tell him Cindy was here to pick up our donation."

"Donation?" Dan is flat out paying his own bills from what I've seen this morning. Why would he be making donations?

"For the soccer club?" Her voice lifts at the end like she's asking me a question. "Dan's our biggest supporter. We rely on him to keep our club going so the little ones can have a team."

"Right, well I don't know anything about that," I say, hoping she'll take the hint and leave. I'm thinking they're not close friends after all. I don't have to play nice.

"He's putting together something special for our annual auction night," Cindy says. "It's soon, and we're counting on him. He said he'd have it this week."

"You'll have to wait until he gets out of hospital." I frown. "I can't help you."

"That's all right. I'll go up and see him at the hospital. What's wrong with him? They don't usually keep you in there more than a day or two."

I really don't like this woman. She's pushy and she's obviously got a thing for Dan. Or maybe she's just using him. Either way I don't like her.

"You'd be wasting your time." I don't want her anywhere near Dan. "He's not allowed to have visitors."

"Now listen here, Missy." Cindy's voice is getting loud. "You have no right to tell me what to do and you can't stop me from visiting Dan in hospital. It's a free country."

"He's in a coma, Cindy," Jake says from beside me and his voice is not friendly. I didn't hear him walk up. "

"What happened? Is he okay?" Cindy's tone has changed and she's sugar-sweet.

"We won't know until he wakes up." Jakes' voice is flat and unfriendly. "We've got to get back to work. See you around, Cindy."

"All right. Bye, Jake," Cindy says. With a final glare at me she turns on her heel and walks out.

"Soccer mums," says Jake, shaking his head. "Nothing scares me quite as much as a soccer mum."

I don't think he's joking. She scared me too.

12 UNUSUAL EYES

I'M HEAD DOWN, BUM UP, SORTING THROUGH YET MORE paperwork—next time my brain tells me the best way to get it sorted is to empty out the entire contents of the filing cabinet I'm not listening—when the hairs on the back of my neck stand on end and I get that unmistakable feeling of being watched.

I look up and gasp. A man is standing at the door to the office watching me.

My hand flies to my chest and I jerk upright.

"Dude. You scared the crap out of me."

He doesn't smile, not even a little. This creeps me out. Something about his eyes creeps me out even more and he looks familiar. He's about my height and his hair is straggly and greasy. His whole appearance says 'unwashed'.

"Can I help you with something?"

I'm not sure where Jake is. It's after four and the other workers, an older mechanic, Mick, and a really young apprentice, Chris, seem to have knocked off already. Mind you, they were already here when I came down at seven this morning so maybe they work builders' hours.

"Looking for Dan," the creepy guy says. He takes a step into the office and I have to steel myself not to back away. Every instinct is screaming at me to get out of there but he's blocking the doorway. I wonder if I can get Jake to put a back door in this office.

"He's not here." Something stops me from telling this guy about the coma.

"When will he be back? I need to talk to him." Innocent words but they come out as menacing. It suddenly clicks where I've seen him before. It's the man from the lookout. One blue eye, one brown. I feel a flicker of fear. Coincidence?

"He's in the hospital," I say. I change my mind in that instant. I need him to leave and the fastest way may be to tell him the truth. "There was an accident and he's in a coma."

The man doesn't look happy about this. "What happened?"

"There was a fire at his home." Just go, just go, I silently chant. "You should come back in a week or two. Hopefully he'll be back on deck by then."

"Everything okay in here?" Jake appears at the office door and I breathe a silent sigh of relief. Jakes eyes flick to mine and he moves into the office, putting himself between me and the man.

"This gentleman is looking for Dan." I feel braver with Jake there. "I didn't catch your name?"

"I'll be back." The words are ominous and echo around the office after the man turns on his heel and leaves.

"Who was that?" Jake asks.

I shiver. "I don't know, but he gave me the creeps." I rub my arms where goose bumps are climbing. "And I'm pretty sure I saw him the other day at the lookout. Do you think he followed me?"

Jake shakes his head. "I've seen him somewhere before. It will come to me. Probably just someone looking for a handout. You ready to finish up?"

He takes in the mess on the desk. It's literally covered in paper. "I think you're going backwards in here. It looked better this morning."

I groan. Much as it pains me to leave a job unfinished I decide I've had enough.

"I'm done," I tell him. "I'm just going to lock the door and start fresh tomorrow."

"Good plan," says Jake.

13 TONIGHT YOU'RE SHARING

THE ALARM BLARES AND I IGNORE IT. I ROLL OVER TO MY stomach, hiding my head under the pillow. We'd eaten and gone to see Dan the night before but it made it a late night after a full day of work.

I sense movement and the alarm stops.

"This is becoming a habit," Jake notes. The bed dips as he sits beside me. Then the bed dips further and I slide towards the edge, colliding with a hot, hard body.

"Oomph." I open my eyes, lift my head and look up to see Jake grinning at me. He's stretched out flat on his back and looks like he's enjoying himself.

"I miss my bed," he says. "I've almost forgotten how comfy it is. I think you're going to have to share."

I feel bad for a nano-second and then come to my senses. "Uh-uh, no way. I've decided I'm keeping your bed."

I expected a reaction, some teasing, maybe a tickling war, but Jake simply closes his eyes. Now I really do feel bad. It's obvious he's not sleeping well out on the couch.

"All right, you win. You can have your bed back. I'll take the couch tonight."

"You're the guest, that wouldn't be right." Jakes eyes stay firmly closed. "My mother would never forgive me if I let a guest sleep on the couch."

I'm up on my elbows watching him, fascinated by his long, silky eyelashes. With his face relaxed he's even more handsome. I study his eyebrows, his cheekbones and his jaw. He's got the sexy stubble happening and I get a sudden urge to run my fingers along his jawbone.

His eyes snap open. We're close. Real close. I was lulled into a false sense of security by his closed eyes and he's caught me staring. My head has a mind of its own and starts sinking towards his face. That mouth! I'm being reeled in and he hasn't lifted a finger. Then his hand moves and he brushes his fingertips along a strand of my hair. He wraps it around his index finger and gently pulls me closer. I could fight it but I don't want to. He hasn't blinked and neither have I. It's intense.

Our lips touch and all bets are off. I melt. His hands tangle in my hair, his leg goes over my thigh, and he flips us so that he's on top. Our mouths don't stop moving the whole time, his tongue wrapped around mine as they dance. My happy place is tingling and my hands have found their way under his shirt. Oh wait, he's not wearing a shirt. Warm skin meets my touch, muscles rippling in all the right ways. His thigh is wedged between my legs creating friction and more tingles. I just cannot get enough of this man. This kiss.

He's on the same wavelength, his hands roaming my body, one firmly on my backside and the other snaking its way up the inside of my shirt, his shirt actually, and caressing my breast. I gasp and throw my head back. His mouth moves away from mine and he's kissing down my jaw and nuzzling into my neck. I couldn't stay 'stop', or 'slow down', if I wanted to. And I do not want to. I want to take it all the way.

Which is when the phone rings.

"Ignore it," I say with a gasp.

Jake freezes. Then he groans. "You'd better get it; it might be the hospital."

Man. I was so lost in the kiss it never occurred to me.

I stretch for my phone and Jake rolls away to the far side of the bed.

I answer without looking to see who the caller is. My mind is fuzzy from Jakes kisses and I'm too slow. The call goes to voice mail.

I sit up and fiddle with the phone to work out who it was. I freeze when I see the name. Work. I'm not ready to talk to my boss yet. No way. Maybe never.

"It's not the hospital. But I'm going to have to listen to the voice-mail," I tell Jake. The moment is broken and I see the realisation hit Jake at the same time. He rolls to his feet and stands.

"Blondie." Jake looks back as he hits the doorway. "Tonight you're sharing the bed."

14 DEFAULT CLAUSE

IT'S LATER THE SAME DAY, ALMOST KNOCKOFF TIME. I'VE GOT TO say, the desk is looking good. Anything over a year old is now in the filing cabinet and the rest is on the desk, sorted into stacks. Bank statements— those are a worry; two stacks of bills— unpaid and not sure; and the invoice books where customers have been billed.

The voicemail from this morning is playing on my mind. It was my boss from the restaurant, Gavin, wanting to know when I'd be back.

The fact that he's doing his rosters so early is not unusual, although he doesn't usually phone staff at that hour. He said I'd over-reacted and asked me to phone him. I'm ignoring him. I've got other things to worry about right now.

I'm going to have to trawl through the bank statements to check if the 'unsure' bills have been paid, which customer invoices have come in and which ones need chasing.

An EFTPOS machine was tucked away on top of the filing cabinet under a pile of stuff, gathering cobwebs. I've pulled it out and it's sitting on the edge of the desk so I can fire it up and start using it.

I've got the booking diary and that's another job. Going through it and making sure invoices have been done for all the work.

There's no shortage of work. The boys in the workshop are busy all day and I've been constantly interrupted by the phone and the customers. People ringing to book their car in, customers dropping off or picking up. Everyone is concerned about Dan and each time there's a ten-minute conversation about how lucky he was and how he's a fighter, and how he'll be back on his feet in no time. I feel like a broken record.

It will take time to get it all up to date and I'm going to set up Xero, an online accounting software, to speed up the process. Gavin used it and swore by it. Part of my job was to enter the bills on a Sunday afternoon when it was quiet.

My heart twinges when I think about Gavin. I miss him and the easy camaraderie we had. Although that was the problem in the end. I'm still hurting about what happened that last night.

It's Dan's bank balance that has got me worried. I can see a lot of payments going out, the wages being the most frequent, and not much going in. The overdraft balance is going up, up, and up. It's way over the overdraft loan limit and, judging by the unopened letters which I'd opened and read, the bank is not happy.

There's a knock on my door and I look up. A man is standing in the doorway. He's good looking, in a polished, professional sort of way, cleanly shaven with short black hair that's slightly longer on top. He wears a white button-up shirt complete with tailored office type pants, shiny black shoes and a pair of trendy black framed glasses showcasing dark brown eyes. The only thing missing from his corporate look is a tie.

In fact, with my white button up, cap-sleeved shirt and tailored skirt, we almost match. Although my skirt is a bit shorter than office professional. My hair is pulled into a high bun and I'm wearing my 'work' makeup, which is just like my normal makeup but with nude lips instead of pink or red.

He blatantly checks out my cleavage, inadvertently on display due to me leaning over the desk sorting paperwork.

It doesn't win him any brownie points.

"Can I help you?" I ask pointedly.

"I'm looking for Dan," he says. He steps into the office and holds out his hand for me to shake, winning back some of the lost points. "Damien Lewis."

I step around the desk to shake his hand. His name is familiar but I've never seen him before in my life. "Alex Vance."

His grip is firm, just this side of too hard, but he's only gripping my fingers. Who does that? You'd think a guy who looks like he shakes hands for a living would know how to actually shake hands.

"How can I help you, Damien?" I want to know who he is and why he's looking for my brother.

"I'm from Best Bank." Aha. He's the one who's been sending all those letters to Dan. My heart sinks as I realise the reason for his visit is not going to be good.

"Dan's been ignoring my letters so I thought I'd come and see him in person," says Damien. "He around?"

"You haven't heard?" I gesture at the disgusting chair in front of the desk to get him to take a seat. I've cleaned the chairs and they're not as filthy as they were three days ago but I think a fire is going to be the only way to fix them for good.

I flinch as I realise what I've just thought. Nope, burning stuff is not the way to go when your parents' house just burnt to the ground.

Damien looks at the chair with distaste but sits down anyway.

I sit the stacks of paperwork on top of each other, turning each separate bundle at right angles to the one below so that I don't lose all my hard work sorting it out. I take the now gigantic paper pile and sit it on top of the filing cabinet.

When I turn back to take a seat Damien quickly takes his eyes off my backside and pretends he's looking at his phone. Jerk.

"What's going on?" he asks. "Where's Dan? Is something wrong?"

"You could say that," I say. "There was a fire. He saved my parents from their burning house but now he's in an induced coma."

Damien leans forward. He almost puts his hands on the desk then thinks better of it, grimacing. Looks like he doesn't want to get his hands dirty.

"Well, that's unfortunate," he says in a hard voice. He's acting like I've inconvenienced him, what with my brother being in a coma and all.

"He's still alive. So that's a plus." I'm trying to control my anger at his lack of sympathy, empathy, or even just simple human understanding. "I'm running things until Dan's back on his feet."

"Alex Vance. Short for Alexandria?" Damien asks. I nod.

"You're a signatory on the bank account, aren't you?"

"I am?" When Dan first set up the business he got me to sign some paperwork. I'm not a co-owner or anything, it was just so that I could access the bank statements and authorise payments as a backup in case something happened. I guess this situation qualifies. It was right before I moved away and I'd just turned eighteen. "I guess I am. Is that good?"

"It means I can talk to you about the loan." Damien smiles but it doesn't reach his eyes. "It means I can tell you that the bank is acting on the default clause and wants the loan repaid immediately."

"What?" I ask, my voice coming out in a whisper. "You can't do that. Dan's in a coma." Maybe he didn't understand me before.

"When did that happen?"

"Last week, last Thursday." My voice is stronger.

"Which was after he'd been advised in writing by the bank, numerous times, that he needed to take action to rectify the overdraft. He's been over the limit for six months. The bank is withdrawing the facility and it has to be repaid in full. I'm only here as a courtesy. The lawyers will be in touch but if the loan isn't repaid the business will be sold under the mortgage contract."

"You aren't serious." My heart is beating a hundred miles an hour and my throat is tight. I blink rapidly to fight the threatening tears back but I can't meet Damien's eyes.

"Is everything okay in here?" Jakes voice fills the room and I've never been so glad to see him as I am now.

Damien stands. "I'm just going," he says to Jake. He turns back to me. "You've got a month."

I sit in stunned silence as Damien pushes past Jake and leaves.

Jake comes into the office and sits in the chair Damien just vacated. He leans forward across the desk and he's not afraid to get his hands or clothes dirty. He's watching me closely. "What's wrong?"

I burst into tears at the concern in his voice. I cover my face with my hands and lean into them to hide. Too late. My body is trembling uncontrollably and I can't stop it. I can't believe what just happened. I can't believe that Dan might lose his business while he's in a coma, unable to do anything about it. I can't let that happen.

Jake pushes back from the desk and comes around beside me. He kneels on the floor and pushes in between me and the desk. His body heat soaks into me as he gathers me into his arms, pushing my legs to the side and sliding me to the front of the chair so he can get close. He tucks my head onto his shoulder and starts stroking my hair.

Gradually my sobs subside and I calm. Jake is sharing his Zen with me and I'm grateful.

"Thank you," I say after a while. He's too close and I suddenly need space to breath. I push away from him and lean back in the chair. He gets to his feet and perches on the edge of the desk, long legs crossed at the ankles and stretched out in front of him.

"Ready to tell me what happened?" he asks.

I suck in a deep shaky breath and nod.

"That was Damien Lewis from Best Bank," I say.

"I thought I recognised him," Jake says. "He's a slime bag."

I couldn't agree more. Good looking or not, Damien is a jerk. I recount what Damien said about the loan and selling up.

Jake's silent when I finish, stroking his sexy stubble chin as he thinks.

I stand and move to the filing cabinet, grabbing the paperwork pile and bringing it back to the desk. I shuffle through the bundles looking for the bank statements. I want to see how much we're talking about. Earlier I wasn't paying attention to the balance. It was just a number at that point. Now it's a number with meaning.

I find the statement stack and flip through until I find the most recent one. Jake has caught on to what I'm doing and is watching closely.

"What's the damage?" he asks.

I swallow hard, in shock. "It's bad," I say. "One hundred and twenty thousand dollars."

"Fuck." I haven't heard Jake swear before. I guess there hasn't been anything to swear about until now.

"And that's just the overdraft. There are loan repayments coming out and I don't know how much the loan is for but I'm betting it's a lot. The repayments are over two thousand dollars a month."

"Dan put the paint shop in about a year ago," Jake says. "That cost him fifty grand. I don't know how much he had in loans before that."

"I've got a month," I say. "I'm going to get these books in order and figure out where all the money is and I'm going to come up with a plan. The bank will have to listen to me."

"I'll do everything I can to help," Jake says. "But you've got to realise it might not make any difference. The bank could sell up anyway."

"Not on my watch," I say. And I mean it. There's no way my big brother is going to wake up from his coma and discover his business has been sold out from under him. No way. I'll do whatever I have to do. Even if it means selling Nanna's house.

"Come on, let's get out of here." Jake takes the loan statements out of my hands and puts them on the desk. He grabs my hand and pulls me from the office, locking the door behind him. "There's only one thing to do in a situation like this."

"What's that?" I ask.

"The sensible response, Blondie," says Jake. "Go out and drink so much that you can't remember what was bothering you in the first place."

"Drown your sorrows?"

"Pretty much." He hasn't let go of my hand and is pulling me out the front roller door towards his ute.

"I don't have my handbag or phone or even my keys." I tug on his arm, trying to backtrack.

"Doesn't matter," Jake says. 'You're not driving, you're not paying, and you're not worrying about anything tonight. We're going to the pub and you're going to have a few drinks and relax. We can worry about this mess tomorrow."

"The sensible response." I smile. Right at this moment I can't think of anything better.

15 SENSIBLE RESPONSE

DESPITE IT BEING TUESDAY NIGHT THE PUB IS ALREADY filling up.

"Why are there so many people here?" I ask. "It's not even six o'clock."

"Two for one Tuesday." Jake grins. "The food is bloody good too."

"So this is your hangout?" I don't really see Jake as a pub type but then, I've only known him a few days.

"Yeah, I guess. Johnno, the owner, is a mate. We're regulars."

I wonder who 'we' are. I guess I'll find out. I follow Jake to the bar and he introduces me to the bartender, Clance. Another one of his mates.

Clance is young. He looks too young to be tending a bar, that's for sure. His dark hair curls at his collar and his eyes are steel blue. I catch a flash at his left ear revealing a small diamond stud. He's tall and his shoulders and arms are muscular, outlined by his polo shirt.

"What are you drinking?" Clance asks.

"Rum and coke?"

"Straight to the hard stuff." Clance grins. He's really quite cute.

Jake puts two fifty dollar notes on the bar. "A beer for me," he says. "And keep them coming."

Clance's eyes widen but he doesn't say anything as he gets our drinks.

Jake hands me a menu. I scan it and can't decide. It all looks so good. I'm starving.

"I'll have what you're having," I say.

"Steak sandwich and chips?" Jake smiles. "Good choice."

He places our order and picks up our drinks.

"Later," he says to Clance. He jerks his head, indicating a row of booths at the back of the bar and walks off. I smile at Clance and follow.

A group of people are already sitting at the booth he approaches. I feel a bit shy. I guess this is his gang.

Jake does the introductions.

His mates Baz and Noah stand to greet us, along with an Amazonian woman called Suze. Noah's wife, Lilly, has just had a baby and I met her mother, the lovely Mabel, at the hospital.

Mabel turns out to be Baz's mother. And Suze's mother. Lilly, Suze and Baz are all part of the Jones family, brother and sisters. Could it be any more convoluted?

A girl called Elise, who looks like she should still be in high school, gives me the eye until she decides I'm not competing for Baz's attention. Baz seems oblivious to her crush.

Another young guy is sitting at the far end of the booth, watching the introductions with a huge grin on his face. I blink, and look from him to Noah. "Whoa you guys are, like, identical."

"Yep." He stands and leans over the table to shake my hand. "Liam Ryan. That's my big brother."

"Let me guess, he's five minutes older?" They're both big guys, but I'd be hard pressed to tell them apart.

"Sixty seconds." Noah's voice comes from behind me.

"And he doesn't let me forget it." Liam's still grinning. This is obviously a running joke between them.

I decide I'm never going to remember all the names and relationships. I mean, I know some of them from school. Baz was one of Dan's mates even back then, but that was a long time ago and I only vaguely knew his family. Clance and Jake are both new to town and the twins went to a different high school.

"Thought you'd be at the hospital, mate," Jake says to Noah, reaching out to do a man-hug back-pat combination. "Congratulations."

"Yeah, just having a feed." Noah shrugs. "It's too quiet at home without Lill."

"What did you call the baby?" I ask. "Is it a girl or a boy?"

"Little girl, Ella." Noah's face lights up. "She's beautiful. I'm heading back up there to see them after I eat."

Jake and I slide into the booth on one side. I end up squashed between Jake and Baz, sitting opposite Suze and Elise. My eye catches Suze's necklace. It's a silver locket, shaped like a heart, on a silver chain.

"Wow, I love your necklace," I tell her. "My mother has one just like it. She's had it forever. Although I guess it's burnt to a crisp now."

"It's titanium. I got it at the second-hand shop yesterday, the one with that dude with weird eyes." Suze shudders. "He's creepy. But I love vintage jewellery so I keep going there. There's just something about getting a piece with some history. Not that I'll ever know the history. Sometimes I like to imagine what it could tell me if it could talk."

She shakes her wrist, which is draped in bracelets and bangles. "These are all vintage too."

It's uncanny how much her necklace is like my mum's. Mum wears titanium as she suffers from an allergic reaction with other metals. She loves silver, so Dad had bought her a titanium necklace with a gorgeous titanium heart shaped pendant, identical to the one Suze is wearing. 'One hundred percent hypoallergenic' he'd told her. Surely Mum wouldn't have hocked it. She loved that thing. Is Suze a thief and just covering up?

"I'm not sure I'd like it if my jewellery could talk," I say, deciding to think about it later. "I think it would freak me out."

The food comes out with more drinks and we eat. The conversations are flowing. They are obviously all good friends, embedded in each others' lives.

I sip on my second rum and coke, still nervous around all these new people but starting to relax. Jake is deep in conversation with Noah. Suze and Elise are discussing some mutual friend and Liam has gone to the bar so I turn to Baz. "How do you all know each other?"

Baz grins. He's another tall, dark and handsome guy. Do they breed them around here? He's got melty-chocolate eyes, close-cropped hair and a goatee beard and moustache. Like the others, he's built. Sculpted arms and shoulders are outlined by his close fitting, moulded T-shirt. I can't tell how tall he is but I feel tiny as I sit beside him.

I feel Jake move behind me, settling his arm along the back of the booth and letting his hand dangle down, touching my arm. He's not talking to me at the moment, but he's making it clear to everyone that we're here together. Suze glances over at me, her eyes alight with curiosity as she notices Jake's hand.

"Tempest Serene," says Baz. I'm not sure what he means and I tilt my head questioningly. "It's our dojo. We're all either teachers or students. Except for Noah. His wife is my little sister, Lilly, so they're automatically part of the crew. And Dan and I have been mates since forever."

I can't imagine hanging out socially with my brother, although we haven't lived in the same town since we grew up, so who knows. I guess if I stay after he wakes up I'll find out. These are his friends, after all. I'm not sure they'd want to be friends with me though, if they knew everything about me.

"Does Dan do martial arts too?" I ask.

Baz laughs. It's a great laugh, booming, filling the space. I can see him and Dan as mates. They'd get into so much trouble together. "Nope. Tried to teach him but it didn't take."

"Doesn't surprise me," I say. "He's always been more of a soccer guy."

"Hey, you should come in and take a beginner's class," says Baz. "You'd like it. It's good fun."

"Totally." Suze chimes in. "Come with me, I'll show you around."

"You do martial arts?" I shouldn't be surprised. Suze looks like she could do anything. She obviously gets her size from her family. She's tall and lean, sinewy muscle showcased on her bare arms. "I'd love to have shoulders like yours," I say. Then my face heats up. "Sorry, that was rude."

Suze bursts into laughter. She's got a great laugh, just like her brother. Not quite a boom but carefree and contagious. "I've been training for the last four years, three classes a week. Looks like my hard work is paying off," she says.

"Four years? Wow." I take another sip from my drink and realise it's down to the ice again. "What sort of training?"

"Tae Kwon Do," Suze replies. "My next grading is for my Cho Dan Bo."

I look at her blankly. "It's the probationary black belt," she explains.

"Wow," I say again. The rum and coke seems to have deprived me of my words. Three classes a week seems excessive, but I keep that to myself.

Clance appears and puts another one in front of me, taking away my old glass. All righty then.

"Hey, what about Clance. Is he a martial arts dude too?"

"Yep," Suze says. "Baz, Clance, Liam and Jake are all instructors. My other brother Tom takes classes sometimes too."

"You have another brother?" Holy shit, how many does she have?

Suze nods. "He's got a security company but he helps out at the dojo. Most of his guys train there and some of them teach part-time as well."

My brain catches up to the other part of what she said and I turn to Jake.

"You didn't tell me you were a martial arts instructor," I say.

"It didn't come up," he replies.

"I would have thought that would be an important part of the whole 'getting to know you' conversation," I say.

Jake chuckles.

"I've seen you in action and I was impressed. I think you'd make a most excellent instructor," I declare.

Jake outright laughs this time. His laugh isn't as good as Baz's, much as I hate to admit it, but it's still a good laugh. "I like your laugh," I say leaning into him. I can feel his body shaking. A thought occurs to me.

"I hope you're laughing with me, not at me," I say.

I reach for my drink and it's nearly empty again.

Clance appears with a glass of water and places it in front of me beside the rum and coke. I smile gratefully. I'm a cheap drunk and mixing it up with water is a good idea. I notice Jake is drinking water now, too. I decide I should try to pace myself so I don't make a fool of myself in front of Jake's friends.

Jake bends his head to talk into my ear. His arm moves around my shoulders as he draws me in. "Laughing with you, Blondie," he says. "And don't worry about drinking too much. I'll look out for you. You just relax and have a good time."

I get warm and fuzzy inside at his words. It's been a long time since I had someone watching my back.

"Hey, Tom," Suze yells. I look up as another man approaches. You can tell he's related to Suze and Baz. They've all got a distinctive look. Tom's hair and eyes match Baz but he's missing the goatee. He's got his arm around a girl who doesn't look happy to be there. He drops his arm and leans over Noah to kiss Suze on the cheek. He fist bumps all the guys and smiles at me. "You must be Alex," he says.

"That's me," I reply. "How did you know?"

"Apart from the fact that you look like Dan?" Tom grins. "Jake's only been talking about one girl lately." He looks at Jake's arm which is still around my shoulders. "Call it an educated guess."

He turns away and grabs a chair from a nearby table, then sits, pulling his girlfriend onto his lap. "This is Bec," he says. "Bec, Alex. Dan's little sister."

Bec nods at me but before she can say anything Noah's standing and saying his goodbyes, telling us he's heading back up to the hospital. Bec immediately hops off Tom's lap and sits in his vacated seat. I'm not sure what's going on there but it's weird.

Clance appears with yet another rum and coke and a glass of water puts them in front of me. I don't remember finishing the previous drink. How many is that now? I've lost count.

Clance greets Tom with a fist bump before returning to the bar with the empty glasses. This is a really close-knit crew.

"I'd better make a move," Liam says. The girls all shuffle out so he can get out of the booth.

"Have fun," Suze says. "He's got a class tonight," she tells me.

"I was wondering about that," I say. "If all of you guys are here, who is at your dojo?"

"There's a couple of other instructors plus Elise's grandfather, Master Lee. He's the owner and he pretty much lives there."

"Wow," I say. "I'm looking forward to seeing Tempest Serene."

I'm starting to feel really comfortable with this crew. The drinks have helped me loosen up, but everyone is so genuine and friendly. Except Bec. I wonder what her problem is. She and Tom don't stay long but the rest of us settle in for the night. It's just what I need after the shock of the bank earlier today.

"What do you do?" I ask Suze a bit later.

"I'm a loansie at Best Bank," she says.

"So you know Damien?" I raise an eyebrow.

"That jerk. He's at head office. How do you know him?" Suze is focused on my answer.

"He came by today to see Dan," I say. "I didn't like him very much."

"Oh." Suze's face shuts down. "He's a piece of work, that's for sure."

I nod, depressed again, and scull the rest of my drink.

"I'm not thinking about that tonight," I say. "Tonight is all about drowning your troubles."

"I'll drink to that, girlfriend," says Suze. "Bottoms up."

16 MORNING AFTER

THE ALARM GOES OFF. I IGNORE IT, CURSING MYSELF FOR breaking the lamp instead of the clock.

A heavy weight rolls almost on top of me and the noise stops.

The weight retreats, then an arm goes around my waist and I'm pulled into a warm, living pillow.

I sigh and snuggle in.

My eyes snap open as I realise there's someone in the bed with me. Someone who is Jake.

"Whoa. Are you in bed with me?" I'm wide awake now. "What happened last night?"

"Go back to sleep, Blondie," says Jake, his voice heavy with sleep. "It was a really late night and I want to stay here for another half an hour."

I roll towards the edge of the bed, intending to get up and put some distance between us until I can figure out what happened. Jake's arm snags me. He pulls me into him, spooning. It feels amazing and I relax for a moment, my eyes closed. I could stay here all day.

Then common sense kicks in and I remember that *Jake's in bed with me.*

Far out, did we sleep together?

I run my hands over my shoulders and find a shirt. Jakes T-shirt, the one I've been sleeping in. Which is not what I was wearing last night. I can't remember getting changed for bed. I can't remember agreeing to sleep with Jake. I can't remember if we had sex or not.

Shit, shit, shit. Did I have sex with Jake? Surely I would remember that.

"Relax, Blondie," says Jake. "We didn't have sex."

Phew! That's a relief. Although it's pretty scary that he knew what I was thinking.

The last thing I can remember is Suze saying 'bottoms up'. Things get a bit blurred after that, but there were many more rum and cokes consumed. There might even have been karaoke.

That's not good.

I squirm until I'm lying on my back. Jake's arm wraps around my waist and he pulls me closer. He's on his side and he snuggles into my neck. His leg burrows under mine until I lift my knees and I end up with my legs on top of his. Oh boy. My happy place is tingling.

Focus, Alex. What happened last night? I'm going to have to ask.

"How did we end up here?"

Jake groans. He unravels himself and rolls onto his back. "You're not going to let me sleep, are you?"

That's it. If he's not going to tell me what happened then I'm not staying here. I roll towards the edge of the bed, and swing my legs over the side of the bed to sit up. I freeze when I get half way. The T-shirt is short and I'm not sure if I'm going to be flashing Jake when I stand up.

"Fuck." Jake sighs. "Come back here for a minute. You don't need to run."

I look over my shoulder. He props himself up on one elbow and pats the bed beside him. "Come on, I won't bite."

He's shirtless and the sheet is draped low over his waist.

"I hope to God you're wearing pants," I say. I hope to God that I am too.

He smiles. "Come over here and find out."

Well, he didn't take long to wake up and start flirting.

I shuffle under the sheet and lay back down. He snags me around the waist and pulls me towards him. This is getting old.

"Stop manhandling me," I say. "I'm getting sick of it."

Jake's smile turns into a full on grin. "That's not what you said last night when I carried you up the stairs. Then you were all, 'Oh Jake', 'I love you Jake', 'take me to bed, Jake'. His voice goes high-pitched as he does an impression of me.

"I did not." I punch him in the arm. It's a weak attempt but I'm at a disadvantage laying on my back.

"No, but I know you wanted to." He thinks he's so funny. "And we did end up in bed together."

"Right." I've had it. "If you're not going to tell me what happened then you can get up and leave me the hell alone."

His eyes go soft and he's still smiling. I realise he thinks I'm cute and I sigh. The fight goes out of me. "What happened, Jake?"

"You were having a great time with Suze. Elise joined in for a while but she dropped out at midnight. You and Suze were playing pool, and dancing to the Jukebox. I think you drank the place dry."

"So there wasn't karaoke?"

"You made your own." Jake's grin grows big. "You were very entertaining."

I groan and put my hand over my eyes. Surprisingly I don't feel hung-over.

"Clance kept the water up to you so you shouldn't feel too seedy." I feel Jake run his fingers lightly over my forehead. "But we didn't get home until after midnight, when they kicked us out."

"They're open pretty late for a Tuesday," I say.

"Perk of knowing the owner," Jake replies.

"So what happened when we got home? You decided you're not sleeping on the couch anymore?"

"Told you yesterday morning I want my bed back. Happy to share." Jake states this like it's a done deal. I guess it is. "But for the record, I turned my back when you got changed and all we did was sleep."

His hand is still trailing lightly along my forehead. Then I feel the bed move and a second later his lips replace his fingers. "Happy to change that," he says quietly.

"Wow." My girly bits are in full quiver and my nipples are at attention. I'm happy to change it too.

I keep my eyes closed and move my hand up Jake's arm, following it all the way to his head. I pull his head down towards me, hoping he'll take the hint and kiss me. He does with bells on.

His lips meet mine and he devours my mouth. His hand, the one he's not leaning on, goes to the side of my breast and his thumb brushes over my nipple. It sends an electric shock straight to my nether regions and I groan. The kiss deepens. He leans closer and moves his leg between mine, his thigh providing pressure right where I need it. I start to grind on his leg, too caught up in the moment to be embarrassed. We're heading into sinful territory and we're heading there fast. I want this. I want it bad.

That's when my phone rings.

I ignore it, but it's persistent. Who would be ringing at this hour?

It better not be Gavin again.

Jake's head lifts from the kiss and he rests his forehead on mine.

"Going to get that?" he asks.

"Don't wanna," I whine. Then I rethink. "I better. It might be the hospital.

Jake rolls off me onto his back and I lean over to the bedside table to grab my phone. I have to stretch and almost fall out of the bed.

I look at the screen. Bri. Why is Bri calling? I swipe to answer the call.

"Hello?"

"Where are you?" Bri sounds out of breath. "I started without you."

"Bri, I'm so sorry. I slept in." I'd completely forgotten our plans to meet up for an early morning beach run. "I had a late night."

"What, you didn't invite me?" she says.

"It was impromptu," I say. "Plus it was with Jake's friends and I don't really know them. It's bad enough me gate crashing."

"Yeah, yeah, I get it. But you've stood me up."

"Reschedule?" I ask. "I'm so, so sorry. Let's do Friday morning instead."

"Deal," says Bri. "Do you want me to pick you up? That way there's no excuses."

"That's a good idea. I'm not sure if my car will be fixed by then." Even if I'd remembered this morning I didn't wake up in time to get down to the beach. It's a good fifteen minute run from Jake's.

We say our goodbyes and I put my phone back on the bedside table.

I turn to Jake. "The mood's gone, isn't it?"

"Well…" He trails a finger along my arm, raising goose bumps in its wake.

My phone sounds again, the alarm this time. I lean over to silence it and look at the time. "It's seven already."

"Damn. Time to get moving." Jake's hand wraps around my arm, pulling me towards him. He dips his head and kisses me, long and deep. My heart is about to burst out of my chest. When he pulls back he rests his forehead on mine. "Tonight, Blondie. It's on."

17 MY WAY

"I've been thinking," I declare. Jake's in the kitchen cooking his breakfast special for me. I'm perched at the breakfast bar with my tea, feeling pretty good for someone who got so drunk I don't remember getting home.

"Dangerous," he teases, a smile twitching the edge of his mouth.

"We've got a month to turn the business around." I take a sip of tea while I organise my thoughts.

"The business is doing really well," Jake says. "You've seen how busy we are."

"So where's all the money? Because the bank balance is going down. In fact it's past down, it's so far down it's going up again."

Jake blinks at me. "That doesn't even make sense."

"I mean the overdraft is going up. That's bad. Dan's got an overdraft and it's overdrawn. He owes the bank a hundred and twenty thousand dollars."

"That's what you said yesterday," Jake says. "I still don't understand how that can be the case."

"I don't either." My stomach is twisting. "But I'm going to figure out what's happening. I've got a feeling it's because the paperwork is such a mess. People not being billed, or not paying their bills. That sort of thing."

"So that's your plan?" Jake tilts his head sideways. "Disappear into the office and shuffle paper?"

"Ignoring the paperwork is what got Dan into this mess." I'm louder than I intended, my temper starting to rise. "What's your big plan?"

"Work harder. Talk to people. Rally the troops and all that."

"Right. 'Cause you don't already work hard and talk to people?" I say sarcastically. I stand so I'm not looking up at Jake. "What good is talking to people going to do? Sure, Dan's got good mates, but he owes the bank one hundred and twenty thousand dollars, plus goodness knows how much the business loan is."

"Did you ever think that maybe Dan has it under control? That he has a plan that you don't know about?" Jake asks.

"Do you know something that I don't?" I put my hands on my hips. "Because now would be a good time to share."

"You need to just leave things to me," Jake declares. "You can sort out the paper but I'll handle the bank. It's my responsibility. I'm Dan's second-in-command."

"I don't think so. This is my brother's livelihood we're talking about."

"Alex," Jake throws his head back and looks at the ceiling. "You need to trust me."

He swings around and takes two steps closer, touching distance, and puts his hands on my shoulders. I look up, meeting his eyes. I think this is the first time he's ever used my name.

"Can you do that?" he asks.

I swallow and look away. No way am I leaving it with Jake to sort out. But he thinks he's got it under control so I'll just continue with my plan and let him think he's in charge. With any luck Dan will wake up in the next day or two and everything will be all right.

"I'll try," I say. I can't meet his eyes.

Jake sighs. He pulls me into a hug.

"Everything is going to be okay, Blondie," he says into the top of my head.

My stomach is still in knots but I nod against his chest. We'll see.

18 WHAT A MESS

I take my laptop downstairs with me so I can get Xero set up.

Seeing as I'm a signatory on the bank account I'm able to organise an online banking login so that I can download the bank statements. Guess that's one thing I can thank Damien from the bank for.

I also set up a free trial of ShoeBoxed. You scan all your bills through and they turn them into Xero transactions. It saves hours of data entry and means I can reconcile the bank and work out which bills have been paid and which ones haven't a whole lot quicker. Which sorts out the expenses.

Then I get started on the income side of things. I take the booking diary and the invoice books and start the tedious process of ticking them off and working out who has been billed and who hasn't.

It turns out there are stacks of people who haven't been invoiced for work done. Then there's the people who *have* been invoiced, and, as far as I can tell, haven't paid.

It's complicated by the fact that chunks of cash have been banked at different times and I have no idea what it relates to. I feel like a detective. I can see which jobs were done the week before the banking and try to mix and match until I come up with the right amount. Sometimes it works, sometimes it doesn't. I feel like ripping my hair out.

I'm going to have to get in touch with all the customers and ask them whether or not they paid their bill. I can imagine how that will go down.

Hi Mrs so and so, it's Alex here from Dan's Garage and I'm just trying to sort out the paperwork while Dan's in hospital. Can you cast your mind back and tell me if you paid us for your car service on the 12th of May last year?

Yeah, awkward.

But the bottom line is, there's been more work done than money banked.

Which explains at least part of Dan's cash flow problem.

The other part of the problem comes to light when I'm talking to Jake later that day about the people who I think haven't paid.

"Oh, Mrs Reid," he says. "She's on a pension and her husband passed a few years ago. Dan never charges her."

"Not even cost?" I can't believe it. "So he's actually paying her to service her car."

"What do you mean? The parts only cost a couple of dollars." Jake shrugs.

"Yeah, but what about the wages? And the power? And the fact that while you guys are working on Mrs Reid's car you're not working on some else's car, someone who would actually pay." I'm fuming. It's all very well to do a good turn, but only if you can afford it.

"I hadn't thought of it that way," Jake says. "But he wouldn't turn her away, Blondie."

"I'm sure she would have paid something. Give her a discount, sure, but don't do it for free. You've got to cover costs. You're going to have every senior in town expecting the same treatment."

Jake looks away. "We do, actually."

I groan in frustration and put my head on my arms on the desk.

I look up at him. "How many? Actually, I don't want to know.

But it goes a long way to explain the lack of cash in the bank account."

"Most of them won't accept a free service. They've got too much pride. Dan's got a pensioner special. He charges them fifty bucks and tells them to pay it forward."

"Let's do the math. How much do you normally charge for a service?"

"It depends."

"On average?" I put my hands on my hips.

"Between a hundred and a hundred and fifty dollars."

"Let's go low and say a hundred. So he's missing out on fifty dollars for every pensioner special."

"So it's fifty bucks. That's a night out at the pub." Jake shrugs in a 'so what' kind of way.

"But then he's got to pay wages. How long does it take to do a service?"

"Anywhere between half an hour and two hours."

"Let's say an hour, at what, thirty dollars an hour for wages? Plus super and insurance. So thirty-five dollars. Plus Parts. Maybe another ten. Then there's the overheads like the lights and phone. Even if you ignore all those things it's still costing forty-five dollars."

"See, he's covering his costs, it's all good."

"You don't get it, Jake." I throw my hands up in frustration. "He might be covering costs on a good day when the work only takes an hour, but he needs the profit too."

"It's just a night out at the pub, Blondie."

"Did you see Dan going out to the pub very often?" I'm betting he wouldn't have been able to afford it.

Jake shakes his head. "I guess not. He comes for a drink but he never eats with us. I just assumed he likes his mum's cooking."

"The 'profit' part is what pays the loan. It pays for the equipment and the extra's. It pays for Dan's time to run the place. And if there's some left over it goes towards Dan's retirement. I bet he isn't paying superannuation for himself, either."

I take a deep breath, getting ready to go into a full blown rant when we're interrupted.

"Yoo hoo," a voice calls. "Hellooooo."

I look out the window and see Cindy Turner standing at the roller door peering in. She's wearing her denim shorts again.

"Christ. What does she want?" Jake sits down in the desk chair and bends his head over the appointment diary.

"Are you hiding?" I ask. "Seriously?"

"Just get rid of her," Jake says. "Please? I'll have your babies if I don't have to talk to her."

A burst of laughter explodes out of me at his words. The tension from before is well and truly broken.

"All right, I'll see what I can do."

I stride out of the office and intercept Cindy three steps into the workshop.

"Can I help you?" I ask.

"I need to talk to Dan." She cranes her neck, looking everywhere.

"He's still in the hospital. Hasn't woken up yet." I tell her.

She deflates a little then starts looking around again. "What about Jake? Is Jake around?"

"Sorry, he's not available. Is there something I can help you with?"

"I need to pick up the donation. For the soccer club? I'm sure Dan has it ready for me. Maybe I can come in and look for it?" Cindy starts walking towards the office.

I step aside and block her. "You'll have to come back when Dan's here," I say. "I cleaned out the office over the weekend and there wasn't anything that looked like a donation. Sorry."

I'm not sorry. This woman sets my teeth on edge. I wish I'd hidden in the office with Jake.

"You might not recognise it. He said it was something special. It will take someone who knows their soccer to recognise it." Her eyes keep darting to the office and I can tell she really wants to go in and dig around.

"I'm just about to lock up. There's nothing here. When Dan wakes up from his *coma*, I'll be sure to ask him about your donation."

Cindy glares at me. I don't think she believes me. "Fine, I'll come back later."

She turns on her heel— three inch stiletto's which do not go with the denim shorts in my humble opinion— and stalks out of the garage.

I feel heat at my back and then an arm goes around my waist. Jake pulls me in to his side and kisses the top of my head. It makes me feel funny inside. Warm, but also a little uncomfortable. The intimacy of the gesture is way too high for the amount of time we've known each other. But I'll take it.

"Thank you," he says. "I owe you."

19 GOOD TEAM

"You know; I think that soccer mum is a part of Dan's problem." It's later that same evening and I'm cooking Jake dinner. I'm making my signature dish, beef strips stir-fried with bok choy, onion, carrot and capsicum and seasoned with my secret ingredients — vindaloo curry paste and honey. There's no bite, the honey offsets the heat of the curry, and it tastes beautiful. I've steamed some rice to go with it and now I'm making the side salad.

Jake's sitting at the breakfast bar watching me. Very domestic.

He frowns. "What do you mean?"

"Between her and the pensioners and goodness knows how many other people he's helping." I shrug. "He's a soft touch. People use him and he's too nice to say no."

Jake frowns harder. "I can see why you think that, but it's who he is."

"It's costing him." I shake my head. "I think what I found today is just the tip of the iceberg."

"Okay, I get it. We shouldn't be doing the pensioner specials."

"I'm not saying that. But you need to be smart about it. Get the apprentice to do the work so it costs less. Have a sliding scale based on the actual costs, so if it takes longer they pay more. If there's extra parts they pay for them. And you need to put a limit on it. Pick a time slot in the appointment diary, say Tuesday mornings, and once its booked out they have to wait for the next week, or pay the normal price."

Jake nods. "That all makes sense. I don't think Dan will go for it though."

"I don't think he's going to have a choice. To be honest, I don't know how he's been keeping the doors open. There's a couple of big deposits into the bank that don't seem to tie back to any jobs, which is weird. But they're the only reason the overdraft isn't double what it is."

"So he's been dipping into his savings." It's Jake's turn to shrug.

"Ha." I huff out the sound on a burst of air. "You think he has savings?"

Jake looks uncomfortable. "I guess not."

"I can't figure out what's going on."

"I didn't realise it was such a mess." Jake runs his hands through his hair. "I'm afraid I'm not much use in the paperwork department. Give me an engine any day."

I smile. "Are you admitting you need my help?"

"I'm saying we make a good team."

20 ALMOST BUT NOT QUITE

We eat dinner together and then go to the hospital to visit Dan.

My parents' car is in the car park when we arrive and I'm not too ashamed to hide.

"Quick, in here." I pull Jake into the chemist. "I've got to buy something."

Jake grins, his smile huge. "That's funny, I have to buy something too. I wonder, is your something the same as my something?"

It's not. It can't be. My something is imaginary and his something turns out to be condoms. Of course, I can't admit I'm really hiding so I scoop up a month's worth of vitamins, some shampoo, and a cute little hand cream and body lotion set.

My parents walk past while we're at the cashier but don't look in, thank goodness. Jakes sees them and gives me a knowing look, but doesn't say anything.

Smart boy.

After we make our purchases we go and see Dan. There's been no change in his condition.

I tell him I'm going to kick his butt when he wakes up due to the mess his business is in. I'm thinking he might wake up and argue back but his heart monitor doesn't even blip.

I'm nervous on the drive home due to the condoms. It all seemed very natural and destined this morning when things were getting steamy but now I'm not so sure.

Jake reaches over to grab my hand and squeezes.

"Relax, Blondie," he says. "We don't have to do anything tonight."

I breathe out a sigh of relief. "So you're taking back the couch," I confirm.

Jake laughs, the sound low in his throat. "Nope." He lets go of my hand to change gears as we turn a corner.

I really don't want to sleep on the couch but fair's fair. "All right, I guess it's my turn."

"Oh no, you don't." Jake's hand comes back. His fingers curl around mine. My hand rests on my leg and I shiver as his knuckles graze my inner thigh.

"We're not talking about it," I say.

"Okay," Jake says. But he doesn't let go of my hand except to change gears the whole way home.

When the car stops Jake moves fast. He's at my side of the car before I can blink and opening my door for me. He grabs my hand and hauls me out, our shopping bags slung from his other hand.

We're parked in the side street which surprises me. He pulls me to a set of stairs at the side of the building that I hadn't noticed before.

There's a gate at the top which he unlocks and we enter. A gantry style walkway stretches across half the building. I glance through the window to my right and can see moonlight glinting off the mezzanine floor in the workshop. Another gate at the end opens to Jakes back balcony. I've been on his balcony but didn't notice the gate.

"I didn't know this was here," I say.

"There's a lot you don't know about," Jake says. "We added it last year so I have a separate entrance."

He'd dropped my hand to unlock the door and now grabs it again.

"Come on." He pulls me towards the bedroom.

I dig my heels in. "No. I'm taking the couch tonight."

He stops dead. "No means no," he says. He changes direction and leads us both to the couch. "It makes no difference to me. We can share the couch if that's what you want."

He sits on the couch, tugging on my hand to bring me down beside him. His feet go up on the coffee table and he grabs the remote to switch the television on.

Guys. My dad is the same, can't be in the lounge room without having the television on. It's like a spot of silence might mean the end of the world.

Jake flips through the channels and settles on some nature documentary about a guy catching killer fish in the Amazon. Then he turns to face me.

"Want to tell me what's going on?" he asks.

"I don't want to talk about it." I fold my arms over my chest. I'm going to play dumb. Not my proudest moment, but I've never been one to face my fears.

"Okay," he says. "But I have something to tell you."

My belly flutters and I suck in a breath. "You do?"

"Yep. The thing is, I don't want to go backwards from this morning. We've got a connection, Blondie. Don't tell me you haven't felt it."

I've felt it, but I don't want to admit it so I say nothing. But Jake wanting to talk about it? He's way more mature than I am.

"This is new for me," Jake continues. "But I like you and I want to see where it goes."

"We've only know each other what, three days, four?"

"Six." Jake's voice is quiet.

"Six days. Less than a week. And we haven't even been on a proper date. I'm not the type of girl who sleeps with a guy she's just met." I cross my arms tighter over my chest. "And what about Dan? I'm still his little sister. Oh, and we're working together."

"That's a lot of excuses," Jake says. "But it doesn't matter. It will be a week tomorrow, I've taken you to the pub already but if you

want a proper date we can do that, and when Dan wakes up he'll
deal. We've already proven we're a good team. That's not going to
change." His voice is firm. This isn't a question, it's just the way it is.

"Now, do you want to sleep out here or in the bed? We don't have
to have sex if you're not comfortable but we're damn well sleeping
together."

Oh boy. The butterflies have turned into rampaging eagles and
they're pounding my insides. Not only that, but they've created
tingles in places down below where I really don't want to be tingling.

If I'm completely honest with myself, I do want the tingles, I
want Jake. But I know I shouldn't act on it. Should I? Why am I
holding back? Just because it's not going to last doesn't mean I can't
have a bit of fun on the way. Dan will be awake and I'll be gone
before Jake figures out that I'm not good enough for him.

But I can't do it.

"No." I'm firm. "I'll take the couch and you can have your bed
back. This morning was a mistake. I'm sorry, it won't happen again.
And tomorrow I'll start looking for somewhere else to stay." Maybe
Bri has room.

Jake goes rigid beside me. His fist clenches around the remote
and his head snaps to look at the television. For a moment I'm afraid
that I've really pissed him off.

Then he sighs and all the tension leaves his body. "All right,
Blondie. You win. But only if you take the bed. Like I said before, my
mum would kill me if I let you sleep on the couch."

I nod. "I can do that."

"And Alex," he says. "Tomorrow night we're going on that date."

21 BREAK IN

"Dan's Garage, this is Alex, how can I help you today?" I'm answering the phone in my best office voice. This place can use some professionalism so I'm doing my bit to help. The guys all answer the phone by saying 'yeah'.

It's been a long day. Jake did not wake me up by hopping into bed with me this morning. I don't want to admit it, but I was disappointed. In fact, I didn't see him at all until I came downstairs to the office. He was already hard at work on someone's car. I'm pretty sure he's sulking. He's hardly said two words to me all day.

"Hey Alex, it's Suze," says the caller. I instantly recognise her voice from the other night. "How are you going? Getting it sorted?"

"Getting there." It's not even a lie. I'm making good progress.

"Don't forget training at Tempest Serene this afternoon," Suze says. "The beginner's class starts at six."

"Did I agree to that when I was drunk?" I ask. Because I sure as hell don't remember it.

Suze laughs, her gorgeous mini boom. "You said you'd think about it. But you should come. It's a lot of fun."

"All right. Thanks for the invite." Suze is making an effort to be a friend and I need friends right now.

"Is Jake about? I need to talk to him," Suze says.

"He's got his head buried in a motor with the other two guys. Can I take a message?" I don't want to interrupt if I can help it. In fact, I don't want to talk to Jake at all. I guess it's not just him who's sulking. I grab a Post-It note from the stash I found buried in the top drawer.

"Sure. Just tell him the paperwork is ready for him to sign."

"No worries. See you tonight." We hang up and I write down Jake's message to give him later.

IT'S NEARLY KNOCK off time, and I'm standing in the door to the office surveying my work. It looks organised. I'm a little bit proud at how much I've got done. A box of unidentified metal parts still sits on top of the filing cabinet but that's it. Jake put it up there saying Dan would have to sort through it when he gets back. Otherwise I'm done. I've almost got the bookwork finished too. By the end of the week I should know exactly where we stand.

I'm about to head back in to turn off my laptop when I get the feeling I'm being watched.

Spooked, I look around the workshop, searching for whatever is giving me the heebie-jeebies. Nothing is out of place. The guys are all head down, bent over an engine on the far side. The radio is playing and everything seems normal.

Movement at the front roller door catches my eye and I see the guy from the lookout. He's eyeballing me. Well, that explains the creepy feeling. I stride over to him, trying to project confidence.

"Can I help you?" I ask.

"Looking for Dan. He back yet?" the man asks. His odd-coloured eyes are darting all over the workshop taking it all in.

"No. Is there something I can help with?" I ask.

"Who's in charge while he's away?" His voice is low and menacing.

"That would be me. I'm his sister, Alex." Maybe I should point him at Jake instead. That would be the smart thing to do. In fact I should never have given him my name. Too late now.

"He owes me. He's had his warning. It's time to pay up." His eyes travel up and down my body, making my skin crawl. "If Dan's not here then maybe I'll get my satisfaction another way."

"What do you mean?" I feel sick in the stomach. This man is serious ick. I don't like the idea of Dan being mixed up with him. Especially not owing him.

The man's eyes catch on something over my shoulder. "Never mind. I'll come back later." He turns abruptly and walks to his expensive-looking four wheel drive. With a screech of tyres he speeds away from the kerb. Jerk.

"What was that all about?" Jake is at my side, his phone in his hand, eyes on the departing vehicle. He seems to have a sixth sense when I'm in trouble.

"Don't know. Something about Dan owing him. I'm sure it was nothing," I say.

"I've got a bad feeling about that guy," Jake says.

"I do too." But there's nothing I can do about it so I'm not going to dwell on it.

"You still mad at me?" Jake asks.

"What? I thought you were mad at me. You weren't there this morning." I thought he'd finally realised he could do better.

"I thought that's what you wanted." Jake frowns. "I can't win, can I?"

"That reminds me." I change the subject, not wanting to delve too deeply into what I want. "Suze phoned before. She said she's got paperwork for you to sign. What's that all about?"

It's none of my business but I want to know. I get the feeling Jake's holding back on something. Nothing I can put my finger on, but it's there.

"Nothing for you to worry about." He won't meet my eyes and I don't like that he's being cagey. "I'll head in to see her then we can go out for dinner. I owe you a date." He looks up with a cocky grin.

Um, no. I don't think so. That could lead to all sorts of possibilities that I'm not ready for. "I'm training tonight. Suze wants me to go to Tempest Serene to do the beginners class."

"That works. We'll have dinner after."

Something occurs to me and I change the subject again. "If you're an instructor there, when do you instruct? You've been home every night this week."

"I do Sunday afternoons and the early class Thursday mornings. Sometimes I do extra if someone's away."

Oh. That explains his absences. "You didn't mention that last night."

"You were waiting for me this morning? Sorry to disappoint." His eyes are warm. I guess he hasn't been avoiding me after all. "I'll make up for it tonight."

I give in with a sigh. "All right. I'll take a change of clothes to the dojo. I assume I can get changed there."

Jake nods. "I'll be back in an hour."

THE GUYS all leave at the same time as Jake. I close the big roller door behind them and head straight upstairs, still feeling a little spooked. I'm digging through the contents of my travel bag, spread out all over Jake's bed, looking for something to wear tonight when I hear an almighty crash from downstairs. My heart leaps in my chest and I jump, stifling a scream. If there's someone down there I don't want them to know I'm here.

I grab my phone so I can call Jake. That's when I realise I don't have his number. I don't have Suze's number either. The only number I have apart from Dan's, which won't do me any good seeing as he's in a coma, is Bri. And I can't phone her. I'm not dragging her into danger.

It's only four thirty and the bank should still be open so I google it and get the number. It takes a while to get put through to the branch, and then Suze, but finally I get hold of her and she gets Jake.

"Jake?"

"What's wrong?" His voice is strong in my ear. "Are you okay?"

"There's someone downstairs," I whisper. "I heard a crash. I know I should suck it up and investigate but I'm too scared." It takes a lot to admit but it's true. There's no way I'm going down there.

"Hold tight, I'll be home in five minutes," Jake says. "It's probably nothing, but wait upstairs just in case."

I decide the best place to watch for Jake's car is the verandah. I go the long way, tiptoeing, checking doors as I go. Four doors. All locked. That's way too many doors for one place. I'm not going to stand out on the verandah; I'm too spooked. I peep through the curtains instead.

Jake's true to his word and roars into the car park out the front in five minutes. I let out a sigh of relief and then go to the kitchen. I pull out the heaviest frying pan I can find, unlock the door, and creep down the stairs.

I MEET Jake downstairs in the office. He tells me he's been through the whole place and there's no-one in here now. Someone's been here though. My nice organised office is a mess.

The papers have been pulled out of the filing cabinet and strewn all over the place. The desk drawers have been upended and the contents tipped out. The box of metal parts is now all over the floor. That explains the crash I heard.

My laptop, strangely, is exactly where I left it.

"They were looking for something." Jakes voice is grim. "Not sure how they got in. But the toilet window was open. Maybe they squeezed in through there."

I'm dubious about that. "It's a really small window."

"It's either that or they picked a lock on one of the doors and then locked it again behind them when they left."

"That could happen," I say, although I don't know how. It just sounds more feasible than someone getting in through the toilet window. "What do you think they were looking for?"

"It doesn't make sense," Jake says. "We don't keep cash on the premises and the only other thing we have here is engine parts. Your laptop is valuable, but it's still here."

This whole thing has me super spooked. First the creepy guy, and now this. "Do you think that guy from earlier has something to do with this?"

Jake shakes his head. "I don't know. But he's been hanging around and he seems to have it in for Dan. I don't like it."

"Neither do I. I wish I knew what's going on." I frown. I have to be missing something.

"I don't like how he was looking at you, either," Jake says. "I'm going to have a chat to Tom and get him to set up some security for us. He's at the dojo tonight."

"I don't know. Don't you think you're overreacting?" I ask.

"You tell me. What exactly did he say to you this afternoon?" Jake's eyes are locked with mine.

I recall the man's words about Dan.

"He said 'he owes me. He's had his warning. It's time to pay up.' Then he said 'if Dan's not here then maybe I'll get satisfaction another way.'" I shiver. "All right, now I'm worried. Who the hell is that guy?"

"I don't know. But I'm going to find out."

22 TEMPEST SERENE

Tempest Serene is only a few blocks away from the Dan's garage. It's close enough to walk, but we take Jake's ute.

From the outside it looks like a big shed but inside it's much nicer.

We walk into the reception which has a small waiting area with a coffee table and chairs on one side and a reception counter on the other. The floor is polished wooden boards. Elise, the young girl I met the other night, is behind the counter.

"Hi Jake, Alex." She smiles, her eyes warm. "You here to try out a class?"

"I'm meeting Suze for the beginner's class. She said she'd show me the ropes." I'm feeling surprisingly nervous about it.

"Is Tom here?" Jake asks.

"Yes, he's got his black belts in the second training room. Should be finished soon," Elise says.

"Come on," Jake says to me. "I'll give you the tour."

"Can I ask a question?" I ask as we enter the wide hallway.

"Sure." Jake

"How old is Elise?"

Jake looks at me funny. "Nineteen. Why?"

"She just looks really young, that's all. I was wondering if she was legal drinking age the other night at the pub but didn't want to be rude and ask."

Jake grins. "She's the baby of the group. Her grandfather owns this place."

I frown and open my mouth to ask another question.

"Clance, Liam and Lilly are your age, twenty-two. Baz is the same age as Dan and I, twenty-four, twenty-five." Jake beats me to it.

"What are you now, a mind reader?" I grin. "And Suze?" I don't need to ask about Tom. It's clear he's a lot older than the others. I'd put him around thirty, the same age as Gavin, my old boss.

"Don't ask her about her age." Jake frowns. "It's a bit of a sore spot for her. She turns thirty next year and she thinks she's over the hill."

"Really? She doesn't look that old." Although she does have that big sister vibe. "Tom's the oldest right?"

He nods and grabs my hand and leads the way down the hallway. "Yep, he's thirty-one. Come on."

Doorways open off each side and the huge double doors at the end are closed.

"Change rooms through there." Jake gestures to our right. "You can leave your gear in there if you like."

I've brought a change of clothes for later. Jake is still insisting we're going on a date. I'm wearing my running tights and one of Jake's T-shirts, not having any other exercise clothes with me. Thongs, five dollar supermarket specials, are on my feet as the classes are all done barefoot.

The change rooms are nice. Open cubby holes cover one wall and I stash my gear in one of them and return to Jake to continue the tour.

Jake's standing in the doorway opposite the change rooms when I come out, chatting to someone. When I peek inside it turns out to be Clance. "Hey," I say. Clance is running on a treadmill and nods his hello.

The room is a mini-gym filled with a couple of weight benches, a variety of cardio-machines, and a cabled contraption looks like it might kill me. Dumbbells sit on a rack, and a metal tree has its branches stacked with plate weights. Hanging from hooks on the wall there's a skipping rope and various handles and chains. A small patch of bare floor features a padded mat, likely used for the skipping. Nice.

"Later," Jake says to Clance. He leads the way down the hall.

"Kitchen, office, training room, another training room." Jake points left and right as we go. I glimpse Tom in one of the rooms, standing at the front of a group of white uniformed men and women, all of them with distinctive black belts around their waists.

Finally we reach the double doors.

"Is it all right to go in?" I ask.

Jake grins. "Yep. Just keep quiet."

He opens the doors and we slip inside.

The space is massive.

A group of about twenty primary school-aged children dressed in the white uniforms with belts of all different colours stand in rows as they are put through a series of moves by an instructor. It's Suze.

"Jake." A man sitting on a wooden bench along the back wall, clearly a parent judging by the school bags surrounding him, nods hello at Jake. There's a mix of mums and dads. Mostly mums. All eyes are on me, curious.

Jake acknowledges the greetings but doesn't stop.

He leads the way to the stairs at the side of the room and we climb up to a mezzanine floor which overlooks the training area.

We stop at the railing along the edge. We've got a great view of the action from up here.

"We can fit one hundred students downstairs on grading days. This is where the spectators come to watch," Jake says in my ear. "They're out of the way but they still feel involved."

I lean on the rail and look down.

Sliding doors downstairs on the left open to a paved courtyard.

"What's through there?" I ask.

"That's the Zen Tranquillity Garden," Jake says. "It's our dedicated meditation space."

"Seriously?" I giggle. "It sounds like something out of a Disney movie."

"It's very nice. We've even got a water feature." He grins. "The kids named it. We thought it would encourage them to meditate when they're out there but all they do is splash around in the fountain."

"I can see that." I giggle again.

Jake puts his arm around my waist and tugs me into his chest.

"I'm going to have to do something about that noise," he says. He touches his nose to mine. "You'll get me in trouble."

He's in a playful mood tonight. I put my hands to his chest trying, unsuccessfully, to push away. "I'll be quiet."

"Too late," Jake says. "There's a price to pay."

He dips his head closer and his lips brush against mine. The tummy flutters are back. I'll have to be rowdy more often.

His kiss is soft and gentle. It's a different kiss to the others we've shared. There's no frantic push, or heat. If anything I'd call it a PG friendly kiss. It's nice.

He breaks away and rests his forehead against mine.

I get the 'eyes on me' sensation for the second time that day and look around. No-one here but us, thank goodness.

I glance down. Thirty pairs of eyes are pointed in our direction. Thirty-one if you count Suze.

"Jake?" I say. But he's seen them. He's grinning, he looks kind of proud of himself.

"Oooooooooooh," the kids chorus.

"Carry on, eyes front," he calls to them.

There's a chorus of giggles but they're well disciplined and turn back to Suze.

"We'll never live that down," he says to me. But he doesn't seem too worried. "And they're all going to want to know who you are. Especially the mums."

"Are they like soccer mums?" I ask.

Jake laughs, causing a few heads to turn back this way.

"No," he says. "Soccer mums don't know how to kick butt."

"Thank goodness for that," I say. "Those soccer mums are fierce."

Then I realise that the karate mums probably do know how to kick butt.

"Should I be scared?"

"Terrified. Some of the kids downstairs play soccer too." Jake grins big. The way he says it I know I've got nothing to worry about.

SUZE FINISHES up with her kids shortly after and we go down the stairs. It's a buzz of parents and kids and nearly every one of them comes up to be introduced to me. It's chaotic and noisy, but it gives me a warm fuzzy feeling in my chest. It's nice to be part of something, even in a superficial way.

"The beginners' class will be in here too," Jake says.

"Why do the kids get the good room and the black belts are stuck out the front in the little room?" I ask. It's not really a little room, but it's all relative.

Jake shrugs. "The black belts don't care where they train. The kids' parents need somewhere to sit and the kids love sliding on this floor. It's all part of the fun."

Suze finishes talking to one of the parents and comes over.

"You ready?" she asks. She's wearing her white uniform and her belt is red with two black stripes at the end.

I nod. "Are we in here?"

"Yep. Clance is your instructor tonight," Suze informs me. "I'm just here to help out if I'm needed."

"I thought you'd be the instructor," I say.

"Nope. I only teach the kids. Grownups like to have a black belt in charge and I'm not quite there yet." She nods towards the women standing near the raised platform at the front, waiting for the class to start. "And we get better attendance with the guys in charge. Especially Clance. He's got quite a following."

"I can see that." There's a good mix of ladies, some my age and some older. A few look to be mother and daughter pairs. "Is it women only?"

Jake grins and Suze outright laughs, her mini boom. She shakes her head. "Not this class. Although it does skew that way. Clance runs a women's self defence class as well. That one is *really* popular."

"I bet." A thought occurs to me. "Does Clance have a girlfriend?"

Jake stiffens beside me and Suze laughs again. "Nope. You looking?" Her eyes flick to Jake and I realise she's stirring him.

I decide to join in. "Maybe. What's his story?"

Jake puts his hands on hips. "Standing right here, Blondie."

I smile. "A girl's got to keep her options open."

"Clance is too young for you. He's still at uni," Jake grinds out.

"Whoa, settle big boy," Suze says, touching his shoulder. My eyes narrow at her hand and Jake grins. "We're just having a bit of fun."

She turns to me. "Clance is all about study and work. He's got two jobs, here and the pub, and he trains hard as well. I don't think he's got time for a girlfriend."

"That's all right, I was just curious." I decide to let Jake off the hook. "Jake's taking me out tonight after this and I'm not a two-timing kind of girl."

"A date?" Suze grins. "That's great."

Jake's arm goes around my shoulders as Clance walks in through the double doors. I guess he's not taking any chances.

Clance nods at us but doesn't stop to chat, walking straight to the front of the room. He's all business. He claps his hands twice for attention and then uses his big voice. "All right guys, let's get started. Everyone who's training come and line up."

"That's my signal to leave," Jake says. "I'm going to talk to Tom."

SUZE SMILES and walks me to the front of the room, showing me where to stand. Right front and centre. I'm not sure about this. I'd rather be hiding in the back not here where everyone can see my klutziness. Suze stands beside me, so at least I don't feel so alone.

Clance leads us through a warm-up which includes jogging on the spot, star jumps, sit-ups and push-ups. I'm pretty fit from my running but have zero upper body strength. I have zero stomach strength too.

Clance demonstrates easier options for the push-ups but even so I'm flat-out doing ten in a row from my knees. I sneak a look at Suze. She's doing proper push-up, up on her toes, and not only that— she's on her knuckles. And making it look easy. Give me five years and I'll be right there beside her. If only. Except by that time no doubt she'll be just levitating. Look Mum, no hands.

Don't be a bitch. I'm big enough to admit I'm jealous. I'd kill for arms like Suze's. And I'll probably kill myself trying to get them. In fact, I'd laugh at my green-eyed monster if I wasn't hurting so much.

After the warm-up I tell myself it can only get easier.

I'm wrong.

It's not that Clance is a bad instructor. He's great. It's more that I'm a complete novice and all the rest of the students are a couple of months into their training.

Clance leads us through a number of choreographed moves. He demonstrates each one, step by step. Then we do it with him. We do each move four or five times. Blocks, punches and kicks, all fairly straight forward.

I'm being lulled into a false sense of security.

After we've done half a dozen different moves Clance calls Suze up the front beside him. They bow to each other.

"Now we're going to put everything together into a pattern," Clance says. "This is the first pattern you'll learn in Tae Kwon Do and most of you are already getting to know it. Suze will lead, just follow along. I'll be walking around the class helping you and correcting form."

The moves are straight forward, the ones we've just practised.

But they're combined with twists and direction changes. I'm lost after the first two steps and stand there like an idiot.

"You're doing well," Clance says from beside me. "If you get lost just stop, centre yourself, and pick it back up with the next move. I don't expect you to get it on your first day but over time you'll find it starts to come naturally."

I nod. I'm not sure I'm going to ever come back so the time thing seems irrelevant. I don't tell Clance that.

After what seems like forever Clance walks back to the front of the class and bows off with Suze. "Now it's time for a bit of fun."

I wonder what constitutes 'fun' in a class like this. Clance tells me.

"We'll be breaking off into smaller groups and practising some of our kicks and strikes."

First, I learn how to do a back fist strike.

It takes some co-ordination. One of the other ladies walks me through it several times before it's my turn to try it on the bag. She has immense patience. "We were all beginners once," she says.

My first attempt I nearly fall over when I spin around and the second time I manage the spin but miss the punching pad completely. It's third time lucky. I spin and connect. Weak, but I'll take it. Go me.

Ten minutes later Clance calls for us to switch activities.

We do elbow strikes, apparently it's the hardest part of the body. Ten minutes after that we learn to escape from a chokehold using a booty slam, backwards head-butt, combination.

"Always run as your first option," Suze says. "Your opponent will be bigger, stronger and faster than you. Run or hide if you're ever in that situation, don't fight unless you have to."

Finally, the whole class comes together for the flying side kick.

The flying side kick is way out of my league. Clance demon-strates. He flies through the air parallel to the ground, both feet up and his knees bent to his chest. His feet fly out and hit the target causing the guy holding it to take a step backwards. Wowsers. The second best flying side kick I've ever seen. The one Jake did the day I met him was better. Maybe.

"That was the advanced version, the double flying side kick," he says. He hasn't even raised a sweat. Show off. "Now I'll show you the single leg version."

This looks exactly the same except only the top leg lashes out to do the kicking.

"That's what you're aiming for. But it takes time and practice to get there. For today, we're just practising getting our launch right and connecting with the bag."

When it's my turn Clance tells me to just have fun with it. So I do. I run and I launch and I fling one of my legs around in the air in the vicinity of the punch pad and actually connect first go. It's a lot of fun, especially when I've got no expectations of myself.

The cooling down activities include another run through of the pattern so we can practise at home if we want.

"How did you go?" Suze asks at the end of the class.

I grin. "That was fantastic," I say. "Same time next week?"

Suze grins back. "I knew you'd like it. Yep, same time next week. If you're still enjoying it after a couple of lessons we'll hook you up with a uniform. That way you can grade later on."

I'd been wondering about that. Some of the ladies were wearing the white uniforms with plain white belts and others were in casual clothes like me.

"Well done, Alex," Clance says from behind me. "You're a natural."

I turn and grin at him. "I know, right?"

I know he's messing with me, but it still feels good.

That last part was fun, and the other women made me feel welcome. I'll feel it tomorrow, but I want to come back again. I smile to myself, picturing my body flying through the air in a perfectly executed flying side kick. I could totally do that.

JAKE AND TOM WALK in through the huge double doors. They each take a door and pin it open and then come over to where Clance, Suze and I are standing.

Holy hotness alert. They've got the attention of most of the ladies in the room. I see the woman who helped me earlier fanning herself. She catches my eye and mouths 'lucky girl'. I smile.

"Hey, have fun?" Jake asks me.

I nod. "Apart from the warm-up. That was brutal."

The guys and Suze all laugh, not realising I'm serious. I decide not to enlighten them.

"You coming back next week, Alex?" Clance asks.

I nod. "I think I will. That was awesome."

"I'm out of here. Later." With a nod of his head, Clance leaves.

"Me too. Catch you around," says Suze and follows Clance.

Tom flicks his head towards the Zen Tranquillity garden and strides that way, obviously expecting us to follow.

Jake grabs my hand and leads me out the side doors. Tom is sitting up on a wooden picnic table in the corner and leaning forward, resting his elbows on his knees. Jake hops up beside him and pats the bench between him and Tom. I look dubiously at the space then decide, what the hell, and squeeze in.

"I'm not sure what's going on but I don't like it," Tom informs me. It's clear that Jake has told him about the creepy guy and the break-in.

"There's been some rumblings about Dan the last couple of weeks and I've done a bit of digging. He's gotten mixed up in some-thing bad. The rumour is that the fire wasn't an accident." Tom's voice is deep and sexy. At odds with what he's saying.

"What?" My gut clenches and I feel sick. "That can't be right. This is Dan you're talking about."

"It's just a rumour, Blondie." Jake puts his arm around my shoulder and pulls me into him. "We'll get to the bottom of it, figure it out. Tom's running the plates on the guy's car from this afternoon and we'll see who we're dealing with."

"The plates?" I can't quite get my head around what's happening. Denial land.

"I got his licence plates. It's the second time he's been at the workshop asking for Dan and I didn't like how he was looking at you. I snapped a photo of his plates as he drove off."

That explains why he had his phone out.

"All right." I shrug Jakes arm off my shoulder and stand up. I need to move. I walk as far away from the guys as I can, which turns out to be a long way. The paved courtyard runs the length of the building.

There is indeed a water feature, a fountain, in the middle of the space. Huge trees lit up with fairy lights and wooden benches are scattered throughout. It would be nice to sit out here in one of the little nooks and read, or think. Meditate, even. I turn back when I reach the picnic table at the end. It matches the one the guys are on. I've got my questions sorted by the time I get back to the guys. They both watch me silently.

"Right," I say when I reach them. "You'll figure out who it is, and then what? Go and talk to him? Report him to the cops?"

"He hasn't actually done anything yet, not that we can prove," Tom says. "For now we'll put in security cameras and a panic button so if he tries anything you're covered."

"Far out. Try anything? What the hell alternate universe is this?" I can feel my heart rate escalating. I've been fairly calm, but now there's a real threat and I didn't see it before. I wrap my arms around my body and try not to cry. Fight or flight has skipped right past and I'm about to lose it.

Then something Tom said unravels in my brain. "Let me check my understanding. When you said the rumour was that the fire wasn't an accident did you mean that the fire was deliberately lit? That someone was trying to hurt my brother?"

Tom nods. "Looks like. If it is who I think it is then they don't care about collateral damage."

He means my parents. They could have been killed too. I might not get on with them but I certainly don't wish them dead.

"On my God, oh my God, oh my God," I chant. I'm starting to hyperventilate.

Jake and Tom exchange a glance and then Jake stands up and comes to me. He wraps me in his arms and walks me back to the picnic table. He sits and lifts me up onto his lap. I only dimly realise this, lost as I am in my chant. Jake wraps his arms tighter, tucking my face into his neck. He strokes my hair gently and I curl into him, hands on his chest.

After a few minutes I calm down, my heart rate slowing into sync with Jake's.

I settle.

"I'm better than this." I lift my head to look at him. "I don't fall into a big heap at the first sign of trouble. I'm a fighter."

"You just found out that someone tried to kill your family. I think you're entitled to a little freak out."

23 DATE NIGHT

"Are you sure you still want to go out tonight?" Jake's hand is warm on my arm.

"I could use the distraction," I say. "Where are we going?"

"It's a surprise." Jake presses a gentle kiss to my forehead. "I'll meet you in the foyer." He turns and saunters to the men's change-room and I watch until he disappears around the corner before going to get myself ready.

I'm lucky that my favourite dress made it into my bag when I ran from the city. It's wash and wear and was draped on top of the washing basket. This dress is the first thing I bought myself when I reached my goal weight. It's a swirly, girly, halter-neck dress with a bare back and skirt that hits mid-thigh. I love it.

I'm wearing my work heels and my hair is in loose curls around my shoulders. It takes me half an hour to get ready, but totally worth it.

Jake takes one look at me as I enter the foyer and drops to his knees in front of me. Actually, that's not quite right.

He launches himself towards me from where he's standing, chatting to Baz and Elise. In a perfectly-timed manoeuvre he hits his knees on the polished floor a metre away from me and dramatically slides the rest of the way. It must kill his knees, but he doesn't miss a beat.

"Be still, my beating heart." He has both hands clasped to his chest.

All eyes are on us. Half a dozen ladies from the beginners' class are milling around, chatting, but they've gone silent. A wolf whistle pierces the air. Baz. He's leaning casually against the reception counter with Elise. They both watch me and I feel my face heating up with embarrassment.

Jake grabs my hand and brings it to his lips and everyone else fades away. His mouth lingers, his tongue touching the back of my hand sending a spark of electricity through me. Then, I kid you not, he levitates.

I think it's a trick of the light.

One minute he's on his knees and two seconds later he's on his feet. It has to be some sort of martial arts move. He dips his body slightly towards the floor then springs upwards and brings his feet underneath him to stand. He never lets go of my hand.

I'm mesmerised. I don't move as his head dips and his lips brush mine, soft, gentle. Then he tucks my hand into the crook of his elbow, scoops my bag off my shoulder, and starts moving us towards the door. I haven't said a word.

Everyone claps and another wolf whistles pierces the air. I glance back to see one lady fanning herself.

My face is hot and I'm sure I'm a lovely shade of red. I can't get out of there fast enough.

"SO WHERE ARE YOU TAKING ME?"

"It's still a surprise," Jake says. We're in his ute driving to places unknown.

We're heading south along the winding beach road and I'm

pretty sure I know where we're going. I'm proven right when we stop at the lighthouse.

Jake pulls the ute to a stop and walks around to open my door.

He offers me his arm and we walk up the stairs towards the light-house. He takes me straight the viewing platform and we lean against the rail.

It's a beautiful night and the moon is full, casting a glow on the water. The last light of the sun is hovering on the horizon.

"It's gorgeous," I say. I shiver slightly as the coastal breeze hits my bare back and Jake puts his arm around my shoulders. His heat hits me and I lean into him for a moment before I pull away.

"Don't fight it, Blondie," he says, dipping his head to my ear. Goose bumps chase along my arms but it's not due to the breeze. I'm fighting my attraction to this man. It's such a bad idea to get involved with him. I've got to cut it short before I get sucked in again.

"This is a great date," I say briskly. "Thank you for bringing me here. Can we go now?"

"Not so fast." He chuckles. "Not going to run on me, are you?"

"This date isn't a good idea." I decide to be honest.

"Just give me five minutes," he says. "If you still want to go I'll take you home."

I sigh. Home is part of the problem, what with him being right there all the time. I really have to find somewhere else to stay.

"Five minutes," I say.

Jake takes my hand and leads me back the way we came. For a minute I think he's given up and is taking me back to the ute. But he stops at the entrance to the lighthouse. He drops my hand while he opens the door, then he takes it again and leads me inside.

I've done the lighthouse tour a couple of times growing up. It's eerie at any time of the day but at night time even more so.

"I really don't think this is a good idea," I say.

"Trust me," Jake says.

He pulls me towards the staircase and we start to climb. I focus on his mighty fine backside instead of the shadows and thoughts of what might be lurking in them.

There's a lot of stairs. After forever we emerge at the top. We're standing on a platform with the massive light suspended above us. Another, smaller set of stairs in the corner would take the lighthouse keeper up to the light itself in days gone by.

On the platform sits a checked picnic tablecloth and basket.

"How?" I whisper.

Jake smirks. "I have my ways."

He waves his arm and does a courtly bow. "Milady."

Following on from the dramatic gesture at the dojo its really sweet.

He reaches out and takes my hand. "I'm really sorry if I embarrassed you before. I got caught up in the moment. I was blown away by how you look in that dress."

I smile. "I forgive you. And your Jedi levitation trick was pretty cool."

I take a seat while Jake opens the bottle of wine and pours two glasses. They're plastic, but it's the quality coloured kind and they're proper wine glasses.

From the basket he pulls out trays of food. I raise my eyebrows. "Sushi? I didn't take you for a sushi guy."

"Do you eat sushi?" he asks. "I should have checked first."

"All good," I assure him. "I love sushi. You've really outdone yourself."

We eat in silence and it gets too much for both of us at the same time and we talk over the top of each other.

"You go first," I say.

"No, it's all right, you go. I was just going to ask if you're going to do another class."

I smile. "I was about to ask you what other types of classes are on offer."

"Didn't like the beginners' class?" The corner of his mouth lifts in an almost smile. "You looked like you were having fun."

"You saw that?" I shake my head. "I was all left feet."

"It can take a while to get the hang of it. It's worth going along a couple of times, unless you hated it. We have boxing and self defence classes as well as the tae kwon do."

I open my mouth to reply when Jake suddenly tenses. His head cocks to the side and he puts a finger to his lips. Then he gets silently to his feet. He bends down and puts his mouth close to my ear.

"Stay here and keep quiet," he says in a soft voice.

Then he disappears into the inky blackness of the stairwell.

I'd forgotten about my initial feelings of creepiness at being in the lighthouse at night but they come rushing back now that I'm alone. I can't hear a thing and who knows what Jake is doing. He seemed alert but not alarmed.

As quietly as possible I pack up the remnants of our meal.

I'm not sure what to do with the leftover wine. I've only drunk about half of mine and Jake's glass is gone. No pot plants up here to do a sneaky drop and run.

Think Alex. Such a first world problem. I'd skull my glass but I'm such a cheap drunk, I'd be useless in an emergency. And this probably counts as an emergency.

I pry the cork out of the bottle and start to pour my wine back in.

A shiver passes up my spine. I'm overreacting, I know it. But where's Jake?

An almighty clanging sound echoes up the stairs. I shriek and the wine glass slips out of my hands, splashing my legs and dress. I've somehow managed to keep a hold of the bottle.

That's when I smell smoke. A trickle of fear slides down my spine and I try not to panic.

The lighthouse is made of brick so what's burning? And where the hell is Jake?

Alex, think.

I grab the picnic tablecloth which is now soaked in wine. You're supposed to use a damp cloth to cover your face, aren't you? I tie it into a bandana and head to the stairs clutching the neck of my wine bottle in case I need a weapon.

I can't see any smoke and the smell is faint, but I'm not taking any chances.

I slip off my shoes so I'm barefoot. I'm kind of proud of myself for climbing up all those stairs in heels, actually, but they're not the best for sneaking around on.

There are a lot of stairs. More than I remember coming up. I'm as silent as possible, as I creep steadily downwards, stopping every couple of steps to listen.

Nothing.

It's so darn creepy. If I was watching this on television I'd have my eyes closed and I'd be chanting 'don't do it, don't do it' to the stupid next victim. But it's different when it's happening to you.

I'm halfway down when I think I sense movement behind me. I whirl around. There's nothing there. Heart pounding, I start down the stairs again. I just gave myself a heart attack over nothing.

I'm nearly at the bottom when I hear something. The smoke is thicker and my eyes are watering. Something is burning but I can't see any flames which is odd.

The noise is a scraping, dragging sound, followed by a whine of metal on metal.

I'm hit by a rush of fresh air and my lungs breathe a bit easier.

The door was just opened, I realise. The clanging I hear earlier, eons ago, must have been the door slamming shut.

I want to call out to Jake but I'm not game. Was it him opening the door? Or is he on the floor passed out somewhere down here?

Something crunches under my bare foot. It's cold and icky and loud in the silence. I freeze, and then slowly inch forward. I reach the bottom of the stairs and keep close to the wall.

The door is open, letting in fresh air and moonlight so that the room is partially lit. Which is good. But it's created deep shadows and smoke is now swirling all around the room. Which is bad.

I want to run outside but I'm too scared. What if there's someone out there? Someone who isn't Jake? And where the hell is Jake?

I whirl towards a noise in the shadows in the far corner and now I'm too scared to stay inside.

Suddenly I'm grabbed from behind, a hand covering my mouth.

I shriek but it's muffled by the tablecloth and the hand.

"Sssh," a voice says low in my ear. "Keep it down, Blondie." It's Jake.

Never have I felt so much relief. I sag in his arms and swat at the hand on my mouth. When he removes it I start tugging at the tablecloth, wanting desperately to get it off my face. The smoke is clearing a little and I can see more of the room.

"What's going on?" I ask quietly.

Jake shakes his head. I see a glint of white teeth as he eyes the tablecloth in my hand. "Later," he mouths.

He moves us underneath the stairs and parks me in the corner, deep in the shadows.

"Hunker down here and stay small. And be quiet." His mouth is on my ear and in different circumstances it would be sexy. "I'll be back."

What? Hell no. I'm not staying here on my own.

But Jake is mist.

Poof, gone.

A shadow moves through the door and I realise he's going outside. Checking the coast is clear? Or hunting something. I decide to stay put and rethink my life choices, for all the good it will do me. Running away seems like it might be a better option but really, where is there to run out here?

We're in town, but there aren't any houses nearby. The lighthouse is at the end of the peninsular. A wooden staircase leads down to the next beach, Lighthouse Beach, and there's houses back along the road and down by the beach, but we're a good two or three kilometres from the nearest house. So running isn't really an option. Guess I'm waiting for Jake.

He saunters back in a few minutes later.

"It's safe now. You can come out," he says.

"Are you sure?" I stand up from my crouch, legs seizing.

"Yep. Saw a car drive off. Did a lap outside but there's no-one here. Whoever it was is gone."

"What was burning?" The smoke has totally cleared and I can't see any fire, or any charred wood for that matter.

"It was a smoke bomb," Jake says. "Haven't seen one of those for years. We used to have them as kids."

"Do you have any disgruntled exes I should know about?"

"Funny, I was going to ask you the same thing."

24 I'M TAKING BACK MY BED

THE SMOKE BOMB ENDS THE PICNIC AND WE PACK UP everything and head back home.

Home. It's only been a week and already this place feels like home.

That's wrong, I realise. It's not the place that feels like home, it's Jake. Jake feels like home.

"What happened back there?" We're sitting on the couch, feet up, drinks in our hands. The bottle of wine made it home unscathed and we split what was left of it, still using the fancy plastic wine glasses.

"I'm not sure. I heard something and went to investigate. I was halfway down the stairs when the door slammed shut."

"I heard that. Scared the crap out of me." My hand goes to my heart.

"I know. I heard you," Jake says. "By the time I got to the bottom there was smoke everywhere. I went through all the little rooms down there in case the person was still inside."

"What if they came back upstairs?"

"I figured I'd hear them. I left my wine glass on the stairs where they'd tread on it." He smirks. He's pretty pleased with himself.

"That was smart." I scowl. "Except it got me instead. Then what."

"I opened the door and rescued you from the big bad smoke."

"You scared the crap out of me, more like. What the hell was the thing in the corner?"

"The smoke bomb. It started rattling when it was nearly empty." Jake reaches over and grabs my hand in his, his thumb stroking across my fingers. "I didn't know what I was walking out into when I left you under the stairs. I was worried it was the person who broke in. That they wanted to hurt you."

"I wasn't the one chasing after them," I say. "We should have just called the police."

"We weren't supposed to be there." Jake shrugs. "I called in a favour from the caretaker. He could get into trouble if anyone found out he let us in."

"Really? You shouldn't have done that. What happened to the traditional dinner and a movie date night?"

"Where's the fun in that?" He grins. "I wanted it to be special."

He drops my hand and I lament its loss until he moves, slinging his arm around my shoulders and pulling me in close to his side. He nuzzles the top of my head and I melt into him.

"That's all right," I say. "I don't need special. I'm happy right here."

He's got me feeling all settled and comfortable and it's nice. Too nice. I've still got questions.

"What about the car. Did you get a number plate? What sort of car was it?" I pull away so I can twist sideways and look at him properly. He won't meet my eyes.

"I'm sensing you don't want to tell me."

He looks up at that. "It was a four-wheel drive. It was too dark to get the plate so I don't know if it was the same one from this afternoon."

I shiver, remembering the man with the odd-coloured eyes. "It could have been him." I don't want to believe it. "But it might just have been kids playing pranks. That seems more likely."

"I saw the four-wheel drive earlier. I thought it was following us when we left the dojo." He frowns. "It disappeared by the time we got to the lighthouse so I decided I was just being paranoid."

"Why didn't you tell me?" I need to know what I'm dealing with. "I'm not a fragile special snowflake who has to be protected."

"Didn't want to worry you for nothing." He reaches for me again but I lean away. He scowls. "Come on, don't be mad at me. I'm trying to keep you safe. I'm not the bad guy."

I sigh. He's right. "You win. And you were very brave earlier. Thank you."

He snickers. I think he sensed my sarcasm.

"I meant it when I said thank you," I say.

"But not when you said I was brave?" He tilts his head with the question and I shrug.

"You'll never know," I say with a wink.

"I'll let you have that secret," Jake says. "But there's something I have to tell you."

I feel a flicker of fear at what that might be. But Jake still looks amused so I push it back down inside. "What might that be?"

"I'm taking back my bed tonight," he says. "And I want you in it."

25 SMOKIN' HOT

"Whoa!" I hold up my hands. "Nu-uh. No way. Not happening."

Jake's lips turn up at the corners and his eyes crinkle. He thinks I'm cute.

I playfully swat at his chest. "And I'm not cute!"

He grabs both my hands with one of his and pulls me into his chest. His other hand goes to the back of my head and threads through my hair.

"Got that right," he says. His voice is low and growly. "You're adorable."

Then he pulls me into his lap and kisses me.

The moment his tongue touches mine I'm gone. If I'm honest with myself, I want this too. Bad. My hands are gripping his biceps and follow the curve of his arms up to his shoulders. Hard, muscular shoulders.

I grab at the neck of his shirt and start tugging, trying to get it off. It's difficult to think about the moving parts when he's kissing me like this, one hand tangled in my hair and the other tracing circles up my bare back.

He breaks contact with my mouth and rests his forehead against mine, breathing heavily. My breathing matches his. I tug at his shirt again. "Off," I say.

He complies, whipping the shirt over his head in two seconds flat. Then his hands go to my halter top and he undoes the tie. Whoosh. Gone. I'm bra-less under the top, the joys of the backless dress.

I don't have time to be embarrassed. Jake's head dips to my neck and he nuzzles a spot just under my ear. His hand returns to my back, wrapped around me like I'm precious. His other hand cups my breast. This hand says I'm precious but in a different way. A sexy way. His thumb brushes my nipple sending a spark straight between my legs. I give silent thanks I picked this dress to wear tonight and groan, the sound unrecognisable as me.

Jake mirrors my groan with his own.

"You're killing me," he says in my ear.

I shake my head, unable to make words. I push his head lower, towards my breast, using my hands to communicate instead.

Jake understands me perfectly. His tongue dances across my nipple and my happy place tingles. The hand at my back curls me in closer. The one on my breast moves to my knee, under the fabric of my dress, and begins a delicate tiptoe up my leg to where things get interesting. His mouth moves to my other nipple and the hand at my back, the one belonging to the super stretchy ninja arms, is now at the breast he was just kissing.

This is too much and I groan again. I'm running my fingers over his back, his arms, his head. I grip him tightly as the sensations build. I want more.

Jake wants more too. I know this from the hardness against my thigh. I wriggle closer and his hand slips between my legs right at the juncture, creating pressure exactly where I need it.

"I want you," Jake says. His voice has gone deep and throaty. "I want you right here, right now."

I nod, words escaping me.

"Say it," he says. "Say yes. Tell me I'm not alone in this."

I nod again then whisper "yes". I'm not sure he's heard me until his mouth crashes into mine. This kiss is hungry, wild. His hands move again and I mourn the loss. But it's temporary.

He stands with me in his arms and moves us into the bedroom. My legs wrap around his waist monkey-style and his arms are around me, one at my back and the other under my backside.

His mouth doesn't stop moving against mine as he walks us to his bed. My hands are frantic, in his hair, on his shoulders. I can't get enough of him.

"Going to christen the couch another day," he says against my mouth. "The first time I want you in my bed."

Oh boy. I don't care where we are as long he doesn't stop touching me. This moment can be my future. My forever. I'm never running again as long as I've got this man in my arms, his mouth on mine and those amazing hands working their magic.

We crash onto the bed, me on the bottom. Jake keeps his weight off me by some miracle, not that I care if he crushes me. I want to feel him against me, all of him. I wrap my legs tighter around his waist to bring him closer.

He places a gentle kiss on my lips, unwraps my legs, and pulls back onto his knees.

"I want to see you, Alex."

My head spins. Finally, I understand why those old fashioned books talked about women swooning.

Jake finds the zip in the skirt of the dress and unzips, then tugs it off over my legs. I'm not sure where it ends up. I don't care. I'm lying there in just my panties. Jakes eyes darken, raking my body. Scorching.

His fingertips reach out and trail down my stomach and up to my breasts. I shiver when he caresses my nipples, his touch fleeting as he continues exploring. Up my shoulders, my neck and finally to my face. I close my eyes as he touches my mouth, my cheeks and my eyelids. He brushes my hair gently away from my face.

"Look at me," he says, voice husky.

I struggle to open my eyes as his hands reverse their journey. They linger on my lips, a finger gently pushing inside my mouth and I suck.

"Fuck." Jake sucks in a breath.

The finger withdraws and he replaces it with his other hand, two fingers this time. I suck hard, an involuntary movement, as the first finger moves straight to my nipple, making circles around and over. The sparks from the movement are a direct hit between my legs, my pussy clenching in anticipation. Yes, I called it my pussy. She's practically purring and demanding to be stroked.

Jake obliges, his hand leaving my breast and trailing slowly down my stomach to caress me through my panties. I'm sucking his fingers so hard I almost choke and he removes them from my mouth. I suck in a breath of air and then gasp as he pinches my nipple between the two wet fingers, simultaneously strumming my purring pussy.

I start to move my hips against his hand.

"Jake," I gasp.

His mouth moves to mine, his body hard against me while his hand continues to strum.

"Come," he growls against my mouth. His hand is suddenly gone but before I can complain it's back, inside my panties this time. The music of our bodies intensifies.

His tongue slips deep inside my mouth as a finger does the same down below. His erection is hard on my leg but I'm too focused on the sensations flooding through me to think about anything but his hand, his mouth, his tongue. I come, a star burst of colour, a crescendo, my body spasming around his hand as I throw my head back and scream.

It's loud and long. I'm not sure what comes over me. I've never been a screamer.

Jake kisses me deep and slow as I come down from my high, his hands running up and down my body feather light.

"Ohmigod." It comes out on a breath as Jake pulls back to look at me. My heart is pounding and I think I'm going to float away. If this is how I feel just from his hands and mouth, I don't think I can handle anything else.

"I take it back," he says. "You're not adorable. You're smokin' hot."

I smile and it's big and lazy. And yet, I'm still turned on.

Jake is propped up on an elbow beside me, his face close, his gaze penetrating. His hand still strokes my body, circling my belly button, then low and gentle over my panties, back up my stomach, my sides, to my neck and then down again. I arch my back as his hand trails past my breast, in a shameless attempt to get his magic fingers to touch my nipples.

When this fails I stretch up to kiss him. He chuckles, deep and throaty, and pulls back slightly.

"Want something?" he asks.

The miscreant hand has reached my panties again and I snap my thighs open, then shut around it. For some reason I've forgotten I've got hands, but I don't need them.

"Gotcha." I smile.

"Now what are you going to do?" An eyebrow arches. He's leaning on one elbow, head propped on his hand, and I've got his other hand trapped so that means he can't touch me. But I can touch him.

My hand that's closest to him is wedged between us so I wriggle and stretch until my little finger touches his erection. I rub him through the soft denim of his jeans.

He sucks in a breath.

Emboldened, I turn my hand sideways so I can caress his full length. I wrap my hand around him and gently squeeze. He's huge, not that I have much to compare to, but still.

His head comes down on mine and he kisses me. This kiss is wild. We've finished with soft and playful, now it's time for something else.

Jake winds his leg around mine and slips the arm he's leaning on behind my head and then he flips us, so that I'm lying on top of him.

"Whoa." I wasn't ready for that.

"Undress me, Alex," Jake says. He's only wearing his jeans but I don't need to be asked twice. I move to the side and unzip them. He lifts his hips and pulls them down, underwear and all, so he is naked beside me. My eyes feast. He is all muscle and sinew and the most magnificent erection I have ever seen.

I run my fingertips along the length of him, and then repeat what he did to me. My fingers glide along his sculpted abdominals, up his chest to his neck and back down again. I make sure I touch his nipples on the way past, and they jump to attention just like his other bits.

I want to take him in my mouth but when I move my head in that direction he stops me.

"Up here," he says. "There's time for that later. Right now I want you to sit on my cock."

My core clenches at that, his word choice awakening something deep inside. I've never been one to like crudity, or dirty talk. Coming from Jake, in this moment?

It's hot.

Jake reaches over to the bedside table and pulls a condom from the drawer. He opens it, eyes never leaving mine, and grabs my hand to help slide it down his erection, slow and sure. He licks his lips and that's all it takes.

I kiss him and this time it's me who is in charge. I slip off my panties with one hand, tossing them in the direction of the dress. Then it's my tongue investigating his mouth, my hands on his erection, and my leg going across his stomach to straddle him. I break away from his mouth while I do this, needing to focus. My bare pussy touches his stomach and his muscles ripple, creating more sparks, as he half-sits to claim my mouth again.

I push him back down to the bed by his muscled shoulders, tearing my mouth away. I take a moment to savour the hard ridges of his abdominals on my bare skin. Then I raise myself up on my knees, position myself exactly right, and lower down slowly.

We both breathe in, deep, shuddering breaths. So good. It's almost too much at this angle.

I move, riding him at a pace that's both tantalising and excruciating. Our eyes are on each other and I can't look away. It's intense. He moves with me and threads his hands through mine. He half sits again to lick and suck on my nipples, first one and then the other. My excitement builds but I need more. I don't know what I need, but I need more.

Jake lies back and pulls me down to kiss me. His arms go behind me and he flips us, still connected, so that he is on top.

This. This is exactly what I need. He pumps inside me and hits that spot, over and over. His magic fingers find my clit and I feel the crescendo building. Jake is almost frantic, his hips buck wildly and he dips his head to my ear.

"Come, Alex. Come with me."

His words send me over the edge and I come. The stars blaze and the music crests and I soar. I have no control, a scream escaping once more. But Jake is ready for it this time and kisses me deep, swallowing my cry and making it his own.

We come together in a burst of light and sound.

I never knew it could be like this.

Jake buries his face in my neck as the orgasm recedes. And then he kisses me. This kiss is light and floaty. It's content and almost sleepy.

Jake wraps his arms around me and rolls to his back, tucking me into his side. The condom is dealt with quickly and efficiently, tied off and tossed in a bin I hadn't even noticed earlier. I'll have to remember to tell him I'm on the pill, have been for years thanks to the severe cramps I get when I'm not taking it.

He strokes my hair gently and runs his fingers down my side, my hip, and my thigh. It's soothing and my eyes grow heavy.

I'm almost asleep, but I could have sworn I heard him say something.

"Falling for you, Blondie." That's what it sounds like.

"I'm falling for you too," I whisper to myself.

The last thing I'm aware of is his lips on my forehead, curved in a smile.

26 STAND & FIGHT

"MAKE IT GO AWAY," I PLEAD. MY HEAD IS FIRMLY HIDDEN under the pillow as the cursed alarm clock bellows its morning greeting.

The bed dips and the noise stops so I relax.

Then an arm goes around my waist and I'm pulled into my own personal cocoon. Jake's breath is warm on my hair as he nuzzles me. My back is to his front, pressing in, and I'm reminded of how happy he is to wake up beside me. Although I think the morning happy is pretty standard for guys.

I roll to face him. His eyes open and he looks into mine from just centimetres away.

"Hi," I say. I feel strangely shy. I shouldn't after last night.

But I do.

"Hi yourself." Jake's voice is husky with sleep. His head dips to mine and he kisses me, morning breath and all. I forget about feeling shy as his lips move on mine. Gorgeous.

He pulls back to look into my eyes.

"We're doing this?" It's a question. "Because I really want to. Say you'll give us a shot, Alex."

I think of all the reasons I shouldn't.

We're working together. He's Dan's best mate. But most of all, I don't deserve him, not after what I did. I'm a bad person, a home wrecker, and if Jake ever finds out he won't want to be in the same room as me, let alone a relationship.

But I want to start over. I want to stop running and have a boyfriend, and friends, and yes, even family. I mean, I've got Dan if he ever wakes up, but maybe it's time to start mending bridges with my parents? I know they love me, even if mum is on my case every chance she gets.

It wasn't always that way. Before Nanna gave me her house we got on pretty well. Yes, I always felt like Dan was the favourite, and yes, the parental expectations used to weigh me down. Nanna's house was my escape route and I took it.

But maybe if I'd stayed we would have worked it out. Maybe it isn't too late now.

It's time to stand and fight.

An idea starts to form about how I might help Dan and win my parents back at the same time. If I sold Nanna's house, I could use the money to pay back the bank. And there would be no reason for Mum to hate me.

Jakes hand brushing my hair interrupts my thoughts.

"Alex? What do you say? Do you even want a boyfriend? I know you're smarter than me. I've never been to uni and you're way out of my league. Hell, you're prettier than me too."

I smile and shake my head. "You're very pretty for a guy."

He smiles back. "We can be good together. Don't you feel it?"

I nod. "I do," I say. "But let's get one thing straight. It's me who's not good enough for you. You're a good person, Jake. One of the best I know."

Jake frowns and looks like he's about to say something but I stop him.

I put my hand to his cheek and cup his jaw. "I feel it, Jake. It's not just you."

He grins big, like I just gave him the moon. "You just made my day, Blondie," he says. Then he gets playful and raises his arm, making a bicep. "I do have more muscles than you."

I shove at his chest and follow when he rolls to his back, straddling his waist and leaning down over him. My hair falls into his face but he doesn't seem to mind as our lips meet. Well, they would if there wasn't so much hair in the way. His hands flail, pulling strands out of our mouths and I giggle.

He flips us so I'm on the bottom and my hair is no longer a problem. Then he kisses me. The kiss is hot, his tongue in my mouth reminding me of last night. His hands are wandering, trailing up my side, my thighs, and they're almost at the best bit when I remember Bri. I freeze.

Jake's response is instant. His hands stop moving and he dips his head to my ear. "You okay?"

"I just remembered something. It's kind of important."

He kisses down my neck and then comes back up to my ear. "Can it wait?"

"Not really." I sigh and push at his shoulders. "I'm meant to be meeting Bri for a run."

"Now? Sure about that?" Jake keeps kissing me and for a moment I let him. I really don't want to leave this bed.

"Let me ring her real quick."

I grab my phone and dial Bri's number, doing my best to ignore Jake as he trails kisses down my arm and across my belly.

"Yo! Everything okay?" Bri sounds wide awake.

"Just checking to make sure you still want to run."

"I'm getting in the car right now. You're not bailing on me, are you?"

"No." A giggle escapes as Jake hits a ticklish spot and I slap my hand over my mouth.

"If you don't want to run with me just say so, no big deal."

"No, no, I do. I'm just having a moment." The kisses stop. Jake's hand snakes around my waist and he pulls me into him. He's still got the morning happy action going on.

"I thought you were ringing because you slept in. Caught up in a moment sounds a lot more interesting." I can hear the laugh in her voice. "I'd hate to interrupt. We can do this next week."

"Too late. The moment's gone now," I say. "Just give me fifteen minutes."

"See you soon, girlfriend." Bri hangs up and I roll onto my back so I can look at Jake. He's resting on his elbow looking down at me, his other hand reaching out to cup my hip. It's like he can't stop touching me and I crave it.

"Sorry, I've got to go. Believe me, I don't want to. But I can't stand Bri up twice in a row."

He flops onto his back and scrubs his hands through his hair, mussing it up and making me want to stay in this bed even more. But if I want to have friends I've got to be a friend, and that starts with going for a beach run when I said I would.

"We could be quick." He rolls onto his side and snuggles in to me, kissing my neck and making me shiver.

"I'm trying to be a good friend," I say. "And I'm already late. Rain check?"

Jake sighs dramatically. "I can see what it's like. You're my girlfriend for two minutes and you're ditching me already."

Jake's girlfriend. I like that. "I'll make it up to you," I promise.

I grab his head in both hands and kiss him lightly on the lips, a goodbye, see you later kiss.

He's not having it. Jake takes control quickly, kissing me deeply and thoroughly. My hands twist in his hair and I try to get closer to him. There's no way I'm leaving this bed now.

He finishes kissing me and pulls back slowly. Somehow we've ended up with him on top, his thigh wedged firmly between my legs, and my arms plastered around him. I make a soft sound of distress, not wanting to lose his mouth from against mine. He smiles, eyes alight with mischief.

"Take my ute," he says. "But tonight, Alex, you're mine."

27 FALLING FOR JAKE

"You know what day it is today?"

Bri and I are jogging along the headland path towards Lazybones Beach. It's a gorgeous morning and the sun is cresting the horizon. The sky is tinted pink and there's a stillness in the air, the smell crisp and clean. I love this time of day outside by the beach.

"What day?" Bri has barely raised a sweat. We're at that comfortable 'steady state' pace where you can still carry on a conversation.

"It's a week since I got back to town. This time last week..." I glance down at my watch. "...it's almost the exact time I met Jake for the first time."

"Is Jake the reason you were late this morning?" Bri rounds the corner to Lazybones just ahead of me.

Now that we're talking about Jake I feel shy. I haven't had a girlfriend for years, since school really. And even then I didn't have anyone I was super close to. I slow to a walk and change the subject. "Feel like doing some sand sprints?"

Bri heads to the boardwalk that leads down to the beach. She grins. "Do you need to burn off some excess tension? Seeing as how I interrupted your 'moment' earlier."

No avoiding it then. "You did interrupt. But I won't hold it against you." I smile. "Is it weird that Jake and I got together so quickly?"

"Do you believe in love at first sight?"

I shake my head. "No, I don't. But there's been a connection since the moment I laid eyes on him."

"Duh, that's what love at first sight is."

Maybe Bri's right. I've never been in love before. I've never felt anything even close to what I feel for Jake.

We hit the beach, sinking almost ankle deep in the dry white sand at the end of the boardwalk. It's hard going and my shoes are swamped in two steps.

"Hang on," I tell Bri. "I'm going barefoot."

I sit on the cool sand and remove my shoes and socks. Bri plonks down beside me.

"Maybe this wasn't a good idea." She stuffs her socks inside her shoes and sits them beside mine. "I usually stick to the walking track. Sand sprints kill your legs."

"Come on, it's good for you." I stand and hold out my hand to pull her to her feet. "Ready?"

We walk to the waterline, stopping just above the white foam deposited by the breaking waves. The wet sand will be a challenge to run on.

"Race you. Up to the big rock at the other end." Bri takes off before I can agree.

I sprint hard, trying to catch her. My arms pump and my legs burn. It's no use. She's way fitter than I am. I don't give up, pushing through until I reach the rock, my feet digging into the sand. I slow down and stop, gasping for air. My heart rate is through the roof.

Bri slaps me on the back. She's already caught her breath and is beaming. "Feels good, doesn't it?"

"Give me a minute," I gasp.

My breathing gradually settles and my heart rate calms down.

"Ready to go again?" Bri nods back the way we came.

"Yep." I take off, getting a head start. I can feel Bri on my heels and take it up a notch. I'm going flat out. Running, just for the sake of running. It feels good to push myself, to feel the strength in my body. To do something just for the joy of it.

And most of all, it feels good to know that I'm not running away from anything anymore. I'm making a stand here, in Tempest Beach. This is where I am now. And come hell or high water, this is where I'm staying.

Bri and I finish in a dead heat at our starting point.

I bend at the waist, hands on my knees, and suck in air.

"That's it, I'm done," I gasp.

"Me too." Bri's face is flushed. "We'll do more laps next time. Ready to head back?"

"Almost. Just give me a minute." I walk down to the water and splash into the shallows. The ocean is cool on my feet. Bliss. The waves run in, splashing my calves before retreating. My feet sink in the sand reminding me of a childhood game I played with Dan, trying to push each other over while our feet were stuck. Loser was the one who got submerged first. Usually me. Dan never took it easy on me just because I was a girl which was just the way I liked it. It made the rare victory even sweeter.

"The tide's coming in." Bri joins me. She puts her hand up to her eyes to shield them from the sun and points out to sea. "Look, dolphins!"

My gaze focuses as I'm pulled out of my memories. A pod of dolphins just past the breakers surfs the waves in, then circles back out to go again. Such graceful creatures, and they seem to be having fun. Enjoying the moment. I could learn something from them.

We stand silently for a couple of minutes just soaking in the beauty of Mother Nature at her finest.

"We're gonna have to get moving." Bri sighs.

"I'm glad I got to see that." I smile at her.

"Me too." She grins. "As good as being 'caught up in the moment'?"

"Almost," I reply. And, strangely, it's the truth.

We walk back to our shoes and scoop them up, walking barefoot up the boardwalk to the path. We take a seat at the top to brush the sand off our feet and put our shoes and socks back on.

"Truth time," Bri says. She finishes tying her shoe and stands, stretching her hamstring out on the seat. "About Jake."

It's time to say it out loud, to admit to my feelings. I might not be worthy, but I can't help that. I can only do my best. I'm not running anymore. For the first time in my life I'm exactly where I'm meant to be.

"I don't know about love at first sight," I tell Bri. "But I'm definitely falling for him."

28 NEW PLAN

It's mid-morning before I get a break to put my new plan into action.

I've decided to sell Nanna's house and to do that I've got to phone the real estate agent back up north. I'm dreading this call.

But I shouldn't have to deal with her. Her being Valencia, my old boss's wife. Or ex-wife maybe. Who knows what happened after I took off.

I suck in a deep breath and dial.

The receptionist answers and I let out a sigh of relief.

"It's Alexandria Vance. My property is rented through you guys," I say. "I'm looking to sell and want to talk to someone and get things moving."

I'm put on hold while she transfers me to Dean, the sales manager.

I've met Dean but don't know him well.

"How much do you want to list the property for?" Dean asks.

"I'm not sure," I say. I really should have been a bit more prepared.

"That's okay. I'll send through a proposal with some comparative sales so you can get a feel for the market." Dean is all business. "We can go from there."

"I want a quick sale. Can you get started straight away?" I want to get things moving.

"Sure," says Dean. "I'll email a contract with some suggested prices. If you sign it and send it back over the weekend we'll list it on Monday. We use electronic signatures to make it easy for you."

"That sounds good." I let out a breath.

"Is there anything else I need to know?" Dean asks.

"What about the tenant?" A family of four has been renting the house for at least five years.

"It will depend on what the lease says. Do you mind holding while I grab a copy?"

"All right." I stand up from the desk so I can pace while I wait. I'm only on hold around thirty seconds before the music cuts out.

"Ms Vance," a female voice hisses. I detect a level of sarcasm, and not the good kind. It's got to be her. "You've got a nerve phoning here."

Yep. It's her. She's not even in sales. Dean must have asked her about the lease, alerting her to my call. My stomach twists in knots.

"I'm waiting for Dean," I say. I'm going to be polite and professional, even if it kills me. "I didn't phone to talk to you."

"I bet you don't want to talk to me, you home-wrecking slut."

"You can't talk to me like that." My voice has a wobble. I'm either going to burst into tears or yell at her. I vote yell.

"I'll talk to you any way I please. After what you did." She's snarling. "Lose weight and go after someone else's man. I don't know how you can live with yourself."

"I didn't do anything. If you'd just take a minute to listen you'd know that." I'm not yelling but my voice is louder than normal.

Go me for not crying.

"You'd say anything. I know you were having an affair with my husband, you little bitch." Her voice drips venom and I'm really glad she's a long way away.

"Just a minute, Valencia. You've got it wrong." My throat is closing up and it's getting hard to talk. She's not getting more tears out of me. She's had enough already. I cried for most of the drive here the morning she made me leave. Was it really only a week ago?

"You don't get to use my name. I saw you. Laughing and flirting. He chose being there with you over spending time with me. He cheated, and he cheated with you."

It's true that Gavin and I got on well. We did. To me, it was just the normal camaraderie workmates enjoyed. Work is supposed to be fun, right?

"We were just having fun. It was perfectly innocent." He didn't even seem to notice my weight loss. His wife obviously did.

"So you admit something was going on."

That's it. I've had enough. I take a deep breath and speak loud and firm into the phone. "I did not sleep with your husband."

Silence at the other end. For a moment I think I've won, and she's hung up. I plonk back down in my chair with relief. Then she's back and she's screaming at me.

"I don't care if you had sex or not. An affair is an affair. Emotional, sexual, it doesn't matter. It's still *cheating*!" This last word is so loud I nearly drop the phone. I see red.

"You bitch! He was my boss! There's no way I'd have sex with him! And I've never even heard of an emotional affair!"

I disconnect and throw the phone on the desk. My hands are shaking and I bury my head in them. I'm obviously not going to win with her.

A throat clears at the door and I look up.

Jake.

"You heard that, huh?"

29 DON'T WORRY

Jake's face is grim. "I've never heard of an emotional affair either. Want to tell me about it?"

I shake my head. "Nope."

"You should talk to someone." He steps into the office and closes the door behind him. Then he takes a seat opposite me at the desk and waits.

The silence stretches and I feel the urge to fill it.

Damn, he's good.

"Apparently I had an emotional affair with my boss and broke up his marriage," I say.

"What the hell is an emotional affair?" Jake's words are clipped. He's angry. Is he angry with me?

"It means he talked to me at work. We had fun together. Hell, the whole team did, but she only focussed on me. Not sex." I clasp my hands together on top of the desk. "I would never."

"I know you didn't have sex with him. Got that part loud and clear. So why exactly did she think that?" Jake leans onto the desk, into my space. Maybe he's not angry with me then.

"She got me the job in the first place when I moved up there. My

Nanna's house is rented through the agency where she works. I guess I was a lot bigger then."

Jake nods but stays silent.

Encouraging. He's calmed down a notch.

"It was such a great job. The team is mostly my age and we had a lot of fun. All of us, not just me and the boss." I'm over-explaining but I can't seem to stop.

"I was rostered on a lot of nights with the boss but I didn't think anything of it. It suited my uni schedule and we got on well. He was my boss. End of story."

"How well did you get on? Are we talking about staying back for drinks after work? Going clubbing together? Hanging out at your house?" Jake lifts an eyebrow. "What exactly?"

"Nope, none of that stuff. We talked. He told me stuff he probably shouldn't have and maybe it was a bit odd. But I never really paid that much attention, you know?"

"What sort of odd stuff?" Jake's voice is conversational, any trace of anger gone. Maybe I was reading too much into his earlier reaction.

"About the business, the cash flow." I sigh. "I thought he was training me to manage the place. I learnt so much from him."

I tilt my head in thought.

"He talked about his kids sometimes. His daughter just had a baby and she's gorgeous. But that was just normal proud granddad stuff."

Jake frowns, then shakes his head. "Was he having problems with his marriage? Did he mention his wife at all?"

"No problems that I know of. He never talked about her. And he wasn't sleazy, nothing like that. He never even asked if I had a boyfriend or anything personal."

Maybe I was stupid, but I honestly didn't get any bad vibes from Gavin. It was all above board.

"You know what I think?" Jake reaches out and takes my hands in his. "I think the wife is insecure and she's overreacting. I don't think you did anything wrong."

"But I must have. I shouldn't have spent so much time with Gavin, trying to soak up all his knowledge. It's easy to see how it could be misinterpreted."

"Blondie, whether he was teaching you about the business, talking about his grandkids, or having fun with you instead of his wife, that's on him. You have nothing to feel guilty about."

"His wife definitely blamed me. She still does. That night, she sat at the bar and watched us. She'd never done that before. I hardly even recognised her, it was years ago she told me about the job. I mean, it was just a normal night. I definitely did not flirt with him. We were a good team and I thought we were friends. I treated him like I treat Dan."

"Did he see you as a little sister?"

"I thought so. But she made a huge scene at the end of the shift. It was two in the morning. She accused me of losing weight to steal her man and told me to leave. Gavin fired me on the spot, said it was the only way to save his marriage. And I just ran, straight back to Dan. My real big brother."

I hang my head, letting my hair fall forward to hide my face. "So now you know my secret. How I ended up here."

Jakes eyes are serious. "I think you've got a case for unfair dismissal. Especially seeing as her claims are unfounded."

"What? No. I don't want to go down that path." It's silly, but I'm too cut up about it. "I still don't believe he took her side." I shrug. "I guess he didn't have any choice if he wanted to save his marriage."

"There's always a choice, Alex. Always."

"Maybe." My voice is noncommittal and I can't meet his eyes.

"I think you need a hug." Jake stands and steps around the desk towards me with his arms out wide. "Come here."

I stand and step into his arms then put my head on his chest. I breathe deep as his arms tighten around me and my hands wind their way around his back. I snuggle in and enjoy the sensation of warmth, of being looked after, loved.

Because Jake treats me like I'm worth loving.

And I've already decided, I'm not running away anymore.

'Don't worry," Jake says into my hair. "We'll figure it out."

LATER THAT AFTERNOON, Dean emails the promised details with an apology that we got 'cut off'.

Yeah, right.

There's been a few recent sales in the area and he gives me some options. The price point to sell quickly versus higher price which might take a while to achieve, but is 'doable', and the highest price which could take up to a year to move the property. He recommends the middle price but I go with the lowest one. I need a quick sale.

It's surprisingly easy and it feels like the right thing to do. Maybe I'll be sad later. But for now I'm just glad to be able to do something to help Dan.

30 BEER STORMING

"Knock off time." Jake sticks his head into the office where I'm deep in reports. "You ready to grab a beer?"

"You got a minute?" I ask. "I need to talk to you about something."

"Sure." Jake comes in and sits down opposite me, leaning back in the chair and stretching one ankle over the opposite knee.

"I've managed to get some figures out for the business." I hand him the profit and loss statement from Xero. "It's bad, Jake. Real bad. I'm not really sure how he's been able to keep the doors open."

Jake leans forward to take the report and studies it intently. He lets out a low whistle.

"I'm guessing that number at the bottom is meant to be positive, not negative," he says.

"Yep. I've printed the cash report so we can see what's actually come in and what's gone out. As you can see there's a lot more gone out than came in."

Jake nods. "I can see that. Where has all the money gone?"

"That's actually not the important question. I mean sure, the expenses are high and I can see a lot of things that he might have overspent on."

"Like the paint room?"

"Yes, like the paint room. But the important question is, where is all the income?"

I hit the print button and then grab the second report off the printer.

"This is the normal profit and loss report. It shows what we've invoiced, regardless of whether it's been paid or not." I point to the revenue figure. "I expected the income to be higher than the other cash report now that I've sent invoices for all the jobs that were done but not billed."

"And is it?" asks Jake.

"It is. But the number at the bottom," I point to the bottom line, "is still a negative."

Jake scrubs his hands through his hair. "This is bad, Alex. What are we going to do?"

"I know. I was hoping you might have some ideas."

"You know what we need?" Jake grins, even though this is definitely not a time for smiling. "We need beer-storming."

"Beer-Storming?"

"Brain storming, but with beers and buddies."

"I don't know," I say. "But I'm not getting anywhere sitting here on my own and trying to figure it out."

Jake stands and holds out his hand. "Let's go."

WE END up at the pub. Of course. Jake spent a few minutes on his phone to gather up the crew for the 'beer-storming' session.

Jake hooks his arm around my shoulders and pulls me into his side as the others start arriving. Tom gets there first, minus the girl-friend. Baz arrives with Clance and Elise. They were all at the dojo when Jake called. Suze will be late as she's still at work.

The waitress comes over and Jake orders beers all round.

"Thanks for coming, guys." Jake is sounding way too serious for a drink at the pub and the others exchange glances.

"What's going on?" asks Tom, voicing the question in all their eyes.

"We've got a problem," Jake says.

"You're not pregnant are you, mate?" asks Baz. He laughs at his own joke.

"Nah, mate. Be serious for a second would you?" Jake's tone says it's not the time for jokes.

"Yeah, yeah. Don't get your knickers in a knot." Baz gestures around the table, taking everyone in. "With the brains trust here there's nothing we can't sort out."

Jake looks to me and nods.

"It's Dan's business," I say. "It's in trouble and I, we, are trying to come up with ways to bring in more money. We need an income boost and it's got to be sustainable in the long term."

"What makes you think it's in trouble? I thought Dan was travelling all right," says Tom.

"Appearances can be deceiving, mate," says Jake. "Alex has spent the last week getting the books up to date. It was a bit of a mess. She's done a good job."

My face grows hot at his words. It's nice to be appreciated. Especially when he was saying he didn't need me a week ago. I don't spoil the moment by pointing that out. See, I can be tactful.

"The paperwork was all over the place. Jobs not billed, customers not being followed up for payment." I look to Jake for confirmation it's all right to talk this frankly to his mates.

"It won't go outside this booth," says Tom, interpreting my look correctly. "Right guys?"

The others all nod in agreement. I take a deep breath.

"The bank wants to shut him down. I've got a deadline and I'm hoping we can turn it around before then and buy Dan some more time. There's going to be a business for him when he wakes up, no matter what."

"So how can we help?" Clance asks. Ever practical.

"Yeah, can we do, like, a Go-Fund-Me page?" Elise speaks up for the first time. "Or a bar-b-que fundraiser?"

"That might help if there's medical costs." I hadn't even thought about that. "But what we really need is ideas to boost the business income. We need other revenue streams, ones that don't need a big investment up front." I look at Jake again. "Jake thought you guys might have some ideas."

There's silence and I have a sinking feeling in the pit of my stomach. This was a bad idea.

Then Tom starts talking.

"The most obvious thing is to get some big contracts," he says. "Approach some of the big companies in town to do the maintenance on their fleets."

"That's a great idea." Baz nods in agreement. "I know a bloke over at the council. I can talk to him and find out what the process is. They probably put it out to tender."

"What about the taxi company?" asks Elise.

"And the bus companies," says Clance.

"Okay, good ideas. I'll start making some calls on Monday," Jake's eyes crinkle at the edges and he almost smiles.

"Hi guys, what did I miss?" Suze breezes in and plonks herself down in the chair at the end of the booth. We fill her in and immediately her face lights up.

"I've got the best idea," she says. "Jake should run classes. Basic car maintenance for chicks. Remember when you broke down, Alex?"

She says it like it was ages ago. "Last week, how could I forget?"

"Yeah, and wasn't it because you didn't do all that maintenance stuff you're meant to do?"

"I did so!" I glare at Jake. "Did you tell everyone that?"

He holds his hands up. "Whoa, not me. But it's pretty obvious if your car breaks down you're not looking after it. Just about everything that can go wrong with a vehicle can be fixed before it actually breaks. If you're getting it serviced and checking 'stuff'." He makes inverted commas with his fingers.

"My point exactly," says Suze. "And how are we meant to know what 'stuff'," she does air quotes too, "we're meant to check unless someone teaches us?"

"You'd get a lot of ladies showing up just because it's you, Jake." Elise chimes in.

"All right, it's a good idea," I admit. "I'd do a class if Jake took it."

The waitress comes over with another jug of beer. "What classes?" she asks.

"Basic car maintenance," says Clance. "Would you be up for that, Stella?"

"I'd be up for any class Jake took," Stella purrs. Then she bursts out laughing. "Sorry, couldn't resist. But sure, I'd do car maintenance. A lot of my friends would too."

"Great idea, Suze," says Tom. Suze smiles at her big brother.

"You need to get on Face Book," says Elise. "I don't think Dan ever did a business page. You could have a car problem of the week, and post tips on car maintenance. People would like that. And some of them would want to know more and would sign up for your class. Easy."

"I can do that," I say. "We'll run the class after work so it's convenient for people. Maybe run it for six weeks. What do you think?"

There's nods and agreement all round but Jake is silent.

"Jake?" I ask.

"I'd do it, but I don't know if people would come." He's shaking his head.

"Do the Face Book page first," Suze says. "We'll get everyone on board to Like the page and see if there's any interest. Then when the course starts you can use Face Book to let people know."

Elise chimes in. "You can even have a signup form online and if you don't get enough takers then you don't run it."

"You could do flyers for the community notice board," says Baz. "The oldies like that. You should advertise in the newspaper too."

"New contracts and a course, even the Go-Fund me, they're all long term ideas," I say. "They're good, but we need something to bring in cash now. They say you should get your existing customers to buy more from you but I don't want to put the prices up, and I'm not sure what else we can sell."

"Car parts," says Jake.

We all look at him.

"Isn't putting the parts in the cars your job?" Baz asks. "Why would you want to sell people parts to do it themselves?"

Jake smirks. "Smart-arse. Not normal car parts, vintage parts. They're hard to source and car nuts spend a lot of money on them. I'd know."

"If they're hard to source, how will you find stock?" asks Tom. Ever practical.

"I've got some contacts from restoring the Chev. I found parts all over the place. I was thinking if we could act as a one stop shop and locate parts for the cars, people would really go for that. Usually when they want a bit they want it straight away. I think they'd pay a bit extra so they didn't have to research it and dig it up themselves."

"You can set up a website," says Elise. "And drop ship."

We all look at her.

"What?" She's turned a bright red. "I've been looking into it for the dojo. I want to sell martial arts gear as a side business and Grandfather has given me a free run with it."

"It's a great idea," I say. "And good on you."

"You need to lift the business profile," Elise says. "Getting active on Face Book will help. Other social media as well. And do up some leaflets, offer people a deal."

"We already do special deals for the pensioners," I say. "It was one of the things sending Dan broke."

"That's not good," says Tom. "What have you done about it?"

"Pensioner Tuesday," says Jake. He listened to me. "We'll keep giving the oldies a discount on their work. Same as has been happening, but quarantined to a Tuesday."

"That's a great idea," says Baz. "You can promote the shit out of it. You'll have them booking you out for weeks in advance."

"It's good PR, too," says Elise. "Taking what you already do and re-packaging it. Genius."

"I know!" says Suze. "You could get the Scouts to come and have a car wash one afternoon. You've got all that car park out front. It would bring people in, and all the Scouts and their families would come to you to get their cars serviced because they know you. Plus, you're doing a good deed, helping them fundraise."

"I think we've done well," I say. "Let's have a toast to Dan's business success."

A chorus of 'cheers' comes from around the booth and everyone is grinning.

"Another successful beer-storming session," Jake says in my ear. "You're one of gang now. Beer-storming is like a rite of passage."

I get that warm fuzzy feeling inside. Like I belong.

And I just know that we can save Dan's business. If only we have enough time.

31 DELIBERATE

"I NEED TO GO AND SEE DAN,"

The night at the pub ended up being a late one.

After our beer-storming we had dinner together and hung out, playing pool and drinking more beer. It was a good night.

We came home and went straight to bed, no hanky panky. Too tired and happy drunk.

This morning was another matter altogether. I woke up with Jake wrapped around me and doing the most amazing things with his magic fingers and then with his mouth and then with his other parts. It all ended too soon. I really could have spent all day in bed with him.

But duty calls.

"I'll drive you." Jake looks up from the stove where he's cooking me breakfast. I could really get used to this. "I want to see him too."

We get to the hospital just after ten. Clance is walking out as we arrive. Guess he's an early bird.

There's still no change. Dan's not looking any better and if anything he's a bit worse for wear. He's still unconscious lying on his back, bandaged and plastered up, with the drip in his arm. The flowers on the bedside table have been replaced by some balloon art but the soccer ball is still there, slightly sooty. He looks thinner, but I guess he hasn't had any solid food a while. It's Saturday, so it's unlikely we'll get any updates until the weekend is over.

We're in and out of the hospital in less than fifteen minutes. It's beginning to feel like a habit. Not one that I want to get used to.

"Where to now?" Jake looks at me, his eyes obscured by his dark sunglasses.

I'm not sure if he's messing with me or not. It's not like I expect him to chauffeur me around all day. But if he's offering, then there's one more place I need to go.

In light of the whole 'I'm not running anymore' decision, it's time. I need to talk to my parents.

"HI, AUNTY JOY," I say when the front door opens.

"Alex!" Aunty Joy pulls me in for a hug and then holds me at arm's length, taking me in. "About time you got around to see me. You're looking well, come in, come in."

Jake clears his throat from behind me.

"You know Jake?" I ask.

"Of course, hi Jake." She leans in to me and whispers confidentially. "Jake's very good with his hands, isn't he?"

My face burns and I blink. I can't believe she said that. Aunty Joy bursts out laughing.

"I'm talking about what he can do with an engine. Not whatever you're obviously thinking about." She grabs my arm and bustles me into the house. "So, you two are an item?"

A shriek comes from further within the house followed by a boy's voice yelling "give it back". A thundering of feet and a little girl of two or three bursts through the doorway from the lounge room and grabs me around the legs. The baby, not actually a baby any more. She's clutching an iPad.

"Save me, save me," she yells.

"Mum! Tell her to give it back!" A teenage boy screeches to a halt just in front of us.

Their mother crouches down beside me and gently disengages the little girl from my legs.

"Sally," she says firmly. "You know you can't take Mikie's things."

"It's Mike, Mum," the teenager says gruffly. His fists clench at his sides and he's breathing heavily, obviously trying to get himself under control after chasing his little sister.

"Hey, Mike," I say. He's really shot up in the four years I've been gone and I'd probably walk straight past him in the street. He nods at me, but doesn't say anything.

Sally begins to cry. "He won't play with me. I want him to play Twister and he won't."

"Why don't you come and have a cup of milo and a cookie?" Aunty Joy ruffles her hair and wipes the tears away. She scoops the little girl up in her arms, snagging the iPad at the same time and handing it to Mike. Sally starts to struggle.

"Put me down, I'm a big girl."

"She's obsessed with Twister at the moment," Aunty Joy says to Jake and I. We follow her into the open plan dining area, separated from the kitchen by a breakfast bar, then she puts the little girl back on the floor.

"Hi Sally," I say, crouching down. I feel ashamed of myself for not making the effort to meet the latest addition to the clan before now. She was born while I was away but that's no excuse. "I'm Alex. Your Great Aunt."

I look up at Aunty Joy. "Is that right? Am I her Great Aunt?"

"Cousin, actually," says a voice from behind me.

I stand up. My heart starts to race as I turn around.

"Hi, Mum."

I TAKE a step in and give my mum a hug. She's stiff and reluctant.

How did it come to this? I remember when I was little I used to love Mum's hugs. They could fix anything. Sore knee, busted toy, broken arm. By the time I needed hugs to fix broken hearts we weren't getting on so well. Not that I had a lot of broken hearts, just one.

Neil Farnsworth in Year Ten. We went out together for a whole term before he dumped me for the new girl who moved in next door to him. I was devastated. I swore off boys and really, I haven't had a serious boyfriend since then. I've dated, had a couple of hook-ups at uni, but on the whole I've been focused on my end game. Get through uni, earn my degree, get some experience and then, when I'm ready, open my own little tea shop.

Aunty Joy is the reason I take my tea so seriously. Ever since I had my first cup of tea with her as a little girl, I've wanted to host tea parties. The dream grew from there.

My job at the restaurant was great experience and all those conversations with my old boss, Gavin, about business and cash flow and ordering and staff, well, I learnt a lot from him. I can't wait to get the chance to run my own show and put it all into action.

It was in high school that I really started to feel the pressure and judgement from my mother. Dan was the golden-haired boy. He could do no wrong and Mum just glowed when she talked about him. Me, not so much.

It was like I was never good enough. It didn't help that I wouldn't do the 'girly' stuff, like cooking and sewing. Mum has very strong views on what a woman should do, and being a good wife and mother is at the top of the list. Old fashioned doesn't begin to cover it.

I like clothes and makeup, getting dressed up and feeling good about myself. But that's as far as it goes with the girly stuff. I'm not looking for a man to make my life complete and I'd rather stand on my own two feet than depend on anyone else for anything.

University was the breaking point. I had my heart set on going and Mum and Dad didn't want me to. I think it was partly the cost. I always knew I'd have to pay my own way. But the main reason was my mother's attitude. She wanted me to stay home and settle down. Find a 'nice boy'. Produce offspring. The circle of life.

But then Nanna passed away and left me her house in the city. It gave me the means to escape and I took it. I ran. The day after I finished high school I left home and didn't look back. I got a job in the city and saved every cent to pay my way at uni. It was tough, but I did it. I haven't relied on anyone except myself for the past four years.

I think if Nanna was still alive she would be proud of me. If she hadn't died she would have let me stay in her house anyway, most likely, but having that asset behind me gave me a sense of security that I wouldn't have had otherwise.

I step back from Mum and look closely at her.

"How are you, Mum? You're looking a bit better than last time we saw you."

She shrugs and shakes her head. "Can't complain."

Uncle Bob walks into the room and drapes an arm over Aunty Joy's shoulders.

"Alex, Jake." He inclines his head in our direction.

Mum takes this distraction as an opportunity to walk away. She goes into the kitchen and starts filling the kettle.

"I've got that, you go talk to Alex," Aunty Joy says. She shrugs Uncle Bob's arm off her and goes into the kitchen, taking the kettle from Mum. "Table, go. You sit and talk. You too, Bob." She shoos Jake, Bob and I towards the dining table as well.

We all obey. The silence quickly becomes uncomfortable once we're all seated. Uncle Bob is the first to break.

"Did you hear about the fire? Looks like it was deliberately lit," he says. "That's confidential information, of course. We're still looking for the person responsible. But I thought you should know."

Well, that sure broke the ice.

"Who would do something like that?" Mum asks, her eyes wide.

"We suspect it's got something to do with that nasty business your brother got himself mixed up in." Bob's eyes drill into me as if he thinks that I've got something to do with it too. I feel guilty and I've done nothing wrong.

"Not sure what you mean, Bob," says Jake.

Well, there is creepy guy and his threats. I haven't told anyone about that and now is probably not the time to come clean. Is it? If this escalates then we might all be in danger.

But he hasn't actually done anything except wave some words around. I'd be making a big drama out of nothing and I don't want to worry Mum and Dad.

Bob sighs. "I was hoping Alex or yourself might know something about it. This isn't an official question, but if there's anything at all you can tell me that might shed some light on it you should tell me now."

Bob's eyes haven't left me and I think he can see me shrink into myself.

"We will. Apart from the break-in I can't think of anything." Jake frowns. "Nothing was stolen, but we've added extra security just in case. There was a shifty looking guy hanging around."

"Let me know if you see anything else." Bob's flinty stare moves to Jake. "Or if you find out what Dan's into."

"All right then." Aunty Joy bustles over with a plate loaded high with home baked cookies which she places in the centre of the table. She scoops up little Sally and plonks her on Uncle Bob's lap.

Sally stretches for a biscuit but can't quite reach. Uncle Bob leans forward and snags it for her. "Here you go, sweetie," he says.

He's a different man when he's in dad mode and the subject of the fire is dropped. Aunty Joy brings over cups and saucers, sugar, a jug of milk and finally a big china teapot. Bliss.

Sally has Milo in her tea cup and she sits up tall so she can dunk her cookie.

I lean into Jake. "I learnt to drink my tea just like that, perched on my dad's knee at Aunty Joy's house. Ever since then I've wanted to host tea parties."

"She was so little," my aunt says, pouring the tea into our cups before she sits down. "But she wanted to join in so badly. We let her have her own special cup and saucer."

I raise my cup in a salute to Jake. "I still use it every time I come here."

"That explains why you like your tea so much." Jake smiles.

"I want to open a cool little tea shop one day. Somewhere with those octagonal window nooks, like Frankie's dress shop downtown. I'd put in tables and chairs for the customers and they can just soak up the view with their tea and cake. I'll have all the different types of tea and do tasting nights.

"There'll be a corner with a display about the different tea growing regions and what makes each one special. And beautiful cups and saucers and teapots so people can enjoy the full experience. I'll do high teas for special occasions, birthdays and baby showers." I sigh, picturing it all in my head. "That's the dream, anyway. When I've got the time and money."

"I'll come and have a cuppa with you, Blondie. Anytime, anywhere."

The conversation flows easily now Aunty Joy is at the table. My dad has wandered in and even Mum loosens up and joins in.

The other kids, all boys, buzz in for cookies and drinks but don't hang around. It's a nice way to spend an afternoon but I still haven't achieved what I came here to do, which is engage my mother in a conversation. A real conversation, a heart-to-heart, even. I take a deep breath. It's time.

"The insurance won't cover us if the fire was deliberately lit, will it, Dave?" Mum is talking to Dad, but her voice carries and all other conversation stops.

"We'll have to wait and see," Dad says.

"It's unlikely," Uncle Bob says at the same time.

"We might have to go back to renting again." There's a hitch in her voice.

"We've done it before, Shirl. We can do it again." My dad scoots his chair closer to Mum's and puts his arm around her. She leans into him.

"Worst case I go back to work fulltime." Dad has been semi-retired for a while now, working three days a week.

"I know," Mum says finally. "I can get a job too if I have to. We've just got to remember how lucky we are to be alive."

Now is definitely not the time. I don't want to upset her even more. Maybe I don't need to have a conversation with her after all? Maybe we'll just slip into a nice, easy mother-daughter relationship. Yeah, right.

"That reminds me," Aunty Joy says. "Bev from church said to bring you down to the opportunity shop. They've had a new shipment come in."

"The church has been really good to us." Mum is talking to me. "They opened the opportunity shop and let us choose all the clothes we wanted. They even threw in brand new underwear." Mum smiles. "Thank goodness."

I smile back. "Second hand underwear would have been pretty gross."

Inside I'm feeling like I've been slapped in the face, and I deserved it. Mum and Dad have lost everything and I haven't given a second thought to whether they've even got clothes to wear. Which has to take priority over the warm fuzzies of 'getting on better'. I'm such a bad daughter. The moment for my deep and meaningful has gone anyway. It's not going to happen today.

I push back from the table and stand up. After gathering all the empty cups, I take them into the kitchen and put them in the sink.

"Don't you wash up. That's what the dishwasher is for," Aunty Joy says. "And packing it is one of Mike's chores."

Mike is at the table with his hand on another cookie. He groans dramatically at his mother's words. Then he trudges into the kitchen and starts packing the dishes away. They're good kids.

Aunty Joy never wanted kids when I was younger but once she

changed her mind she went all in. I don't think I'd be able to cope with four kids, especially twins. But she makes it look easy.

Who knows? Maybe one day that will be me.

I wonder if Jake and I had kids would they have his hair?

I give myself a mental shake. Too soon to think about that, Alex. Even if Jake does have great hair.

32 VINTAGE

"So, that was a bust." I sigh. Jake and his great hair and I are at the beach grabbing burgers and chips for lunch. The sun is shining, the sky is a brilliant blue, and the sand looks inviting. It's a perfect Saturday afternoon.

"What do you mean?" Jake stakes a claim at one of the big wooden tables, timing it perfectly as a family gets up to leave.

"I didn't get to have my D and M with Mum."

"Deep and meaningful?" Jake shakes his head. "You'll get your chance, don't rush it."

He's right so I don't argue and we settle into a companionable silence while we eat. Surfers are visible out off the point. Closer to us, the breakers are rolling in and the surf patrol is doing their thing. There are heaps of people swimming between the flags. Makes me wish I brought my swimmers.

"What do you want to do now?" Jake scrunches his burger wrapper into a ball and pegs it carelessly at the bin. Perfect shot. Is he good at everything? "Cos if you've got nothing on, the Chev is ready to take for a spin."

My eyes widen. "Seriously? I thought it was weeks off being finished."

Jake grins. "The final part came in this week. She's running smooth and I want to take her for a test run. I thought we could go for a drive up the coast road, take the scenic route to Diamond Head."

"I thought you'd want to go inland." I smile so he knows I'm teasing. "You know, so you don't get any salt spray on the car."

Jake mock gasps, his hand on his heart. "Are you saying I wouldn't wash her and polish her after I get her home? I always look after my girls, Alex. If you don't know this, then I haven't been doing a very good job with you."

He leans across and swats my hair playfully. "I've been doing my best. You have to tell me if I need to try harder."

"Oh, you're good all right." I fan myself as I flash back to this morning. "Real good." I lower my voice to a sexy purr, then burst out laughing. "Come on, let's go take the Chev for a spin before I ask you to look after me right here."

Jakes eyes go dark and he leans in. His hand goes to my hair and his mouth comes to mine, kissing me long and deep. When he pulls back he leans his forehead against mine.

"You're killing me," he says, voice low and gravelly.

A seagull picks that moment to swoop in and land on the end of the table. It hops toward us, eyeing the leftover hot chips.

"I think that's a hint." Jake's voice is back to normal as he pulls away. He stands and takes the rest of our rubbish, scattering the last of the chips on the grass. The seagulls swoop in, the one on the table leading the flock.

Jake walks to the bin with a sexy swagger. I could watch his backside all afternoon. He turns around after depositing the rubbish and catches me, a slow smile lighting his face.

'Gotcha', his look says.

And he does. He has me heart and soul, and I never want to let him go.

WE DRIVE BACK to the workshop and swap cars. I dash upstairs for a quick bathroom break. I put my bikini on under a pair of denim shorts and an old Rip Curl singlet top, in case we end up going for a swim. Jake comes out of the bedroom wearing boardies and a sleeveless muscle shirt so we're obviously on the same wavelength.

The Chev is a lot of fun to drive. It's a ute for starters, so there's fantastic visibility. The seats are leather and it's a bench seat which means I can sit as close to Jake as I want. Maybe we'll snuggle up together later, but for now I sit by the window in the passenger seat and get comfy.

Surprisingly, despite its retro look, it's got Bluetooth and Jake hooks his phone up so he can play his music.

"Tell me about the car," I say. It's obviously his pride and joy, and despite knowing nothing about cars I want to show an interest.

Jakes eyes light up.

"She's special. She's got new suspension with a CPP front disc-brake upgrade kit and a new booster, master cylinder and two inch drop spindles. I've lowered and tuned her to give her a better ride and handling. The engine's a four bolt Chev 454ci big block and it's all been redone. There's an Edelbrock carb and intake manifold... and, I've lost you, haven't I?"

"No, no, keep going." I smile mischievously. "It's sexy how you talk about your car like it's alive."

"I'm just getting to the good part."

"The good part?" I roll my eyes. "Let's hear it."

"The good part is the two point five inch custom TIG-welded exhaust system. It's a work of art. And," he smiles. "The transmission's got a 2400 RPM stall converter. Useful when you're driving in busy traffic."

I look around and wave my hand at the empty road. "Like this?"

"Exactly." Jake grins and pats the seat beside him. "Get over here. You can test out my bench seat."

"I think the bench seat is the best bit." I undo my seatbelt, slide over to the middle and re-buckle. "And I love the colour." It's two toned, sky blue roof, bonnet and tonneau cover and a soft cream bottom.

Jake shakes his head. "That would be right. Surrounded by all this superb machinery and you like the leather seat and the colour."

I shrug. "What can I say? I've got simple tastes."

JAKE DRIVES with one arm resting on the window sill and the other on the steering wheel. It's such a macho pose I can't help but laugh.

"What?" he asks.

I shake my head. "Just you. And your arm. Can you be any more of a guy?"

Jake flicks his eyes to me, then back to the road. He moves the hand resting on the door to the steering wheel. Then he moves the hand that was on the steering wheel to my knee. "Is that better?"

Butterflies tumble in my stomach at his touch. I smile. "Yeah," I say. "That's better."

We wind our way down the coast road, Jake's eyes on the road and his hand on me. It moves slowly up my leg towards my gooey centre. The butterflies are doing cartwheels now.

I have no choice.

I put my hand on *his* leg and start sliding it closer to his not so gooey centre. Two can play at that game. His hand stops mid-thigh and his other hand clenches the steering wheel. My little finger brushes his erection through his jeans.

"Fuck," Jake mutters. "You're killing me."

I smirk. "You started it."

His hand moves again, slipping right up the inside leg of my shorts and touching my panties. He presses lightly with the side of his hand and I gasp. My fingers clench the muscle of his thigh, all play-fulness forgotten. He twists his hand so he cups me and those magic fingers lightly touch a sensitive spot.

"Oooooh." I can't stop the sound that escapes me. I lift my hips a little, hoping he won't notice, and press my legs together to keep his hand right there. We stay suspended like that for long seconds, and then I roll my hips into his hand ever so slightly. I can't help it.

Jake growls. He rips his hand away from me, grabbing the steering wheel with both hands and wrenching it sideways. We careen down a shady dirt track until we're out of sight of the highway and he jams on the brakes. The car stops and he opens his door, grabs my hand, and pulls me out the driver's side with him. He drags me around to the back of the car and picks me up by the waist, sitting me on the hard tonneau cover. He moves into me. His mouth descends on mine, his hands wrapping in my hair. My legs wind around his waist and I kiss him back. It's wild, it's hungry, and it quickly gets out of control.

He breaks away from my mouth and kisses his way along my jawbone to my ear. "You're smokin'," he tells me.

I murmur something incoherent in response as his mouth descends down my neck. His thumb strokes my nipple and then his mouth is there, kissing me through my singlet. He pushes my top up and the kisses trail lower over my stomach. I wrap my hands in his hair, holding tight.

Jake puts gentle pressure on my stomach, pushing me backwards to lie on the tonneau cover, my head and back supported by his arm. My legs are still wrapped around him but move to his shoulders when he lays me down. His mouth, that magic mouth, lowers until it is right there, putting delightful heat and pressure on that sensitive spot through the denim shorts.

My legs curl around his head, pulling him in. I'm so lost in the bliss that I don't notice he has my shorts unbuttoned and unzipped until he starts tugging them down, lifting his head to manoeuvre better, and I feel the cold metal on my bottom. He hooks one knee and slips my leg up and out of the shorts. The air hits me, in a place that has never been exposed to raw sunshine before.

"Jake," I say. I don't know whether to stop him or help him. It feels so good and it's going to get better. But we're outside where anyone could see us.

"Ssh." He puts a finger to my mouth and I suck it in. How did he know that was just what I needed?

My shorts and panties are hanging off the other leg and Jake's free hand drags them to my foot and off, tossing them up over my head. His mouth dips right to the heart of me.

For a moment he just rests there, all breath and heat, and my heart lurches. The tingles are off the charts. His hand is on my bottom and he squeezes gently. He has my total attention. Between his hand and his mouth, I'm too scared to move lest he thinks I'm trying to pull away. I think I could live in this position forever.

Then he starts kissing me. There. I've never been kissed there before and if you told me my first time would be outside on the back of a ute I would have told you to stop dreaming. I'm not that kind of girl.

I would have been wrong. I'm totally that kind of girl.

He kisses me there like he would my mouth. His mouth and tongue move on me, licking, sucking, and nibbling. My legs wrap around his head tighter and my hands clench and unclench at my side. His finger is still in my mouth and I suck on it frantically. He slips another finger inside my mouth and at the same time sucks my clit. My hips jerk violently and I gasp. Then his fingers withdraw from my mouth and I lift my head chasing them. They go to my nipple and tweak. Between that and his tantalising mouth I feel like I'm about to explode.

His hand on my bottom moves, a finger sliding inside me. His tongue laps at my clit and I can feel the crescendo building.

"Jake." I grab his hair and start pulling frantically, desperate to get his mouth to mine. "I need you."

He lifts his head and his eyes have gone dark. He leans up to kiss me, an arm moving behind my neck and the other going to my waist. I'm frantic and my fingers fumble at his waistband. I try to untie the drawstring on his board shorts but then start just shoving.

He pulls me upright, tight against him, and finally helps get rid of those boardies. At last I can touch him.

I slide down his body. I guide him into me and let out a sigh as we fit together. Arms, legs, wrapped around him, locked tight. His arms tight around me and the feel of him inside me, filling me up. Home. This feels like home.

And then he starts moving, rocking against me, his lips still on mine. The music swells and I'm frantic again. I buck and his hand goes between us, producing magic. I'm going to burst.

"Jake," I gasp.

"Come, Alex, come with me," Jake says. His hips are pumping and then he tenses and we explode together. Nothing compares to this feeling I have with Jake, right here, right now.

I'm never going to let him go.

"Never letting you go either," Jake says in my ear.

I'm not even embarrassed that I said that out loud.

With a sudden roar of its engine noise a car zooms past us, stirring up dust. Music blares, the windows are down and the car is full of guys and girls a couple of years younger than me. High schoolers, still on their P plates. The horn honks and there's cheers and catcalls. 'Get a room', and 'put on some pants'.

Jake presses my head into his shoulder and holds me close. He's shaking, laughing I realise. His body hides me from sight but the carload of kids would have had a fantastic view of Jake's backside. Lucky them. It's pretty obvious what we've been doing. I melt in closer to him, too blissed out to care.

The music fades into the distance as the car keeps driving. Thank goodness.

"Well," says Jake. "I guess we better put on some pants."

33 TICK TOCK

Sunday morning I borrow Jake's ute so I can hit the beach for an early morning run.

Our Saturday night had been tame compared to our afternoon, the frantic edge missing. We took our time, savouring each other. More sexy times followed this morning, early. I didn't want to leave our bed, but when Jake mentioned he was missing a planned martial arts session I made the snap decision to go for a run while he trained. I'm not going to be responsible for him losing his edge.

The beach is glorious; I love early mornings. The clouds are tinged pink as the sun's first rays peek over the horizon. The air is cool, but not cold this time of year. Absolutely perfect.

My run has been magic. There aren't many people out, but there are a few. Joggers like me, and dog walkers. Even one pram walker, the baby's adorable cries making me smile, happy I'm not the one having to cope with that sort of stress.

I'm on the home straight, heading back to the ute, when I think I see the creepy dude. Actually there's no doubt. It's definitely the creepy dude.

He's sitting on one of the benches near where I parked and looking intently both ways up and down the path. When he sees me he smiles. And not in a good way. His smile doesn't meet his eyes.

I have a split second as I jog past to decide whether to stop as planned or keep going and run all the way home. But what harm can one creepy guy do? It probably isn't even me he was looking at, right? Right.

I pull out my phone as I slow to a walk and stop the timer on my running app. I take my usual finish line pic of the beach with the sun rising over it. Beautiful.

"Ms Vance," he calls. I'm tempted to ignore him; to pretend I didn't hear him. But manners are too firmly ingrained into me and I turn around to face him. He stands up from his bench and walks towards me. I keep fiddling with my phone, sliding the iPhone camera from photo to video and hitting record so that there'll be a record of this encounter if he tries anything. I really don't have a good feeling about it and am wishing I'd kept running. My heart is pounding. I try to act casual with the phone loose in my hand so he won't realise what I'm doing.

"How's your brother?"

Anyone else asking that question you'd think it was polite. Nice even. But not this guy. Coming from him it gives me chills. Goose bumps marching up and down my arms. I don't answer.

"I hear he hasn't woken up yet." Creepy dude is getting closer. He stops three steps away, far too close for my liking. "And that's a problem."

I still don't say anything and the man smirks. It scares the shit out of me.

"Specifically, it's your problem." He takes a step closer and I shift half a step back. He outright grins, taking obvious pleasure in my discomfort.

"What do you mean?" I ask. I can't see what Dan waking up, or not, has to do with this guy. Or maybe I can, but I'm in denial.

"Dan owes me, quite a bit of money, and his deadline is Thursday. Either he pays me, or you do." He points at me with his index finger to emphasis the word 'you'. "I don't care, as long as I get paid. Then I can pay my boss, and we're all happy."

"You'll have to talk to Dan when he wakes up." I shake my head. "I don't know anything about it."

"No, love. You don't get it. The deadline is Thursday seven a.m." He steps closer to me and I back away another half step. "I'll be by the workshop to pick it up. Cash, or a cashier's cheque is fine. And make sure that Jackie Chan boyfriend of yours goes to his kiddie class like usual, or he'll be the next one in a coma."

I gulp. What the hell? Is he saying he put Dan in a coma and Jake's next, or is he just threatening Jake? Either way it's not good. I suck in air as I realise he must be watching us if he knows Jake isn't there on a Thursday morning. Hell, I didn't even know about that until last week. I have to get rid of this guy.

"How much money are we talking about? Because I don't exactly have cash lying around." I can probably scrape up a couple of hundred dollars, maybe even a thousand. Any more would be pushing it. Not that I want to pay this scumbag, but if it will get him off my back and away from Dan, and Jake, then it will be worth it.

"A hundred thousand. You're lucky I'm not charging extra interest." He smirks. "I'm a gentleman and I keep my word."

I'm not sure that I heard him right. "One hundred thousand dollars?" My voice rises to a super high pitch on the last word. "I don't have that sort of money."

"I'll spell it out, seeing as you're not getting it." He stares at me, eyes cold, pure evil. "Your brother, Dan Vance, borrowed money from me. Money I got from my boss. He was meant to pay it back two weeks ago. He missed his deadline so he paid the price to get an extension."

He shakes his head. "It's a shame his house burnt down in the process, but them's the breaks."

My chest feels tight and I'm getting light headed. Uncle Bob's words echo in my head. Deliberate.

Creepy dude continues.

"The extension runs out on Thursday. The repayment price is one hundred thousand dollars. He's lucky I didn't double it for all the trouble he's causing me."

What the hell? What would Dan have done with one hundred thousand dollars? I feel faint.

He steps right into me, his face close to mine, and his breath is rank.

"And I give you my word, if you don't have it by seven on Thursday you'll be sorry. Your brother won't wake up." Then, I kid you not, he leaned closer and licked my cheek.

Licked. My. Cheek. I was too stunned to move. Frozen, the proverbial deer in the headlights. "Don't worry, you'll still be paying. If you don't have the cash then I'll take it out of your hide. Love."

He pulls back, turns, and walks away.

My breath came back in a big whoosh.

Then he turns and looks back over his shoulder. "No police. I'll know if you tell them and you'll regret it." He makes a shooting motion with the two fingers and thumb of his right hand, then says, "I'll be back. Thursday."

It would have been funny, a bad Terminator impression, if I wasn't so freaked out.

I stand there until he disappears around the corner then I run and lock myself in the ute. Not that it will do any good to keep the bad guys out. The bad guy has just bailed me up and nothing about the encounter was good.

I burst into tears, clutching the steering wheel.

I'm not sure how long I sit there.

I finally remember my phone and stop the video recording. I'm too shaken to play it back. I don't think the picture will be any good but the microphone is awesome and should have picked up the sound. Don't know what I'm going to do with it. Proof, I guess.

Did he say what I thought he said? Dan owes him one hundred thousand dollars. How or why I don't know.

What the hell am I going to do?

One thing's for sure. I've got three days to figure it out. And I can't tell Jake. He'll just want to jump in and fix everything. There's no way in hell I'm letting him get hurt.

Maybe I could ask Uncle Bob for help, but if Dan is involved with something shifty I don't want to be the one who gets him sent to jail. Nope, Uncle Bob is out, at least for now.

I GET BACK from my run, still shaky, to find Jake practising his martial arts, just like the first day I saw him. His body is liquid motion. He's shirtless and gleams in the morning light filtering in through the high windows. I still can't believe he's real, with all those muscles, and not some actor or model.

Is it really just over a week since I first laid eyes on him? It seems incomprehensible that Jake wasn't part of my life before then. It feels like he's always been here, he belongs. We belong together. Which is why I need to protect him.

Suddenly he shoots towards me in his signature flying side kick move. Yep, straight out of the movies.

I squeal but hold my ground as he lands mere millimetres from where I'm standing.

His messy, wavy hair falls across his forehead and he flicks it out of his eyes with the sharp, sideways move I've seen a thousand times in the last week. I thought it was vanity at first but now I know he just hasn't bothered to get it cut. Maybe he'll let me do it for him?

"Hi," Jake says. His arms go around my waist and he head dips his head, pulling me close as he kisses me.

Oh boy. I'll never get tired of this.

He lifts his head. "You okay?" His hands are still on my waist and he holds me slightly away from himself so he can look at me.

I nod, unable to speak. I give myself a mental shake. Two minutes and he's already on to me. I'm going to have to do better than this if I want to keep him safe.

"Lunch at the pub?" I ask. I go up on tiptoes and kiss his cheek.

"What was that for?" He sounds suspicious.

"Just because." I smile. "I'm going to get changed."

34 BABY BLUES

Jake drives us to the Pub.

"You're quiet. You sure everything's okay?" he asks.

"Yeah," I nod. "Just worried about Dan." Although not for the reason Jake thinks I'm worried.

"He'll wake up. We just have to give him time." Jake's eyes cut to me before hitting the road again. He reaches over and squeezes my hand. "Hang in there, Blondie."

The gang's all there when we arrive except for Noah, who's home with his wife Lilly and their new baby. Suze tells us they might swing by later.

"I'm looking forward to seeing the baby," says Elise. She squeezes in next to Jake, making me shuffle along to the end, almost bumping into Suze who's claimed the top spot at the back of the booth. I still haven't totally warmed to Elise but she's focused on Baz who's sitting opposite her. "How does it feel that your baby sister has a baby?"

Baz shrugs. "Lilly always had the hand-me-downs growing up. It's kind of nice that she gets to be the first to do something."

Suze is silent, her gaze focused on her menu. Which is weird. They eat here so often that nobody needs a menu anymore.

She grabs a paper napkin and dabs at her eyes, turning to face the back of the booth to do it.

"Allergies," she mouths when she see's my curious look. But I wonder what her feelings are about her baby sister having a baby. She's a doting Aunt, but if it was me, if I had a little sister, I'd probably be a little jealous. And I don't even like babies. It must be hard for Suze to be nearly thirty and not even have a boyfriend.

We order our food and everyone chats, talking about their week. To my surprise, they've got an unofficial visiting roster worked out. At least one of them calls in to see Dan every day so he'll never feel left out, even if he doesn't know they're there. I've run into various members of the gang when I've been visiting, usually just leaving, but never realised how planned it was.

"We're trying to spread ourselves out," Tom explains. "If you're there, then we don't need to be."

Clance, perched on a stool he's dragged over to the open end of the booth, nods. "We all work so we can't have someone there all the time, but we're doing our best."

I get a warm, fuzzy feeling in my chest as this sinks in.

They're a family, I realise. Not all related by blood, but they care about each other and look out for each other. Maybe I should tell them what's going on with me.

"You all right, girlfriend?" Suze asks quietly. We're almost knocking knees, at right angles to each other. Her brother Tom is sitting beside her, deep in conversation with Liam, who sits opposite me. Baz, next to Liam, is chatting to Jake and Clance.

I put my back to Jake, facing her, and it's about as private as you can get in this place. I open my mouth, not sure what I'm going to say. Tom turns sharp eyes to me and I snap my mouth shut.

Suze sees my indecision.

"Come and have lunch with me tomorrow," she says. "We can talk about whatever's bothering you."

That might be a good idea, I realise. If anyone can help me come up with that sort of money it will be the Suze, loans officer. I'll tell her it's for the business.

"That would be good," I say. "What time do you have lunch?"

Jake's arm goes around my shoulders as we make our plans and he pulls me back against his chest. I try to relax into him. I'm afraid they're onto me. Tom or Suze or even Jake is going to call me out, make me tell them what's going on.

The loan shark's threat rings in my ears. I can't say anything, it will put them in danger. I have to deal with this myself.

"How's tomorrow afternoon for the Scouts?" Suze is talking to Jake now. She's quite the organiser. The way she takes care of everyone I can tell she's the heart of this group. "I saw my friend, she's the Scout leader. They have a car wash and bar-b-que planned for their meeting but nowhere to hold it. They usually use the service station on the main street but there's been some last minute maintenance thing which means it's out."

"That was quick work." Baz grins. "Did you put the servo up to it?"

"Just good timing." Suze grins back. "We put it out into the universe on Friday at our beer-storming session and the universe has provided."

"In that case tomorrow arvo will be perfect." I twist my head around to look at Jake and he's smiling as he speaks. "We can't piss off the universe, can we?"

"That would not be smart," Suze agrees.

Jake ruffles my hair. "See, Blondie? It's all going to work out. We're getting the business on track and Dan will wake up soon. Everything will be fine."

I look around the table and they're all smiling and nodding their encouragement at me.

They think I'm worried about Dan. And I am. It's just that I've got so much more to be worried about now.

"Hey, guys," a soft voice comes from beside Clance. It belongs to a pretty girl, maybe my age, with a pram. She bends over the pram and scoops out an adorable little baby, dressed in a cute pink jumpsuit.

"Oooh, she's wearing my outfit." Suze's face is wistful. Maybe her biological clock it ticking? "I knew it would look good on her."

Liam shoves on Baz's shoulder. "Let me out, I want to say hi to my niece."

"She's my niece, buddy." Baz mock-glares at Liam, but he moves so Liam can get out. "Lilly's *my* little sister, in case you've forgotten."

"Don't be a jerk, Baz," says the slim brunette. I cannot believe she gave birth a few days ago. "Ella, say hello to your Uncle Liam."

She hands the baby to Liam as he pushes out of the booth. His face melts as he looks down in the little girl in his arms. "Hey, sweetheart, how are you?" he says softly. "You look just like your mummy."

"Lilly, this is Alex," Jake says to the brunette. "She's Dan's sister."

Lilly beams at me. Her eyes are a brilliant baby blue. "Hi, I was hoping I'd get to meet you. I've heard all about you."

"Oh boy, that can't be good," I say.

Lilly laughs. "Just my mum doing her bit to keep the town gossip engine alive. She told me about the breakdown and how she sent Jake out to rescue you."

Her eyes move between Jake and I with curiosity but she doesn't say anything else.

Baz holds his arms out to Liam. "My turn," he says. Liam kisses the baby's forehead gently before carefully passing the baby to Baz. These big tough guys are so adorable. I suspect that little Ella is going to be spoilt rotten. And probably won't ever get to date.

LUNCH FINISHES NOT LONG after and we swing past the hospital to visit Dan.

There's still no change that I can see. The friendly nurse is on duty and she says the doctors are happy that the swelling on his brain has gone down. She thinks they're planning to bring him out of the induced coma this week. That's got to be good news. Now it's up to me to make sure that the creepy guy doesn't finish what he started.

Jake drops me back at the workshop on the way to his class at the dojo. Even if I changed my mind and decided to talk to him about what happened at the beach this morning I don't get a chance. Not that I tried very hard.

35 BUT WAIT, THERE'S MORE

It's midday Monday and I meet Suze at Best Bank. We plan on walking the two blocks to a little cafe she suggested.

I come to a halt when we get to the corner just up from the bank. This is where Frankie's dress shop is. Or was. It's a fantastic spot, right opposite the beach. The shop still has two octagonal window nooks on each street front, but right now they're covered in newspaper and you can't see in. The corner entry way doors are closed.

"What happened to Frankie's?" I ask.

Suze stops beside me. "Miss Frankie retired. She's gone to a better place, the Tempest Beach retirement village."

"Do you know what's happening with the building? I'd love to open my tea shop here. You know, if I had the time and money to do it."

"I think the owner is renovating." Suze cuts me a look. "What are you doing working in a garage if you want to open a tea shop?"

I sigh. "Time and money. Plus, Dan needs me right now."

Suze nods and we continue on to the cafe. Cute glass water bottles are on the tables. Ours is emerald green and there's reds and blues on the other tables. The effect is summery and cheerful.

My mind drifts back to this morning with Jake as Suze chatters on about her work. I'm falling for him in a big way, and it's not just the sex although that is rather fantastic. He's kind, thoughtful, and always seems to know the right thing to say. He looks after me, acts like he really cares. It's been a long time since I had that.

I vaguely hear Suze say she's worked at Best Bank since she left school and focus back on the conversation. Friends listen to friends when they talk, and I really want to be friends with Suze.

"I've worked my way up through the ranks to be a loansie," Suze sees the question in my eyes. "Loans officer to the uninitiated. It's been hard work, sweat and tears."

"Not too many tears, I hope," I say.

"Hardly any," says Suze. "And I love it. Just being able to help people to buy a house or a car. I'm like their fairy godmother. Can you just see me with the wings and wand?" She lets out a loud laugh and it's contagious. I giggle, picturing Amazonian Suze with delicate fairy wings.

We order our food and drinks. Suze gets a cappuccino and I ask for a pot of Earl Grey tea. Then Suze reaches out to touch my hand. "Right, spill. I know there's something up with you and I want to know what it is. I also want to know about that dreamy smile. Let's start with the smile."

I grin big, unable to contain it. "I've never met anyone like Jake before," I confide.

"He's one of a kind," says Suze. "And it's obvious he's fallen for you."

"It is?" Is it really possible he feels the same way I do? I'm not exactly a catch. I'm just waiting for the moment he figures it out and kicks me out of his apartment. And his bed.

I give myself a mental shake. I've never been one for self doubt and I'm not going to start now.

"Look at you!" Suze waves her chocolate croissant at me. "You're gorgeous. Plus, you've got the smarts to back it up."

I shake my head but Suze hasn't finished. "I've seen the way he looks at you. Like he can't look away. You've captivated him, Alex. That boy is hooked. It might even be *lurve*." She drags out the word, a mischievous glint in her eye.

"Do you really think so?" I smile. "It might be *lurve* for me too. But he hasn't said anything." Except for that time when I was half asleep. Does that count?

"Have you?" Suze's gaze is direct and I look away and pour a glass of water for each of us. Then I shake my head.

"We've only known each other a week. Can you believe it? But I think I knew the moment I first saw him."

"Love at first sight." Suze clasps her hand over her heart and sighs dramatically. "I wish it would happen for me."

"Give it time," I say. "It will happen when you least expect it."

Suze gives me a look. "That's what everyone says. And I'm nearly thirty. I'm running out of time."

"You're not nearly thirty. Are you?" I tilt my head sideways and look quizzically at her. "You don't look that old."

"See!" It's a shriek. "Even you think it's old! I'm turning thirty next year. Over. The. Hill. And I don't even have a boyfriend, let alone a husband and baby." She slumps down in her chair.

"You do realise it's not a competition, don't you?"

"Yeah, tell that to Lilly."

I think of the gorgeous brunette I met last night. "Lilly's sweet. I don't think she's competing with you, Suze."

"I know, I'm just being a bitch. Not that I even want babies, you know. I want my Black Belt first and that's my focus right now. And my career. But you and Jake are so cute together, and baby Ella is gorgeous. I feel like I'm missing out." She picks up her coffee mug and takes a sip. "Now, enough about me. What's going on with you. I can tell something's bothering you and it's not just Dan."

"How do you know it's not Dan?" I ask.

"Because Dan's improving a little bit every day, we've come up with some great ideas for the business, but you're looking more and more stressed out."

"Oh." She's a lot more observant than I expected.

I find myself telling her about my run in with the guy at the beach. I didn't intend to, but she's a really good listener and keeps asking questions. Little by little the whole thing comes out. When I finish she's pale.

"You've got to go to the police," Suze says. "You can't let this blasted loan shark win."

"No!" My fist clenches. "I can't go to the police, it's just my word against his." I remember the video on my phone. It's proof, right? But he'd say he was just mucking around. His threat rings loud in my head. "He made it pretty clear what would happen if I told anyone. I shouldn't even have told you."

"You did the right thing telling me." Suze looks firmly into my eyes. "Don't worry, I'll help you come up with a plan."

"I just want to give him the money and make him go away."

"I think you should tell Jake." Suze points a finger at me. "You can't do this on your own. You don't have to."

"No! I won't drag Jake into this. He's at risk too." I close my eyes and put my head in my hands. This is all too much.

"I'm pretty sure Jake can hold his own. He's a big tough karate kid." I look up to see Suze smirk. "You've seen him in action."

I shake my head as I picture Jake doing his martial arts moves. "That's not going to help when the bullets start flying, or his house burns down. This is a bad guy, he doesn't fight fair."

Suze picks up her mug and takes a sip of coffee. Giving herself time to think, I realise.

"If you won't talk to the police or Jake, what about my brother?" she says.

"Baz?" I frown. He's such a jokester, I can't imagine him being able to help in this situation.

"No, my other brother. Tom."

"Tom?" It hadn't really clicked for me that Suze had two brothers.

"Yeah. He's got a military background. They both have, actually.

But Tom set up his security company when he got out and this is the sort of problem he specialises in."

"I'll think about it," I say, just to shut her down. "But you can't say anything to anyone else."

"All right, settle down. I don't agree with you but I'm here for you, okay?" She grabs my hand and squeezes. "Have you got any other ideas?"

I nod, smiling. "I have, actually. I'm selling Nanna's house which will give me the money I need."

"To do what?" Suze tilts her head. I can almost see the gears ticking over in her head as she thinks.

"I've got to choose, haven't I?" I pick up the paper napkin and start tearing it into long, thin strips. "I've got to choose between saving Dan's business, by paying out the bank loan. Or saving his life, by paying off the loan shark." Either way I'm paying Dan's debt. "If I have enough time to turn the business around I might be able to do both. Selling the house gives me options."

"There's two problems, sweetie." Suze takes the napkin from me, drawing my eyes to her face. Her eyes are intent on mine. "It's going to take between four and six weeks for the sale to go through. After you find a buyer. And you need the cash by this Thursday, right?"

I nod. "I know, that's a problem. I'm going to talk to him on Thursday and beg for more time, hope he sees reason."

"I wonder." Suze is frowning, thinking hard. "Maybe you could get bridging finance. It's a loan designed for people who want to buy a new house but the sale on the old one hasn't gone through yet.""

I sit up straight and lean forward. "That's a great idea."

"Except you need to have sold the house first."

"Oh." I slump back down in my chair. "Well that doesn't help."

"And then there's the other problem."

"But wait, there's more?" My attempt at humour falls flat. But it can't possible get any worse, can it?

Suze looks away and won't meet my eyes. I guess it can.

"I shouldn't tell you this, but I'm pretty sure Damien's started the sale process for the business."

"What? He can't do that!" My voice comes out shrill. "He said we had a month."

"They can do whatever they want, sweetie. The loan's been in default for a while." She takes a sip of her coffee. "I know it's not fair, but they'll be lining up potential buyers."

My throat feels tight and I blink hard to stop the tears from coming. I reach for my water and gulp it down.

"If you pay out the bank loan before they find a buyer you'll be able to save the business," Suze says. "But I'm not sure you'll be able to do that if you pay this loan shark. You won't get enough from the house sale to do both, and the bank won't lend you money on a business that's already been proven to have problems. Not without any security."

"So I really do have to choose between saving his business or his life." I swallow.

Suze nods. "Looks like it. Unless you can come up with another idea."

"It's a no-brainer, isn't it? If I pick the business, then the bad guy kills him."

"It might just be a threat." She sounds hopeful.

"You didn't see his face. His eyes." I shudder. "He's evil. It wasn't just a threat."

"Then you need to get the cash to pay him."

I rub my eyes, feeling my throat tighten as tears threaten.

"Think about talking to Tom," Suze says. "I'm sure he can help."

I nod, unable to meet her eyes. I'll think about it, sure. There's got to be a way to come out of this without having to make that final choice. But the less people involved the better. I don't want anyone to get hurt because of my actions.

36 OFFICIAL BUSINESS

I HEAD BACK TO THE WORKSHOP AFTER LUNCH WITH SUZE feeling less alone. It's good to know that someone else knows. The burden feels less, somehow.

I've got my head deep in the computer, working on the invoicing, when there's a knock on the door. I look up to see Uncle Bob. He's wearing his police uniform and has his cap clenched in one fist.

"Uncle Bob!" I spring up and round the table to give him a hug and a kiss on his cheek. He hugs me back somewhat awkwardly.

"Come in, sit down. Is everything all right?" I tug on his arm and point him towards the visitor chairs in front of the desk. I've thrown out the decrepit monstrosities that Dan had. The new chairs are from the second hand office place but they're in good condition and were cheap. Win, win.

"It's official business, Alex," he says. "I'm here unofficially, of course. They won't let me investigate my own family. But I've got some questions about your brother and if you can help me you'll be helping Dan too."

"Oh." I breathe out in a rush as I sit back down behind the desk.

Uncle Bob is still standing which makes me edgy. "Should I get Jake?"

"I want to talk to you first. Then I'll get to Jake." He goes to the door, shutting and locking it. He glances at the window before he sits. The window is shut making the room somewhat soundproof so I guess he doesn't care if anyone sees him. The fact that he locked the door makes me uneasy. Whatever this is, it can't be good.

"What is it, Uncle Bob? You're scaring me." I decide to be honest.

"We know the fire was deliberately lit." Uncle Bob's eye contact is maximum. "What we're trying to work out is who lit it, and why."

I blink. "I don't know anything about it."

So much for honesty. I've got a pretty good idea who lit the fire, and why. But there's no way I can get Uncle Bob involved, even unofficially. Is there?

"I'm hoping you might have seen something. We think Dan was involved in something pretty serious. We're not sure what, but he owes a lot of money. Jake might be implicated too." Uncle Bob holds the eye contact and it's getting hard to keep meeting his gaze. I feel like if I look away he'll think I'm hiding something. Which I am. "What can you tell me, Alex?"

And there you have it. What *can* I tell him? Nothing about the unofficial debt, that's for sure.

"What do you think he's involved with?" I'm stalling, hoping I'll be able to come up with something useful without getting into more trouble. In all honesty I'd like nothing better than to hand it over to the police to deal with. But I remember the look in that guy's eyes. He meant it when he said no police. There's no way I'm risking it.

"I'm hoping you can tell me. Give me something. You've been here the last week and you've basically taken over the business. What doesn't look right?"

This I can share.

"Well, he owes a lot of money. The bank wants to shut him down." Uncle Bob already knows about the money and I think it's safe to tell him about the bank. "His invoicing system was a mess. I'm starting to get on top of it now."

Uncle Bob looks frustrated. "Any idea what he's been spending all the money on?"

"I think it's just bad decision making. Nothing sinister. He put in a paint shop and bought a couple of old cars to restore. Expensive ones. They're sitting out the back and to be honest it's hard to tell they're even cars. But Jake says they cost a lot.

"Plus he's way too generous. He gives discounts to all the pensioners, and that money really comes out of his own pocket. Money he doesn't have. He donates to the soccer club and goodness knows what else."

"So he's Mr Goody Two-Shoes," Uncle Bob says sarcastically.

"Well, yeah." I roll my eyes.

"Anything else?" Uncle Bob never was a quitter.

"He's got a great group of friends. Jake's one of them. They're all getting involved with helping me save the business." I smile. Getting to know Dan's friends is the one good thing that has come out of all this. "They're great."

"Even Jake?"

"What do you mean by that?" My smile falls away. "Jake is especially great."

Uncle Bob frowns. "I meant is Jake helping?"

"Of course Jake is helping." I'm frowning too. I'm getting a tad bit annoyed at this line of questioning.

"Right. Helping Dan or helping himself?"

That's a cryptic comment, and not very nice, but I'm pretty sure he's just trying to rattle me into giving something away. It won't work. Apart from the dodgy borrowings Dan has nothing to hide. And I'm not saying shit about the loan shark. "I don't know what you're saying, Uncle Bob. Jake's been a real godsend since I got here."

"I bet he has," Uncle Bob mutters to himself. "Right. I'd best talk to Jake then."

"Hang on, I'll go and find him for you." I want Uncle Bob to wait here so I can give Jake a heads up.

It's not happening. Uncle Bob is right on my heels as I move to the door.

I always thought he was a good guy, a good cop. I guess he is a good cop. He's doing an awesome job right now. I wish I could tell him everything. An idea starts to form in my mind.

"Uncle Bob," I say hesitantly as I turn and face him, one hand on the doorknob pulling it open. Through the window I see Jake striding towards us. I don't have much time. "I might need your help with something. But I can't really tell you anything at the moment. Just giving you a heads up, you might be getting a call from me in a couple of days."

Uncle Bob frowns. "I don't like this, Alex. What's going on?"

I shake my head. "It might be nothing."

He sighs. "There's some really bad stuff happening and I don't want you getting caught in the crossfire. If you know anything, now's the time to tell me."

"Tell you what?" Jake's there.

"Jake." Uncle Bob reaches out and shakes his hand. He's not as warm as he was the other day at his house and I wonder what's changed.

"I'm here unofficially, looking into Dan's affairs. Trying to figure out exactly what he's got himself into."

I turn to go back to my seat. Uncle Bob puts his hand on my shoulder. "I need to talk to Jake alone. Can you give us a minute?"

"Sure." I swallow. "Can I get you a coffee?"

Uncle Bob nods. "Just black, thanks."

"Jake?"

Jake shakes his head. "No thanks, Blondie. I'm good."

His arm wraps around my waist as I squeeze past him to get out the door. He lifts his hand to my cheek. "You okay?"

I nod. "All good."

It's another lie. But really, what else can I say?

37 SOCCER MUMS ATTACK

Jake won't tell me what Uncle Bob said to him. He came out of the office at a fast pace. He walked straight through the kitchen, where I was still making the coffee, and out the back. He ignored me when I called his name. Maybe he didn't hear me. Maybe he just didn't want to talk. Then I heard clanging and a giant crash. It sounded like he hit something, hard enough to knock it over.

Uncle Bob stuck his head in the kitchen to say his goodbyes, his eyes focused down the hall in the direction Jake went. When I asked what they spoke about he just shook his head and said he had to get going. Then he left. He didn't drink his coffee. In fact, I think he forgot I'd even made it for him.

I sigh and pick up my coffee, heading out the back to find Jake.

"I don't want to talk about it," Jake says. I take the hint and go back to my office.

The afternoon drags after that, until four when the Scouts turn up. I walk out the front to meet them.

Suze's friend, the Scoutmaster, is a bubbly brunette full of energy.

"Hi," she says, striding up to me with her hand extended. "I'm

Michelle. Thank you so much for letting us set up here on such short notice. The kids are really excited."

Something catches her eye and she puts her fingers in her mouth and whistles. "Beau! You're meant to be unpacking the gear!"

A boy in his early teens turns around. He's got a hand on the tap, the hose in his other hand and pointed at one of the younger boys. Fortunately, the tap hasn't been turned on.

He drops the hose and puts his hands in the air. "Yeah all right. I'm going. We were just mucking around."

Michelle turns back to me shaking her head. "You've got to have eyes in the back of your head. They're good kids, but their idea of fun can get out of hand sometimes."

I grin at her. "Is there anything I can do?"

"You bet. Do you know your way around a bar-b-que?"

I don't, but I'm a quick learner. The older kids have pulled the barbie off the back of a truck and set it up, off to one side. The first batch of sausages is already half done.

"And there's our first customer," Michelle says, her hands on her hips.

A dusty Land cruiser wagon rolls up. It's Tom. He walks over to where we're standing, leaving the dirty vehicle with the kids.

"That will give them a run for their money." He hands a twenty dollar note to Michelle. "Think that will cover it?"

Michelle takes the cash. "I'll get you some change."

Tom waves her off. "No worries, it's for a good cause."

He heads into the workshop, no doubt looking for Jake.

"What are you fund raising for?" I ask.

"The money from the car wash is to buy camping equipment." She smiles. "But the bar-b-que is mainly for the kids. We'll eat together after we finish."

More cars arrive and soon there is a line up. Beau and a girl called Becky are helping me with the food. I was surprised to see there are girls in the group but apparently it's been a thing for years.

A lot of the customers are parents and family of the Scouts but we're getting our fair share of randoms as well. Not bad for a Monday afternoon.

Michelle sends Jake and Tom out to buy more sausages and bread when we run out. I can't even guess at how much money they've raised so far but they must be doing well.

A CAR DOOR slams and I look up to see Cindy the soccer mum approaching, flanked by two other women. She's wearing her little denim shorts, with stiletto's, as are the other two. All of them look pissed off.

"What the hell?" I look around for Jake but remember he's off buying more meat. I'm on my own, except for Beau and Becky. And Beau's over at the tap, re-filling buckets for the younger kids. Just me and Becky then.

I don't want a teenage girl exposed to the antagonism that's fast approaching.

"You might want to go and help Beau," I say. Becky is staring at the soccer mums. At my words she turns the heat down and backs away. Smart girl.

Cindy skids to a stop in front of me.

"So," she says. "You let the Scouts come and do a car wash. When is it our turn? Because Dan said no to us."

"I'm sure he had a reason." I stay calm. "You'll have to talk to Dan about it."

"He promised us something unique for our charity auction fundraiser instead." Cindy has her arms crossed over her chest and she's frowning, clearly unhappy.

"Well there you go." I roll my eyes. "He's showing his support in other ways."

"That would be true if he'd actually given it to us." Cindy's volume is increasing. She picks up a tomato sauce bottle from the table and points it at me. "But he hasn't. I don't even know what it is. And our event is next weekend."

"You realise Dan is still in hospital, right?" My hands go to my hips and I take a step forward. I'm starting to get mad. The Scouts don't need a rampaging soccer mum making a scene at their car wash. "He's probably got your donation stashed somewhere safe. But I don't know anything about it."

Cindy's face softens. She drops the sauce back on the table next to the napkins. "He's not out yet? I thought he'd be back at work by now."

I shake my head. "Not yet. We're hoping it will be soon."

The fight goes out of Cindy. I can almost see her deflate. One of her friends whispers in her ear, gesturing violently. Cindy turns to face her, says something inaudible, then grabs her arm and tows her away without another word. The third woman gives me a dirty look and then follows her friends.

I breathe a sigh of relief. That could have gotten really bad and for a moment I thought Cindy was going to start a food fight. Thank goodness it didn't come to that.

JAKE and I are sitting outside in the soft night air with Michelle and some of the parents, drinks in hand, a lot later on.

"Looks like you had a good afternoon," says Jake.

Michelle nods. "We raised a lot of money. I was a bit worried when the soccer mums turned up though. They've got a reputation for stirring up trouble. They think they're losing kids to the Scouts. Of course, a lot of kids do both."

"Apparently Dan's promised a donation for their big fund raiser. It's next weekend and they're getting a bit antsy about it." I shrug. "I don't know what it is, or if it even survived the fire. They left when they realised Dan is still in hospital."

"Just as well," Jake mutters. He really doesn't like Cindy Turner.

All's well that ends well. That's my new motto, and I'm sticking to it.

38 SAY WHAT?

I wake up to an arm going around my waist as I'm pulled into Jake's warm, hard body. He nuzzles my neck, a hand trailing up my side.

I snuggle deeper into my pillow trying to ignore him, not ready to wake up yet.

"Morning, Blondie," Jake says into my ear, sending a shiver through me. I'm awake now and decide not to fight it.

"You've got my attention," I murmur.

That's all it takes. He rolls me to my back and starts kissing his way down my neck, his hand trailing softly along my belly, my hip. My skin pebbles as goose bumps rise up everywhere he touches. I will never get enough of this man.

He comes up on one elbow and looks down on me, face close. When he catches my gaze he moves in to kiss me full on the lips.

This kiss is amazing. Soft and slow, he's telling me he loves me without words. I'm telling him I love him right back. Surely it's too soon for that? But the spark was lit the moment I set eyes on his hard body flowing through his martial arts moves, gleaming in the morning light. The moment he came flying through the air towards me. When he playfully showcased those gorgeous muscles and then laughed at himself. The moment he first called me Blondie. I can admit it now; it was love at first sight. And even though it's only been a week and a half, I'm this close to just blurting it out.

We make love, and it's soft and slow, just like the kiss.

Afterwards he holds me close to his heart, his hand stroking my hair and back. My hand is on his chest and my thumb strokes gentle circles on his skin. I could live in this bed, with him, forever.

IT'S mid-morning and I'm at the desk. I've made good progress sorting out Dan's mess but I'm starting to hate paperwork.

A loud rap on the door startles me and I look up to see Damien Lewis from Best Bank.

"Damien." I get up and knock a bundle of paper to the floor as I stand. I crouch, scrambling to pick it all up again. By the time I do, Damien has come in and shut the door behind him. He's sitting in one of the visitor's chairs with his left ankle crossed over his right knee, grinning. Great. I amuse him.

"What?" I say. I sound defensive but I can't help it. He's the last person I want to see.

"Didn't you get my email? You're acting like you didn't know I was coming."

"What email?" I haven't even turned the computer on this morning.

"I sent it yesterday, about five." He smirks. "To give you a heads up that I'd be calling in today."

"It's been a little busy around here." I still sound defensive but I'm not telling him I was bar-b-que-ing with the Scouts. It's none of his business. "How can I help you?"

Damien straightens in his seat and leans forward, forearms on the desk. He's acting all buddy, buddy and I don't trust him. "I've got some bad news, I'm afraid."

"What do you mean?" I remember Suze saying Damien was starting the sales process for Dan's business and clench my fist. *Not yet.*

"We've got a buyer and the bank has decided to protect its investment by activating the default clause immediately."

Suze was right. But I'm not going down without a fight. "What? You said I had a month. It's barely been a week!"

"I'm sorry, Alex. It's out of my hands. I tried to get them to hold off. Suze told me how hard you've been working to turn things around. But the buyer's finance has just been approved and head office wants to proceed with the sale."

My stomach clenches. I can't believe this is happening.

"Look, there might still a chance if you can pay off the loan by the end of the week. There's a cooling off period for the buyer. If you can make the payment before then I might," he stresses the word might, "be able to get head office to decide in your favour. They'd have to at least look at it again."

It hits me then. I mean, I've known all along but the knowledge settles in me like warm seafood on Melbourne Cup day. You eat it thinking it's going to be okay, it hasn't been sitting out that long. You know you shouldn't. Then you start to feel sick and before you know it you're puking your guts up. Let's hope I don't start puking all over Damien's shoes. Although he deserves it. He's a bit of an arsehole, actually.

I clench and unclench my fist. It really has come down to two choices. Pay the bank or pay the loan shark. A flash of guilt sears through me when I think of my parents. There's nothing I can do for them if their insurance doesn't come through. But I know they'd choose their son over themselves.

Dan's business or his life. I can't save both. I thought I could, if I just had more time. But I can't.

And what if I choose his life and he wakes up and doesn't want to go on without his business? I'll have failed. Maybe if I pay the bank and save the business I'll get lucky, and the bad guy won't go after Dan.

Or me either, for that matter.

But I haven't had a lot of good luck lately.

All my life my big brother has looked out for me, been there for me, and the one time he needs me to come through for him and I've failed him. No matter which way I go, I've failed him.

It's all too much and my throat tightens. I can't break down in tears in front of Damien. I just can't. Sure, he's just doing his job, but right now I don't care.

"I think you should leave," I say, standing up to shoo him out the door. I need time to think.

"I'm only trying to help. Don't shoot the messenger." Damien gets to his feet. He looks out the window and we both see Jake striding towards the office door. He's seriously pissed off.

"Oh look," says Damien. "Here's the lucky buyer now."

The the floor drops out from under my feet. My whole world just tilted. I grab hold of the desk with both hands and hold myself up by leaning on my arms. This can't be right. Damien can't mean that Jake's the one buying the business. *Tell me it's not true.*

My mind flicks back to his caginess about certain things. The 'not my story to tell' that first morning. The 'trust me' and the 'let me handle the bank' later on. His meeting with Suze to sign some paperwork, all 'nothing for you to worry about'.

It doesn't mean what I think it means. It doesn't mean that Jake's a backstabbing, business-stealing bastard. It can't. There'll be a logical explanation.

Don't panic, Alex. Jake will be able to explain.

Jake is rattling the door handle. "Unlock this door, dammit."

Damien strolls casually to the door and unlocks, then opens it. "Jake, buddy. I was just telling Alex the good news. Well, bad news for her, good news for you isn't it?"

Jakes fists clench at his side but he doesn't deny it.

"Jake?" I say. Then I crash back down in my chair, my legs unable to hold me up any longer.

"I'll leave you to it. Good luck kids, don't kill each other." Damien is in full arsehole-mode as he saunters off, leaving me with Jake the snake.

39 BETRAYED

Jake closes the door and walks over to the desk. He sits in the seat just vacated by Damien, his jaw clenched, hands curled into fists on his legs. He looks like he wants to hit something. "That fucking Damien. He's a prick."

"I agree. He's an arsehole." I can't help a small smile before I remember what Jake has done. Tears well in my eyes as I look at him. "Tell me it's not true, Jake. Please tell me it's not true."

His anger leaves him in a rush of air. He leans forward on the desk and rests his forehead on his hands. He looks deflated, defeated.

Then he lifts his head and meets my eyes. He sighs. "It's just business, Blondie. You weren't meant to find out like this."

Sucker punched. And I'm the sucker. I rise to my feet so I'm on not looking up at him. *How could he?* "It's not just business. You've betrayed me, you've betrayed Dan."

"You don't know everything." Jakes eyes are so sad he looks like he's about to cry.

"Then tell me." It comes out as a whisper. I want to give him a chance to explain. To make it right.

"I can't. It's not my story to tell." He shakes his head and rubs his hand over his face.

"It's not my story to tell." I mimic him, my voice high-pitched and singsong. It's becoming obvious that he's not going to make it right. Or maybe he just doesn't want to.

"Please, I just need more time. I need Dan to wake up."

"Whatever. I can't believe a word that comes out of your mouth." My throat goes tight again. The tears start and I blink hard to stop them. I need to get out of here before I become a blubbering mess.

I stab at the mouse to shut the computer down before I remember I haven't turned it on this morning. I open the bottom drawer and grab my handbag and keys then push away from the desk.

"That's it. I'm out of here. We're done."

Jake is sitting in silence, stunned.

"Alex, don't go. Please don't walk out like this." He reaches out, snagging my arm as I storm past and I wrench it out of his grip.

I'm furious. I cannot believe he would do this to me, to Dan.

"Don't you dare talk to me. Don't you touch me. I don't ever want to see you again, Jake Lawson. You're a lying, cheating, backstabbing, jerk of a bastard. I thought you..." I stop and take a deep, shuddering breath. "I thought we..."

I can't go on. The tears stream down my face and I can't talk. That last little burst took it all out of me.

Jake looks like someone has ripped his guts out. His hand is outstretched and his mouth is open, like he wants to say something but can't spit the words out. Can't think of another lie quick enough, most likely.

"Blondie..." He gets to his feet and steps closer, but I'm done.

"No. Don't 'Blondie' me." I turn to the door, unlocking and opening it for the fiftieth time this week, and storm through. The workers are standing beside a car on the far side of the workshop and have obviously heard the yelling. They hurriedly turn back to the engine. I guess they don't want to be caught staring. Too late, guys.

I power through the workshop and up the stairs, into the apartment. It takes me ten minutes to shove everything into my bag. Ten minutes to clear myself out of Jake's life.

I can't believe it's come to this. Only this morning I thought I was in love with him, and now this? I still don't understand what's happened.

I wheel my little bag to the back balcony and use the side entrance to leave so I don't have to go through the workshop again.

I'm all the way downstairs and on the street when I realise my problem. Not only do I have nowhere else to go, I don't even have a car to get there.

I'm tempted to walk to the Greyhound bus station and get the first bus out of town. To run far, far away from here and let someone else sort it out.

To never have to see Jake again, or my parents or even Dan.

A fresh start.

But if there's one thing I've learnt since coming back to this town, it's that you can't run from your problems. They have a way of tracking you down no matter how far you run. It's time for me to stop running and face my fear.

My problem.

Reluctantly I pull out my phone. There's really only one phone call I can make. I'm going to have to suck it up and face the person who made me leave town in the first place.

My mother.

40 ELEPHANT IN THE ROOM

My dad pulls up in the familiar white station wagon ten minutes later. I've pulled him away from his weekly bowls game but he doesn't seem to mind. I'm lucky that today is his day off.

"We were all done bar the presentation, and lunch of course. You're a lot more important than lunch." Dad is shutting the rear door having just put my bag—singular—in the back. He tilts his head, questioningly. "Is this all you've got?"

I nod and get into the car. We drive in silence for a couple of minutes.

"Do you want to talk about it?" Dad asks eventually.

"Not really. Not yet." I sigh. "I'm trying to get my head around everything that's happened."

"We're here when you need us, sweetheart." Dad reaches over and pats my knee awkwardly before putting his hand back on the steering wheel. "We always have been, even if you didn't think so."

"I've been a bit of a bitch to Mum, haven't I?"

Dad winces. "I wouldn't put it quite like that. Things haven't been easy between the two of you though."

"I need to talk to her and get things straight." I glance sideways at Dad's profile. "I've had a bit of an epiphany."

Dad smiles. "I think your Mum has had one of her own, what with the house burning down and all."

We pull into Aunty Joy's driveway and go inside.

Mum is in the kitchen with Aunty Joy, making sandwiches. I'm assuming Uncle Bob is at work.

"You're just in time for lunch." Aunty Joy smiles big. "Come in, you can set the table. I've just boiled the kettle."

I let myself enjoy the rhythm of life in the household. We sit at the table and eat chicken and salad sandwiches with a much appreciated cup of tea. Conversation is light, everyone avoiding the elephant in the room.

Me.

When Aunty Joy stands and starts clearing the table I decide it's time.

"Mum, can I talk to you outside for a minute?"

Mum looks up with a puzzled expression. She doesn't say no, so I walk to the sliding glass door and open it before heading out to the back verandah. I pause at the door and look back. Dad is nodding encouragingly at Mum, and she pushes back from the table with a dramatic sigh.

I walk to the railing and lean on it, waiting for her to join me. I'm not really sure what I'm going to say.

The door slides shut and then Mum comes and leans on the railing beside me. "What's all this about?"

I turn so I face her, leaning a hip against the rail. She mirrors me with her arms folded. I realise how defensive it looks and uncross my arms, putting one elbow on the rail and forcing the other down by my side.

"This is really hard, Mum." I take a deep breath and let it out, and then I spit it out. "I'd like for us to get on, like a proper mother and daughter."

"We do get on," Mum says. "You're my daughter and I love you. It goes without saying."

She says it automatically, like it's the required response. I shake my head.

"Really? Because when we met at the hospital, my first day back in town, I got the distinct impression that you'd like me to go away again and not come back. And nothing has really changed since then."

"That's not true, Alex. It was just unexpected seeing you there." Mum uncrosses and recrosses her arms, obviously uncomfortable.

"Would you have told me about Dan?" I speak softly, almost afraid of the answer.

"I was going to phone you as soon as we knew what was going on. I didn't want to tell you what happened until we knew he would be okay." She won't meet my eyes.

"So I still wouldn't know, seeing as we still don't know when he's going to wake up." I huff out a breath of air. "For the record, next time I want to know as soon as something happens, not after he's been in a coma for a month and then wakes up."

"Hopefully there won't be a next time, but if there is I'll make sure to tell you right away." She looks me in the eyes and reaches out to touch my arm. "I'm sorry, Alex. I just didn't want you to worry."

I nod. "All right then."

Time to address the other elephant in the room.

"Are you still mad at me for getting Nanna's house?"

"What? No!" The shock in Mum's voice is real. Her hand goes to her mouth in denial. She takes a deep breath and lets it out slowly, like she's working up her courage.

"I know you don't think so, but your father and I were happy that you and Dan received your inheritance from Nanna. Dan got the deposit for his workshop and you got to go to university. We couldn't have done that for you. Nanna could, and she did. University wasn't my first choice for you, Alex." She clenches the railing and draws in a sharp breath. "I pressured you about that and I'm sorry. I didn't want to lose you to the city. But I'm proud of you. I hated it when you wouldn't answer my calls when you moved away."

I turn to face the backyard. Is it possible I was over reacting? I left town in a bit of a rush. I thought I'd get trapped if I stayed and just assumed that Mum was mad at me. That's how I would have felt if someone else got what was mine.

I squeeze Mum's hand. "I'm sorry too."

Mum smiles. "Nanna had a big heart. She helped your father and I when we were first married, you know, with the deposit for our house."

"I didn't know that." The house that I grew up in was filled with so much love. And now it's gone.

"Your house..." I turn to face her again. "Were you able to save anything?"

Mum shakes her head. "There wasn't much left, and what was had too much smoke damage. It's all gone."

"That's terrible. I thought you might have been able to salvage some things."

Although what would you pick, I don't know.

"We all survived and we have to believe Dan will pull through. We've just got to wait for the police to finish investigating before the insurance company will pay up."

I remember what Bob said earlier. "Did they decide if the fire was deliberately lit? Insurance won't cover it if that's the case."

"We'll cross that bridge when we come to it." Mum pats my arm uncertainly. "Everything will work out, I'm sure of it."

"If there's anything I can do you tell me, right?" I step in and put my arms around her tightly, suddenly overcome with emotion. My throat is tight and I blink rapidly to stop the tears.

Mum hugs me back and it's a good hug. I breathe her in. I've really missed her. And to think it was all my own silliness and jumping to conclusions. So much lost time, and it's all my own fault.

"I love you, Mum," I say quietly.

"I know." Mum steps away from my hug and puts her hands on my shoulders. She looks me right in the eyes. "I'm sorry if I've been a bit distant since you got back. It's not about you. I want you to know that. You're my daughter and I'll always love you no matter what."

I nod. "What's been worrying you?" I haven't been a very good daughter for the last four years. It's time to start making up for it.

"It's just everything built up. Your Dad being semi-retired and hanging around more, not that I don't like spending time with him, but it's taken us a while to work out how we fit together."

"Hence the lawn bowls?" I smile.

"Hence the lawn bowls." Mum smiles back. "I told him he had to get a hobby. I don't want him underfoot all the time, or worse, stopping me from doing my CWA and water aerobics."

"You do water aerobics?" This is news to me.

Mum nods. "Three times a week."

"What else has been going on?" There's got to be more to it than Dad retiring.

Mum sighs. "Nothing really. I had a health scare which turned out to be a false alarm. And, Dan's obviously in trouble and wasn't talking about it. You've been living away and not knowing what you're up to is hard. I'm a mother. Worrying is part of the job description."

'Health scare?' I look at her closely, noticing the gray at her roots and the fine lines around her eyes, deeper than before. "What happened?"

"I had a lump in my breast. The results came back yesterday and it was all clear. Nothing to worry about. But it's kept me distracted on top of everything else."

"You've got to tell me these things." I frown. "Especially when it's your health."

She nods, eyes glistening, and I step in to hug her again. "I'll try to be a better daughter from now on. And I'm working on getting Dan sorted."

Mum hugs me back tightly, then steps back.

"All right." She smiles brightly and blinks away any trace of tears. "Let's get back inside before they send out the search party. There's another cuppa in there with my name on it."

41 TOO LATE

I help Aunty Joy with the dishes and then go back outside to sit on the verandah. I need to think things over, try and come up with a way out of this mess.

My phone rings as I sit on the hanging chair that lives in the corner. I take it out of my pocket to answer. The caller ID says it's the real estate agent and I feel a lump in my throat. I don't want to talk to Valencia right now. Or ever again, actually.

"Hello?" My voice is shaky.

"Hi, Alex, it's Dean."

That's a relief.

"Hi Dean, what's up?"

"Good news. We've got a buyer for your property. They didn't argue on the price; in fact, they've already paid the ten percent deposit."

I get to my feet and walk to the railing, a surge of adrenalin hitting. "That's fantastic!" It means I've got options. With the sale of the house I have options. "What do I need to do?"

"Your solicitor will be in touch about the contract. You'll need to sign it, then settlement will be four weeks after exchange. Assuming you're happy for it to go through a bit faster the normal."

Hell yeah. But...

"What about my tenant? Don't I need to give them notice? Did you ever get a copy of the lease?"

"That's the good part. The tenant is the buyer. They came and made an offer yesterday, straight after we put the 'For Sale' sign up."

"Wow. That was fast." It was only Friday that I'd spoken to Dean about putting the house on the market. I'd signed the buyer's agreement electronically on the weekend and sent it back, but today is only Tuesday.

"We don't muck around." Dean chuckles. "Although it normally takes a lot longer than this to get a result."

"Thank you," I say. "It will be good to get it settled."

Dean clears his throat. "There's one other thing I need to talk to you about."

I nod, but he can't see me. "Okay," I say.

"It's about Valencia. I'd understand if you want to make a formal complaint about her behaviour on Friday. It was unacceptable and we've issued a formal written warning."

"Oh." I'm gobsmacked. "How did you know about that?"

"The whole office heard it." Dean chuckles but this time he doesn't sound amused. "The only reason she wasn't fired on the spot was because of extenuating circumstances. She had asked for time off to deal with some personal issues and we said no, because we were too busy. Hindsight's a wonderful thing."

I return to the swinging chair and sit, rocking it with my foot, my other foot tucked up underneath me. I don't know how I feel about Valencia. Her outburst was nasty and she deserves to be punished. I still feel a bit rattled by her attack.

But I can sort of understand where she's coming from. If I thought someone was flirting with Jake then I'd probably react the same way, and we aren't married. Hell, we aren't even together anymore and I'd still likely want to kill anyone who flirted with him.

"I don't want to make a formal complaint or anything," I say. It's too much hassle, and life is too short. "She should apologise to me though. And I know you can't do anything about it, but I'd like to be able to have a conversation with Gavin without being accused of anything. He was a good boss and I didn't even get to say goodbye."

"Leave it with me," Dean says. "The apology goes without saying, of course."

We talk about a couple of other details, logistics for the settlement, and hang up. I kick back in the chair thinking things through. The sale of the house came through right when I needed it. Divine intervention? I'll have to make an effort to get to church with my parents this weekend assuming I make it that far.

I can use the money to pay either the bank or the other debt, and I've already decided to save Dan's life and pay the loan shark.

I feel like a weight has lifted off my shoulders. In some ways, Jake has done me a huge favour. I don't have to worry about the business anymore. Dan can sort it out with Jake after he wakes up.

I think about Jake's eyes, the way he looks at me like he sees me. Was it all a lie? A way to get me to help him turn the business around? He didn't want me to have anything to do with the business at all, in the first place. My office clean-up project was probably just a way to keep me busy. Bet he was glad though. I scoff. Without me getting the paperwork sorted out there's no way the bank would have lent him any money. The business was just not profitable on paper.

Then again, maybe he doesn't need to prove the business is profitable. I remember Bri mentioning that Jake has a property with the agency where she works. Ironic really, Jake having a rental property too. We had a lot in common. If he was to use his property as security it wouldn't matter what the loan was for. I realise I don't actually know much about Jake Lawson. He could be a secret millionaire for all I know.

Thinking about Jake isn't getting me anywhere. What I need is a plan to deal with the loan shark. And first things first, I need to get an advance on my house proceeds. I'm going to need cold, hard cash for my meeting on Thursday morning.

I pick up my phone and flick through the contacts to find Suze. With any luck she'll be able to get the bridging finance for me, now that the house is sold. I just hope it's not too late to get things organised for Thursday.

42 TITANIUM

Suze answers the phone on the first ring.

"What's up, Chickadee?" Suze says. Obviously she hasn't heard about my fight with Jake.

"I need your help." I tell her that the house has sold and I need an advance on the money. "Can you do the bridging finance?"

"How about you come in and see me. I don't think the bank will want to give money out to pay a pawn shop, but I'll see what I can do."

"Oh." I debate my transport problem for a moment and decide I can't call on my parents to play taxi any more than they already have. "Can you come and get me? I'm at Aunty Joy's."

"Girlfriend, you are going to owe me big time." Suze lets out a huff of air and for a moment I think she's going to say no. "I'll come and do an onsite meeting. They occasionally let me out of the office for one of those. It's a good thing it's official business."

"Thank you," I say. "I appreciate it."

"You owe me a beer," she says. "See you soon."

I'm still sitting out the back when the doorbell rings fifteen minutes later. In fact, I think I dozed off. I push out of the chair and head for the front door but Mum has already beaten me to it.

"Hi Suze," says Mum. She's standing in the doorway staring at Suze.

"Hi Mrs V," says Suze. "I'm here to see Alex."

I'd forgotten that they already know each other, Suze being friends with Dan and all. "Mum, are you going to let her in?"

Mum is frozen and her hand has gone to her throat. She's blocking the doorway and she's not moving.

"Mum, what's wrong?" She's lost all the colour from her face.

"Suze," Mum says slowly. "Where did you get that necklace?"

Suze's hand flies up to touch the heart shaped pendant at her neck. "My titanium necklace?"

Mum swallows hard. "Yes," she says. "Your titanium necklace."

"I got it at the second-hand shop down town. Alex said you used to have one that looked like it."

"Can I have a look at it, please?" Mum holds out her hand, palm up. Her hand is shaking.

Suze and I exchange glances.

"Why don't we all go and sit down inside. Then Suze can show you her necklace."

Mum nods, ashen-faced, and we all go to the kitchen table. Aunty Joy is bustling around in the kitchen, making brownies from the looks of things.

"Hi Suze," she says. "Good timing. I'm just about to put the kettle on."

We sit and Suze takes off her necklace, handing it to Mum.

Mum studies it closely, turning it over in her hands. It's engraved on the back with a date. Mum runs her thumb over the date and looks up at Suze and I.

"That's our wedding anniversary," she says. "I'm pretty sure this is my necklace."

I gasp and Suze's face goes white.

"I got it from the second-hand guy, I swear," Suze says. "That creepy dude with the weird eyes."

"When you say weird eyes, do you mean that they're different colours?" I ask.

Suze nods. "Yeah. Why?"

"Can we just focus for a minute, please?" Mum says. "What I want to know is, how did my necklace end up at the second-hand shop?"

"They're supposed to keep records," Suze says. "We can probably find out who they bought it from."

Mum shakes her head and sighs. She seems to wilt in the chair. Aunty Joy comes over and puts a hand on her back, rubbing gently.

"It looks like your suspicions were right," Aunty Joy says to Mum. "I know you didn't want it to be true, but this proves it."

I look from one to the other. "What are you talking about?"

"Your brother was having money troubles," Mum explains. "He was constantly selling things we had lying around the house. The old stereo, the PlayStation and all the games. The push bikes. Even the drinks' fridge, not that it was worth much. All his old stuff, and we didn't pay a lot of attention. It's just his way, you know."

Mum sighs and pushes her hair back from her face. "We were suspicious, but it was nothing you could put a finger on. Like Dad's chainsaw. He never used it much but when he needed it he needed it."

"He thought he'd lent the chainsaw to Bob," Aunty Joy chimes in. "They nearly came to blows."

"Then it turned up in the back of the shed." Mum shakes her head.

"It was really weird," says Aunty Joy.

"I wasn't game to tell your father about my necklace," says Mum. "I was sure I'd put it in my jewellery box when I went out for a night and wanted to wear something a bit fancier. I never took it off other-wise. When I went to put it back on the next day it was gone."

"I'm so sorry, Mrs V," Suze says. She reaches out and closes

Mum's hand around the necklace. "You keep it. I'm glad I can return it to its rightful owner."

Tears fill Mums' eyes as she stands and hugs Suze. "Thank you. You have no idea how much this means to me."

I'm still hung up on her suspicions about Dan.

"So you think Dan was hocking stuff?"

"You tell me, love. You've been at his business for nearly two weeks."

"That's the thing. He's made some bad decisions, and things weren't running smoothly. But it isn't so bad that he'd have to resort to stealing." Something hits me. "Did he have a drug problem? Or a gambling problem maybe?"

Mum shakes her head. "I think we'd know if that was the case. He just never seemed to have any money. I can't believe that he'd take my necklace. It's the only valuable thing that's gone missing, that I know of."

Suze jangles the bracelets and bangles on her wrist. "These aren't yours, then? They came from the second-hand shop too."

"No," Mum says. "I'm not a bracelet person."

"Thank goodness. But I'm only buying new jewellery from now on."

"Probably a good idea," I say.

"Maybe it wasn't Dan who took your necklace." Suze frowns. "Maybe someone broke in."

"I guess we won't know for sure until Dan wakes up and we can ask him," says Aunty Joy. "I think it's time for a cuppa."

She bustles around making our tea and brings it over to the table.

"Right." Suze stands and grabs her tea cup. "Alex and I have some business to sort out. Is there somewhere we can go to talk?"

I lead the way back out to the verandah. A little two-seater table and chairs are wedged along the wall next to the hanging chair and we settle in with our tea.

"Okay," says Suze. "What's happening?"

43 DECISION TIME

"First things first," I say. "Tell me about the weird eyes."

"The pawn broker?" Suze pulls out her phone and opens the web-site. "This is him. He's got one blue eye and one brown eye." She shudders. "Creepy."

I take her phone and inspect the photo. Icy fingers crawl down my spine and the hair on my arms rises as goose bumps break out. "This is him. The guy from the beach."

"He's the owner of the Pawn Brokers, Lenny White." Suze reaches for her phone and looks closer at the photo. "I always get a bad vibe from him. He sold me your mum's necklace."

"Well that explains a lot. If Dan was going in there hocking stuff it's an easy next step to take out a pay day loan. But why would he do that?" I still can't wrap my head around it.

"I didn't want to say anything in front of your mum, but Dan's been known to bet on the horses when he's had a few drinks." She shakes her head. "I can't believe he would steal from your mother, though. Things are pretty messed up if he's doing that."

"Even if he did, he's still my brother. I'm going to do whatever it takes to help him. He was always there for me growing up. Always."

There was the time he took the rap for me when I broke the windscreen of Mum's car. We were playing basketball on the front driveway and I was trying to prove that I could make an overhead backwards basket. I missed. I missed so badly that I hit Mum's windscreen and shattered it. She would have killed me if she knew that I did it. Grounded for a month and never allowed to play basketball again.

But because she thought it was Dan he only got a slap on the wrist. He had to pay for it, apologise and promise to be more careful. That was it. Dan wouldn't even take my money when I offered. He said that he had a part time job and I didn't and that was the end of it.

It's nothing compared to what's going on now, but at the time it was huge. I mean, a month stuck at home when you're fourteen is a life sentence.

He's definitely the best big brother ever.

Suze reaches out and takes my hand. "Hon," she says. "I get that you love him and he's a great brother. I've got two of them and nothing can beat that. But it's not up to you to save him. You don't have to take that on."

"I know," I say.

And I do. I pull my hand from her grasp and shove my hair back off my face. "But it doesn't change anything. One way or another I'm going to save him. And if that means paying off this Lenny White with the money from Nanna's house then that's what I'll do. I'm just sorry I can't pay off the business loan as well. Jake the jerk has beaten me to it. He's betrayed Dan and now the business will be his." I shake my head. "I can't believe I fell for his act."

My heart hurts thinking of Jake. I miss him so much. If only he had been honest with me. But then, I haven't been completely honest with him. I haven't mentioned Lenny, have I?

Suze squirms uncomfortably in her seat. "About that."

I look sharply at her. "What."

"Look, I can't really say much without breaching confidentiality.

In fact, I shouldn't be talking about it at all. But I'm trying to be a good friend. It's a fine line between business and friendship."

"Just spit it out," I snap. I should have more patience, she's trying to help, but it's wearing thin.

"I don't know the full story, but I know Jake would never betray Dan. They're like brothers." She takes a deep breath and lets it out slowly. "You know that I did the loan for Jake?"

I nod.

"All I can tell you is that this all started way before the accident."

"What do you mean?" I'm really confused. "Just tell me."

"Maybe," Suze says carefully, "this was planned. Maybe, this is what Dan wanted."

I STAND up and start gathering the cups to take back inside, my movements jerky. I'm not sure who I'm most angry with. Suze, for dropping hints but not actually telling me anything. Jake, for knowing all along that the business was in trouble and not saying something. Oh, and don't forget how he was doing deals with the bank behind my back. Or Dan, for getting into this mess in the first place.

"I'm not leaving yet," Suze says. "We've still got things to talk about."

I ignore her. She's the one I'm angriest with right now, I decide. She's the one in front of me, one problem at a time.

I walk into the kitchen and put the cups in the sink. I feel like going for a run. I just need to escape for a while. Get outside, be free. Better still, leave town and don't look back.

No. That's the old Alex. I take a deep breath and let it out, shaking out my arms and hands.

The new Alex stands and faces her problems. Even when that problem is someone who is supposed to be her friend.

Logically, I know she can't say anything because of her job. And she was friends with Dan and Jake first, so of course she's going to be loyal to them. She didn't have to say anything at all to me, but she did.

That says something. Maybe, she's trying to be a friend to me too. Calmness settles over me as that sinks in.

I go back outside to find Suze leaning against the verandah railing. She turns her head to look at me.

"You okay?" she asks.

I nod. "Getting there. There's a lot to take in, you know. And I feel like you're not on my side."

"Oh, honey. I'm trying to help you." Suze puts an arm around my shoulder and gives me an awkward hug. It's mainly awkward on my part. She's a lot more touchy-feely than I'm used to.

I sigh. "I know."

She turns back to lean on the railing. "We'll figure it out. You're the best thing that's ever happened to Jake and I'm pretty sure he's in love with you. I just can't see him throwing all that away. And I don't think you want to either."

"When did this become about Jake and I?" I ask.

"Since you rocked into town two weeks ago." She grins. "We've just got to get the rest of this mess sorted out. Then I can go back to playing matchmaker."

I'm gripping the railing tightly and take a deep breath, relaxing my hands. "That can wait. Back to the real problem. Can you help me with the money?"

"That I can." Suze flicks her hair over her shoulder. "We can do bridging finance now that the house is sold. But I'm going to have to get creative about the reason for the loan, and the fact that you want cash."

She turns to face me and reaches out to touch my arm. "Are you sure you want to do this? It feels dodgy, even though you're doing it for the right reasons."

I nod. "I'm sure. But I don't want you to get into trouble."

"It should be fine. At the end of the day it's your money, and it's up to you what you do with it. The loan will be repaid in four weeks when the sale goes through. It will raise a few eyebrows if anyone looks at it too closely though."

I frown. "If there was any other way I'd take it."

"You could still go to the police. Talk to your Uncle. I'm sure he could help."

"I can't risk it, Suze. What if Lenny comes here and starts shooting? What if someone dies because of me?"

Suze sighs. "I get it. But I want you to think about backup."

She puts her hands up as I start to protest. "My brother, Tom? He's really good at this sort of thing."

"I don't know." I shake my head.

"What happens if you give Lenny the money and he decides he wants more? What if he wants all of it? Or he decides to rape you and kill you? He could kill Dan anyway. What then?"

I hold up my hands to ward her off. "Whoa, I don't want to think about all that. I'm in denial. And anyway, he wouldn't. We have a deal."

"And you trust him? You trust this creepy weird-eyed dude who licked your cheek? It grosses me out."

I shudder. It grosses me out too, big time.

"I can see your point. But what can Tom do?" I spin my hands out to the side, palms up in the traditional 'what' gesture.

"I don't know, Alex. Maybe he can't do anything. But we should at least go and talk to him." She pushes away from the rail and heads for the door.

"Now?" I follow her back into the house.

"Have you got anything better to do?"

44 BACKUP

We say our goodbyes to Mum and my Aunt and hop in Suze's car. She texts Tom to make sure he's at work and then we're off.

She drives me to offices in the industrial area, not in the central business district as I'd expected. We're not that far from Dan's workshop. The building is five storeys and stands out amongst all the industrial sheds and two and three storey buildings.

"Tom bought this place when he got out of the army," Suze explains as we park in the underground car park. "It was rundown and he practically rebuilt it. They usually go out onsite to meet their clients so they don't need a flash office."

"I don't know. This looks pretty flash to me."

"Tom lives on the top floor. He's got an apartment that takes up the whole floor." Suze grins. "You can actually see the ocean from up there."

"He's doing all right for himself then."

"Yeah. He is. Mostly it's just convenience though. Everything he needs right at his fingertips." She nods at the elevators. "Let's go up."

She uses a key card to access the elevator and again to activate the control panel once we're inside.

I scan the control panel. "There's a gym?"

"Yep." Suze points to each button on the panel. "Ground floor is retail, first floor is the gym, second is TJ Security, three has a couple of apartments, and four is the penthouse where Tom lives."

"What sort of retail?" I ask, picturing a pool shop or landscape builder. I didn't notice any signs when we drove in.

Suze grins. "Retail security systems, home safety gear and other gadgets. Tom doesn't own it, but I'm pretty sure he's a silent partner."

"And the gym. Can anyone train there?" Tom seemed like the entrepreneurial type when I met him, but I had no idea his empire was this big.

"Not really. It's mainly family and friends. Invitation only. It's not staffed, people just go in and do their own thing. You're invited though, if you want to. You're practically family."

"I prefer to run outdoors," I say. "But I'll keep it in mind."

Tom meets us in the reception area and takes us through to his office. It's nice, with a real timber desk and a conference table off to one side. We sit and Tom asks the question.

"What's going on?" He's frowning at us.

Suze and I look at each other and I want to giggle. I feel like a naughty schoolgirl. I hold it in. I'd probably burst into tears in the next breath, something I want to avoid.

"It's a long story," I say.

"I've got all night." Tom leans back in his chair and crosses his legs at the ankles, completely relaxed. "Let's hear it. Start from when you arrived in town. And Alex," He looks at me pointedly. "Don't leave anything out."

I take a deep breath to centre myself and let it out slowly. Then I do as Tom asks. I start at the start and I don't leave anything out.

This takes a while. Tom frowns when I mention my run-in with Lenny White at the beach.

"I don't like how much this has escalated," he says. "You should have come and told me straight away. In fact," he points his finger at me, "didn't I tell you that when we set up the security cameras?"

"Security cameras?" asks Suze.

Huh. I guess I didn't tell her everything.

Tom ignores her. "So what's your plan? I assume the fact that you're here means you're not going to the police?"

"I'm going to give him the money. That's it. There is no plan except to get an advance on the sale of Nanna's house and pay Dan's debt."

Tom's still frowning. "I don't like it. He sees you as an easy target and if you can get hold of one hundred thousand in a week then he's going to try and get more out of you."

"I'll just tell him I can't. I'll pay what Dan owes and that should be the end of it. Simple."

Tom laughs, a harsh, barking sound. "It's not going to be that easy, Alex. He's a bad guy, his nickname's 'the Shark' for a reason. His boss is even worse."

"What am I going to do? I can't just let him kill my brother." My heart is beating loud in my ears, my pulse racing. I push away from the table and start pacing. To the door, back to the table, to the door again.

"Whoa, hon. That's why we're here, remember?" I turn to see Suze glaring at Tom. "And you don't need to be so nasty about it."

"Sorry, Sis. I just don't want to see Alex get hurt." He looks at me. "Or Dan either. Although, if Dan ever wakes up I'm going to kill him myself for getting mixed up in this shit."

"So what do you suggest?" I ask. "You've heard my plan. If you've got a better idea then I'm all ears."

Tom smiles then. It's a slow, cocky smile and I feel my heart leap at the sight of it. He's an attractive guy, and if I wasn't head over heels for Jake the jerk, Tom is exactly the sort of guy I'd go for.

"Alex," he says. "How do you feel about being bait?"

"No," says Suze.

I ignore her. "How does that work?"

"You stick to the plan you've got now, with a few modifications. You'll have us as your backup. And if everything works the way I want it to, we'll be able to put him away for a long time."

"He said no police. I hinted to Uncle Bob that I might need his help, but that's a last resort. I can't risk Dan's life."

"Alex, no!" Suze is not happy. "We came to see Tom so you could be less involved, not more. I was hoping Tom would be the go-between and do the money handover for you."

Tom shakes his head. "It won't work. For starters, Alex wasn't supposed to tell anyone else. If he sees me there he won't engage. He'll walk away, and, being the bully he is, he'll want to teach Alex a lesson. He'll most likely go after Dan straightaway and then he'll come for Alex."

I shiver at that thought, fear snaking through me.

"I was going to face him anyway and give him the money." I put my hand on Suze's shoulder to get her to look at me. "At least this way I've got a safety net."

"We've got your back." Tom nods at me reassuringly. "And if you decide you don't want to face him then we'll find another way."

"A way that won't end up with Dan dead? Because that's my biggest fear. The whole reason I'm doing this is to keep Dan safe."

"No guarantees, sorry." Tom shoves his hand through his hair, messing it up in a way that manages to look rugged and sexy. "Even with us as backup there aren't any guarantees. But it's the best I can do."

I nod. "I understand."

Tom looks at me, straight in the eye. "I want the whole team involved, Alex. And that includes Jake."

45 BABY SITTING

"Now," says Tom. "Where are you staying? I know you ran out on Jake."

"Is that what you think? That I ran out?" My hands clench at my side. "Is that what he told you?"

"I'm just calling it like I see it." Tom folds his arms across his chest.

We've moved into the kitchen to grab coffee after working out the details for Thursday morning. Tom's leaning against the sink to wait for the jug to boil and Suze has gone to the ladies. It's just me and him.

"There's no way I could stay after he backstabbed me like that." I fold my arms over my chest and scowl at him.

"Overreact much?" Tom smirks. "Look, the only reason I'm asking is because one of the apartments upstairs is free if you need somewhere to stay. It's fully furnished. You can have it for as long as you need."

"Oh." I've been sucker punched, the air rushing out of my lungs. "I was going to sleep on Aunty Joy's couch, just for a night or two. I'm leaving town as soon as I get this sorted."

"How are you going to avoid Bob's questions?" Tom raises an eyebrow. "He's going to try to pin you down, especially since you flagged that something's going on with you."

I could kick myself. I shouldn't have told Uncle Bob that I might need his help. "I didn't think of that," I admit. "I could couch hop. Suze and Bri both offered me beds."

Tom sighs. "Just stay here. I would have offered when you first came to town if I knew you didn't have anywhere to go."

"Why didn't you mention it when you found out?" I ask.

"Didn't want to interrupt a good thing." He grins. "You and Jake were getting on so well."

"Yeah well, that's over now." I sigh. "It was good while it lasted. I'm going to miss him."

Tom frowns but Suze walks back in before he can say anything.

"What did I miss?'

SUZE PLAYS taxi and takes me back to Aunty Joy's to pick up my bag. Then we grab a pizza, chocolate and wine take it back to the apartment. It's a little one bedder with an ensuite bathroom and a balcony off the living room. Ocean view if you get on your tiptoes while you stand on the pot plant. Not that I tried.

"Girls' night," Suze declares.

We have a good night, watching an old Brad Pitt movie, *World War Z*, and scoffing ourselves on pizza and chocolate, washed down by a very nice Chardonnay. It's late when Suze leaves and I tumble straight into bed, no time to think.

THE NEXT MORNING I wake to banging. My arm gropes for the alarm, but can't I reach. I roll over to stretch it, and then remember I'm not in Jake's bed. I'm not even in his apartment. The events of the previous day come flooding back with a rush. My throat tightens with regret as tears threaten. Who'd have thought I'd miss that stupid alarm clock?

The banging comes again.

It's the door, I realise. Who's here this early?

I let out a yelp as I look at my watch and realise it's not actually early. It's eight o'clock. I need to hustle; I've got a lot to do today.

The banging comes yet again and I drag myself out of bed. Maybe it's Jake. I feel hopeful, even though he's a jerk bastard.

Tom left strict instructions not to open the door without checking through the peephole first. And further, not to open the door unless it was him or one of his 'guys'.

I look through the peephole and see Liam, holding two paper takeaway cups. I don't know Liam very well. Out of all the gang, he's the one I haven't really interacted with.

"Coffee?" I ask brightly as I open the door. I'm trying not to let my disappointment show but judging from the look he gives me it's not working.

"For you." He holds out a cup. "And you might want to go take a look in the mirror."

My hands fly to my hair and I run for the bathroom, leaving him standing holding the coffee. His chuckle follows me.

I grab a change of clothes and jump into the shower to wash away all evidence of last night's decadence. I really should have gone for a run this morning, not slept in. Oh well.

When I come back out, feeling somewhat human, Liam is sitting on the couch, feet on the coffee table, watching television. It's Sunrise, a news show I haven't seen for ages. My coffee is on the end of the table so I scoop it up and sit in the single armchair, at right angles to the couch.

"Thanks for the coffee." I wait for him to enlighten me as to why he's here. "So..." I prompt after a couple of moments silence.

He looks over and smiles, but doesn't take the hint. He's a cutie. Way too young for me. Or maybe not. "How old are you?"

"Same as you. Twenty-two."

Not a baby then.

I decide to focus on Liam's appearance at the apartment. "So, why are you here this morning?"

"Boss's orders." The smile turns into a grin and it's dazzling. What is it with the guys around here? They're all stunners. The muscles outlined by the too tight sleeves of his cotton T-shirt don't hurt either. Then he drops the bomb. "Babysitting."

His words sink in a second after he says them and my jaw drops. "What?"

"Don't shoot the messenger," he says, hands up in the 'surrender' position. "Boss-man doesn't want you left alone until after the plan goes down. Too risky."

He grins again. "And I'm your ride."

Right. I still don't have a car. Getting it fixed just got bumped to the top of my list. Right after getting the money and paying off the loan shark. I'll probably have to call a tow truck and take it to a different mechanic. It's unlikely Jake will fix it for me now. I frown as I think about Jake.

"What's up, Buttercup?" Liam asks. The grin is back. "Jake liked playing chauffeur but it's my turn now."

"Huh." I never thought of that. But until now, not having a car hasn't been a problem. Jake was always there with an easy grin and a set of keys, either letting me borrow his ute or driving me around himself. I miss him.

"Don't call me Buttercup," I snap at Liam. Then I sigh. "Thank you, I guess."

Liam shakes his head. "No need thank me, I'm just doing my job. And right now that job is keeping you safe." He looks serious, the frown out of place on his face. "We're not taking any chances."

"Won't Lenny get suspicious if I'm with someone all the time?"

"Nope. He's got to know you don't have a car and if he's been watching you then he knows you and Jake had a fight. You've been hanging out at the pub with Suze and I for the last two weeks so the natural assumption is that you'd called your friends for a ride."

"If you say so."

The cocky grin is back. "We've just got to act natural," he says.

LIAM DRIVES me to the bank to see Suze. He tells me to text him when I'm done. I consider ignoring this, but then think better of it. What else am I going to do? It's not as if I can call Jake. And I don't want to take a cab with that much cash on me. Even in hundred dollar notes it's a lot of money.

I could have gone for the cashier's cheque option but Tom said that Lenny 'the Shark' White would be more distracted by cash, and less likely to notice anything amiss. So cash it is.

The loan process is quick and painless. Suze got me to phone my solicitor, who faxed a copy of the sale contract and proof the deposit had been paid.

She'd ordered the cash the day before for overnight delivery to the branch. Who knew you had to do that?

I text Liam to meet me at the bank so he can carry the heavy bag to the car.

Now there's nothing left to do but wait.

"Can we go see Dan?" I glance over at Liam as I ask the question. I need to see my big brother.

"No *problemo*." Liam takes everything in his stride. We detour past Tom's office so he can 'secure the cash' – his words – and then go to the hospital.

The nurse is smiling as she tells me they expect him to wake up soon. Finally, some good news.

I give Dan the censored version of what's been happening. This version doesn't include Lenny, or Damien, or Jake so it doesn't take long. Liam stands at the window and stares at something outside to give me some privacy.

I hug Dan hard, which is easier now that there's less tubes and things, and try not to cry all over him when my emotions nearly get the better of me as we leave.

Afterwards, we head back to the apartment and spend the rest of the afternoon watching television. Boring.

I'm tempted to phone Bri, but I don't want to drag her into this mess.

Suze, Tom, and Tom's girlfriend Bec join us after work. The vibe between Tom and Bec is weird, like they're fighting, until Suze pulls out Cards Against Humanity. They call it the card game for 'horrible people' and it's a lot of fun. I've haven't laughed so much since forever. I just wish Jake was here too.

I miss him.

So much.

"He wants to see you," Tom tells me. "He wanted to come tonight."

"No," I say. "I can't."

Tom frowns. "It's your call." But I can see from his expression that he doesn't think it's the right one. Tom's almost ten years older than me, older than my real big brother. I don't like disappointing him.

But I can't see Jake. I'm hurt and pissed at him for his betrayal and at the same time I miss him so much. It's confusing. And if I were to see him again I'd probably forgive him. So it's simple. I need to keep the hell away from Jake Lawson.

46 SURPRISE

I ARRIVE AT THE DAN'S WORKSHOP AT SIX THIRTY THE NEXT morning, dropped off by Liam. I unlock the normal-sized door next to the roller door and prop it open. I kept my keys when I stormed out of Jake's life, thank goodness. Liam carries the duffle bag with the cash into the office and then I walk him back to the door.

"You sure about this?" he asks. His hand comes up to my face, a tender moment set up for anyone watching. I think. We didn't rehearse this bit; we're just playing it by ear. We're pretty sure the loan shark would have staked the place out to make sure Jake left and I'm here alone.

"I'm sure. It's the only way." I reach up and rest my hand over his. "Thank you for yesterday. Even if you were just doing your job. I appreciate it."

He nods. "No *problemo*." He takes a step back, breaking the moment. "You're up, Buttercup. Good luck."

He walks back to his car and I watch until he's out of sight. Then I walk into the office to wait. My stomach is a mess, the butterflies fighting each other instead of fluttering.

The lights are on in the office but the rest of the workshop is still dark with the roller door closed and the sun not yet up. I feel like I'm in a fishbowl. It's just on seven when I hear a sound and look up to see Lenny 'the Shark' White standing silhouetted in the office doorway. My heart skips a beat. He's here. It's time. Now I've just got to do my bit.

"Have you got it?"

I'm not supposed to know his name so I just nod. Tom's words echo in my head.

Draw him out.

Get him to admit everything if you can, but don't put yourself in danger.

"Can I get you to sign something?" I ask.

He looks at me in disbelief, then laughs. The sound slides down the back of my neck and into my gut.

"What, like a receipt?"

"Yeah. Proof that Dan's debt is paid."

"The only proof that you'll get is the fact that your brother's still breathing."

"But..."

"Look here, bitch. Do we have to go through this again?" He talks as if I'm simple.

I stop the eye roll, barely. His posturing is meant to be scary but it's like he's got his lines from a gangster movie. It makes me feel less afraid.

"Your brother, the fuckwit Dan, owes me money. Money I've got to pay back to my boss who isn't as nice as me. I'm keeping the interest, of course."

I wait for the evil laugh but it doesn't come. Maybe he's not so much the cardboard cut out.

"He's had one extension already and you know the price he paid for that. "

"The fire?" My voice is steady. Go me.

"Yeah, the fire. Now hand over the hundred k or you're the one who's going to pay. Right here. Right now."

I'm laughing at him on the inside. At least that's what I'm telling myself. My hand shakes as I reach over to unzip the duffle bag to reveal the hundred dollar notes bundled up inside. So maybe I'm more scared than I want to admit.

"All right, it's here. You can count it if you want."

In fact, I'd be terrified if I didn't know Tom and Liam, and maybe even Jake, are out there somewhere. "Good luck with it. It weighs a ton. I can't lift the stupid thing."

I realise my mistake when his eyes squint. "How did you get it in here? Stupid bitch. Ever heard of a cashier's cheque?"

"I thought you wanted cash. That's what you said at the beach."

"No. I said cashier's cheque. Now answer me. How did you get it in here?"

"As if you weren't watching." I'm getting kind of annoyed. "A friend carried it for me."

"You tell him what's going on? And don't lie, I can tell."

I shake my head. "I didn't, I swear." It's even the truth. Technically I told Tom and Tom told Liam.

"Want to tell me why he left and then came back here?" He's got a cunning look on his face, like he knows something that I don't.

"What? No he didn't." There's lead in my belly and it starts churning. This just got real.

"Yeah, he did. But don't worry. He's not going to be a problem. I sorted him out good."

I gasp. What the hell? "What did you do to Liam?"

"Don't you worry about that. He's not coming to save you though. Is that what you're counting on? Is that why you're giving me lip?"

If he saw Liam, did he also see the other guys? I don't even know where the other guys are, or who exactly is out there. Tom just said there would be back up and not to worry.

Too late. I'm worried.

"Tell me you didn't hurt him." It comes out as a whisper. Dammit. Tom told me to act confident. Showing fear will egg him on.

"Aren't you just the slut of the town. First it's Jackie Chan and now it's the baby. Hey, here's an idea. It's my turn now." His eyes, which were flitting around nervously, now lock on my chest and travel down. It's as if a thousand spiders are crawling over me and I shiver. My skin feels clammy and my heart is racing at a thousand miles an hour.

I lift my chin. Show no fear.

"You've got your money, it's time for you to go." Wow. I sound like some cheesy quiz show host. The new plan is to run for the door when he gets the bag. I'm sure he won't try anything. He's all talk. But just in case I'm getting out of here as fast as I can. "

And what did he do to Liam? Is Liam going to be okay? I'll never forgive myself if he got hurt because of me.

"Slide it over here."

"What?" Focus, Alex.

"You heard me."

I grab the handle of the bag and tug half-heartedly. It doesn't budge, not even a little. I tug a bit harder and it still doesn't move.

"I can't," I say. "It's too heavy."

"I'm getting sick of this, you little bitch." Lenny steps fully into the room and I back away. I'm looking for my chance to push past him and run. "It's payback time, and I'm going to make it hurt."

"Oh no, that wasn't part of the deal." I back away, hands up as if to ward him off. "You've already got your payback. My brother's in a goddamned coma!" My voice is getting louder. It's either yell or cry and I'm too angry to cry right now. I'll do that later.

He laughs and shakes his head. "It's not up to you, bitch. If you want your brother to wake up, then you're going to do exactly what I say."

He thrusts his hips forward and back, a bad version of the JT sexy dance, and licks his lips. "You and me baby, what do you say?"

My jaw drops. "You can't threaten me and then ask me if I want to, what? Get it on? I wouldn't get within ten feet of a pea-sized, flea-infested penis like yours."

Oh, no. I didn't just insult his penis. Way to go Alex.

His fists clench at his sides and his eyes go glittery. "You fucking slut."

He advances, moving through the walkway between the side of the desk and the wall. I shuffle back putting the chair between him and me. Now I'm scared. No, I'm terrified. I keep waiting for the backup to burst through the door but it's not happening.

Any time now would be good, boys.

Lenny comes around the side of the desk and moves fast. It's unexpected. Before I realise what's happening his fist connects with my cheek. So much for the chair protecting me. The blow hits hard but I don't get the full impact because of the angle. It might have knocked me out otherwise.

I go down anyway, stunned, unable to think. The pain of the hit is unexpectedly crushing. I'm going to be rethinking my martial arts career if I survive this.

I force myself to ignore the pain and crawl under the desk. The chair and the desk drawers are blocking Lenny from getting to me but not for long. I grab hold of the chair and hold tight. Lenny's down on the floor trying to get hold of me.

We're having a tug-of-war with the chair. He's stronger than me so he'd win if he had both hands on the chair, but he doesn't. He's pulling it with one hand while the other is trying to get hold of me.

He grabs my foot and I kick out. I connect with his nose. At the same time I shove on the chair, hard. The chair connects with his face as well, the momentum of my shove combined with his pull on it launching him backwards. He slams into the wall, the chair hitting his nose in the exact same spot as my foot. My shoe is clutched in his hand.

How do you like being hit in the face, scumbag?

"You bitch!" He screeches, the chair now sideways on top of him. His hand is on his nose, blood streaming everywhere.

I take advantage of the moment and wriggle out from under the desk on the side closest to the door. It has those stupid courtesy panels. I have to get on my belly to crawl out but I do, banging my head.

Once I'm out I take a second to check where Lenny is. He's getting to his feet, murder in his eyes. I don't think, I run.

Panic and the pain from my cheek blind me, stop me from thinking clearly. Instead of going out the front door to the street, where it's safe and maybe has backup I run towards the kitchen and the back. I sprint down the hall to the paint and panel workshop door.

"Come back, you fucking bitch!" Lenny yells. No doubt he's chasing me. I hoped he would've just let me go, but no. The insult to his manhood was too great. You had to insult his penis, didn't you, Alex? He's probably not too happy about his bleeding nose, either.

I grab hold of the doorframe and swing around the corner into the paint and panel workshop. I'm heading for the back door, the laneway outside and freedom. Then what? He's faster than me and he'll catch me in seconds.

My only chance is to misdirect him. I fling open the back door and then double back to the corner where the huge frames are. They still have the car parts all over them and the door to the secret room is not visible. I push in behind the frame to get to the door. New plan, hide in here until the backup comes. Lenny will think I've run outside and will follow me out there and meanwhile I'm safe in here.

I open the door as silently as I can. It squeaks as it comes free of the door frame, opening towards me a few inches, just enough room for me to squeeze through the gap. I can hear Lenny in the hallway opening cupboards. Thank goodness I didn't try to hide in there. I hold my breath as I wait to see if he heard the door squeak.

"Come out, come out where ever you are." Lenny singsongs. He's opening the toilet door at the end of the hall. His next stop will be Jake's garage or the paint and panel workshop. If I run for the outside door now he'll definitely see me. It's too late to second guess myself.

I creep inside the secret room, my breath coming in gasps. My heart is about to explode out of my chest. I should be safe in here until Tom comes to rescue me. Oh God, I hope so.

I stop just inside the door. It's pitch black in here. Tears blur my vision, my eye still watering from the punch to the side of the head. It should be hurting more, but the adrenaline masks it for now. I move further into the room to hide on the far side of the wrecks. I want something between me and the door just in case. My shoeless foot connects with something, crippling me and making a god-awful noise.

"I can hear you. I'm going to find you, and you're going to pay, bitch."

He sounds close. He's in the workshop and he didn't take the bait of the open door. Damn it! It was a good plan too.

Where the hell is my back up?

My eyes have adjusted and I hobble as fast as I can to hide behind the wrecked cars, avoiding the spare parts that litter the space. From my spot in the dark he won't be able to see me, assuming he even finds the secret door. Of course, I didn't shut it for fear of making more noise so the odds are good that he's going to find it. My shitty luck is holding strong. I cross my fingers that the backup arrives before he finds me.

I hear the back door shut. "Nice try, bitch, I know you're in here somewhere. Come out, come out and I might go easy on you."

I close my eyes and hold my breath, not daring to breathe. I feel something trickling down my face and touch my cheek with my fingertips. He must have cut me with his ring, or his nails, when he punched me. Judging from the coppery smell I'm pretty sure it's not tears.

A sliding noise comes from the workshop and my eyes fly open, pinned to the doorway. He's going to find me, no question.

An idea begins to form.

It took my eyes a few minutes to get used to the dark in this room.

If I can lure him in far enough I might be able to sneak back out the door without him seeing me. I might even be able to trap him inside.

I grope blindly on the floor nearby, not taking my eyes off the doorway. My fingers connect with something solid. Two somethings solid. I don't care what they are, they'll do. I pick them up, one in each hand. Timing will be everything. I begin edging closer to the door, hugging the bonnet of the wrecked car.

The sliding sound from outside has stopped.

"Gotcha!" says Lenny. "Thought you could hide from me, you stupid cow."

For the second time today Lenny's body is silhouetted in a doorway. I heft the object in my right hand and throw it away from me, aiming for the second wrecked car. It connects with an almighty crash.

Lenny is obviously not thinking of anything except revenge. I mean, if it was me I'd be moving away from the noise, not towards it. But he heads straight towards the source of the noise. His eyes seem to have adjusted a lot quicker than mine, he avoids the parts on the floor easily.

"Come out, come out wherever you are," he sings again. It's creepy as hell.

I'm moving slowly and silently around the front of the chassis and am only a couple of metres from the door. I take a deep breath and peek over the car bonnet. Lenny is about as far away from me as I can hope for, two car lengths and he's facing the other direction still looking for me over there. It's now or never.

He must sense me, or he's got eyes in the side of his head like his namesake, the shark. He turns as I stand to run and lunges for me. I toss the heavy car part and it connects with his crotch with a crunch. He goes down in a heap, screaming blue murder.

I sprint for the door, out and through, and slam it shut. I lean on it and wonder what next. There's no lock.

"Alex! Where are you?" The voice is coming from the front of the workshop and is faint. Tom maybe?

"Blondie!" Another voice joins in and I know it's Jake. Of course it's Jake, no-one else calls me Blondie.

"Jake! Help!" I scream it as loud as I can. "Paint shop. Hurry!"

The door shudders as something bangs into it and it partly opens. I'm leaning on it and immediately push back. "Help!"

There's another thud and it opens again, instantly shutting as I push back again as hard as I can. My feet are slipping. I don't know how much longer I can hold it. "Jake!"

Jake rounds the corner into the workshop at a sprint at the same time as the third almighty crash on the door I'm leaning on. It flies open. I'm flung backwards, straight into Jake's arms and we go down in a heap. Somehow I end up on top, my elbow hitting him in the solar plexus as we land.

Lenny launches forward, carried by the momentum of his final assault on the door. He lands on top of me and starts laying into me and Jake with his fists, not caring who he connects with. He's rabid.

I don't think, I just react. My elbow goes back sharply at the same time as I do a backwards head butt. I connect with his groin and his nose. Again. He rolls off me and curls into a little ball, cupping his manhood with one hand and his face with the other.

If I get out of this alive I'm going to thank Clance for his martial arts moves and sign up to get my black belt just as fast as I can.

I roll off Jake on the side away from Lenny and look up, over my head to see Tom and Liam standing there.

"Way to go, Buttercup." Liam holds his hand up and mimes a high five. There's nothing visibly wrong with him so Lenny must have been lying about 'sorting him out'. "You took out two men, twice your size, in one go. Ain't nothing like an overachiever."

He walks to Lenny and puts his boot into his back, rolling him onto his stomach. Lenny's face hits the floor as Liam pulls his hands behind his back and handcuffs them. Lenny groans. Liam might have pushed a little too hard on his back, making other injured parts connect with the floor as well.

Or maybe that's just wishful thinking. He pats Lenny down,

searching for weapons, and takes a knife out of a holder strapped to his thigh like some sort of military guy.

"Alex, are you okay?" Tom walks over and grabs my arm, pulling me to my feet. He does the same to Jake. Then he takes a step back and gives me a little shove towards Jake. I hit Jake in the chest and his arms go around me. We don't hit the ground this time.

Jakes' arms tighten and I breathe him in. I wrap my arms around him tight. I'm never letting him go.

His hand goes to the back of my head and holds it to his chest. I listen to his heart, pounding just as hard as mine. He doesn't say a word. He doesn't have to.

47 WRAPPED UP

Tom's the one who calls Uncle Bob to tell him the good news.

Uncle Bob turns up about ten minutes later with two other policemen. We've moved from the paint and panel workshop out back to the main workshop in the front but Jake hasn't let go of me, even for a second. He's leaning against the workbench and I'm wrapped up in his arms, face tucked tight against his chest. A tea towel full of ice cubes is jammed between us on my injured cheek. His hand is stroking my back and my hair.

I'm still shaking.

Tom is on the phone with Baz, who, it turns out, was in the control room back at the TJ Security office this whole time. Tom's voice is heated and he looks like he wants to punch something but I can't make out his words.

Jake tells me that Baz was watching everything on video and keeping Tom informed. Even Clance was roped in, and he doesn't work for TJ Security. He's been up at the hospital with Dan in case Lenny tried something funny. Jake's words, not mine.

Liam dragged Lenny from the back workshop out here, then

threw him face down on the concrete again. He still has his boot on Lenny's back, holding him in place. I'm still not sure what Lenny did to him, but he's looking no worse for wear. Although he might be leaning on his boot a little harder than strictly necessary.

Uncle Bob makes a beeline for me and yanks me from Jake's arms to smother me in a hug of his own. I clutch my ice-filled tea towel in one hand, the other going around my Uncle's back.

"Why didn't you come to me for help, Alex?" He says this into my hair, his arms tightening. Finally, he lets me go. Jakes snags me around the waist and pulls me back into him again. He lets me face forward this time but he's got one arm tight around my middle and the other wrapped along my chest at shoulder height. His chin rests on top of my head. You'd think I'd feel smothered, and in another life-time I might. Right now I'm enjoying feeling safe. Because it can't last. Even now, I can't forgive him. My brother comes first and he's betrayed Dan in the worst possible way.

"I couldn't, Uncle Bob. He was going to kill Dan."

Lenny is glaring at me from the floor and I flinch back further into Jake. Liam catches it and uses his boot to scoot Lenny around on the concrete so he can't look at me.

Uncle Bob shakes his head. "You're going to have to come in to the station and give a statement. Make sure you don't leave anything out, Alex. We need everything."

The two uniformed police officers with Uncle Bob move in and pull Lenny up off the floor. One of them takes each arm and they half-walk, half-carry, him to the waiting police paddy wagon. He gets put, none too gently, into the back of the vehicle. I've seen inside the back of the paddy wagon and it's not comfortable. I don't care. Lenny deserves every scrap of pain he gets.

"We've got video footage of everything that happened today," Tom says to Uncle Bob. "The whole place is wired. We put cameras in after the break-in last week."

"Thank goodness we did that straight away," Jake's voice is close to my ear. "Thanks mate, I owe you one."

Tom nods. *De nada*, no worries, his expression says.

"I've got some video on my phone from the beach the other day," I say.

All the eyes snap in my direction.

Tom knows what happened, but I didn't give him all the ins and outs of it.

"The beach?" It's Uncle Bob who asks the question.

I sigh. "On Sunday." Jake goes rigid behind me. "He approached me after my run. I was a bit nervous so I hit record on my phone video. I don't think the picture will be any good but the sound should be all right."

"What happened?" Uncle Bob again.

"That's when he told me that unless I paid him the hundred thousand dollars that Dan owed him he'd make sure Dan didn't wake up. He said he'd put Jake in a coma too if I told anyone."

"What if you couldn't come up with the money? One hundred thousand dollars is a lot of cash to get your hands on in less than a week." Jake's voice is low in my ear.

"He said he'd make me pay, one way or another." I shudder, thinking how differently this could have all turned out.

"I'm not sure how admissible it will be, but let me have your phone and we'll check it out." Uncle Bob is all business and I hand him my phone. He puts it in his pants pocket. "If nothing else, it will help us piece together what's happened. The fire, Dan's coma, the break-in, and today... we need to figure out how they're all connected and if we can link it back to Lenny. Or better still, his boss. We don't know who his boss is."

I've still got a question and I'm hesitant to ask. I mean, I'm safe, and everything turned out all right in the end. But it was a close call. I spit it out.

"What took you guys so long to come and help me?"

Jakes arms tighten and Liam can't meet my eyes. Tom answers.

"I'm so, so sorry Alex. We came in as soon as Baz saw you take off for the back."

"That doesn't make sense." It was maybe five minutes from when I ran for my life and when the guys showed up. It felt like five hours.

"The cameras are recording here, onsite, and a live feed goes back to the control room. Sometimes, if there's an internet problem, we get a delay. That's what happened today. We thought we had a live feed but it turns out there was a couple of minutes lag time."

Well, that explains his raised voice on the phone earlier.

"Baz just finished watching the whole thing. He says bits of it are pretty funny, if you can put aside the fact that you nearly got killed, or worse."

We all take a moment to think about what the 'worse' could have been. I shudder. Then the rest of what he said hits home.

"Funny?" I glare at Tom. "You've got to be kidding me."

Tom shrugs. "That whole bit when the door partly opened three times then you went flying into Jake and Lenny landed on top. I caught the tail end of it."

He holds up his hands when I throw daggers at him with my eyes. "It was only funny on the replay, when he knew you took out Lenny with the moves we taught you at the dojo. Nice work by the way"

"I think Clance takes credit for that." I unclench my fists, trying to relax.

"Baz also said that we only just made it in time," Tom continues. "Lenny had a knife strapped to his thigh and was reaching for it when you connected with the head butt."

I didn't know about the knife. I bury my face in Jake's chest and take a deep, shuddering breath. It's all too much but I refuse to cry. Jakes arms tighten around me.

My phone rings from inside Uncle Bob's pocket. I turn, holding my hand out for it so I can answer it, but he's already got it up to his ear. His eyes move to me. "Okay, we'll be there in ten minutes."

"Who was it?" I ask.

"The hospital," Uncle Bob says. "Dan just woke up.

48 AWAKE

"Hey Alex, you forgetting something?" Liam is standing in the doorway to the office swinging the duffel bag full of cash.

Show off.

"I can take it back to the bank for you if you like," he says.

Uncle Bob looks from the bag of cash to me. "That's evidence. Sorry, Alex. But I'm going to have to take it back to the Station."

"I'll get it back, right? I mean, it's my money."

My uncle frowns. "We'll need to see the paper trail. It should be fine, but it might take a while to process."

"Sorry," Liam mouths.

I walk over to Liam, going up on tiptoes to kiss his cheek, one hand resting on his muscular shoulder. "Not your fault. And thank you."

Liam blushes. Actually blushes. He mumbles something under his breath, sounds like 'no *problemo*'. It's kind of like his catch phrase. I smile and walk back to where Jake is standing with his arms folded over his chest, looking cranky. He probably saw the 'tender' moment earlier too. Oh well, that's his problem. I'm allowed to have friends. In fact, I'm going to need them to survive our break-up.

UNCLE BOB DRIVES me to the hospital. It was the easy choice. Part of me never wants to be separated from Jake again but the realist in me knows that the sooner I let him go the sooner I can start getting over him. Jake wasn't happy about it but he let me go.

He and Tom follow in their own cars. My money went to the police station with the uniformed officers.

Suze was excited when I spoke to her on Tom's phone, but said she'll have to wait until she knocks off work to come up to the hospital.

Dan's been moved to his own private room and is sitting up at a forty-five degree angle in bed. He's surrounded by people. Mum and Dad are there with Aunty Joy. Clance has already arrived, and Baz walked in with us from the car park. With Jake, Tom, Uncle Bob and me crowding into the room it's a full house. The nurse hasn't noticed yet or she'd be kicking everyone out, I'm sure.

Clance claps Dan on the shoulder and says something to him. Dan nods and Clance walks out, nodding at Tom, Baz and Jake as he goes. Dan's eyes follow Clance to the door and light up when he sees his mates. His face splits into a huge grin.

"Get over here," he says.

It's so good to see him awake. He's thin and pale and still has tubes inserted, but his eyes are alert and aware.

My big brother is back.

The guys move to the bed and the rest of the family shuffle back to give them room. Shyness fills me and I hang back on the periphery of the crowd and patiently wait my turn.

"Had to see with my own eyes, mate." Tom moves in for a manly hug and shoulder pat. "It's good to have you back with us again."

"It's been no fun without you." Baz does some complicated knuckle and handshake combination with Dan, then they high-five each other. "Tom's resorted to playing card games, for goodness' sake."

The brothers move aside to make way for Jake.

"Dan, bro," Jake says. He and Dan clasp forearms in a more inti-mate form of a handshake. Jake does the shoulder pat as well. His voice is scratchy, emotion filled, and if I could see his face I'm sure there would be tears.

"Missed having your ugly face around. Had to make do with your sister."

The room goes silent as Dan drops Jake's arm. His eyes scan the room. "My sister's here? Where is she?"

Mum is standing in front of me and at Dan's words she turns and pulls me forward. She passes me to Jake who puts his arm around my waist and hauls me the rest of the way to Dan. Dan doesn't miss a thing, from the intimate way Jake touches me, to my blush.

"Am I going to have to kick your arse, mate?"

I'm not sure if Dan's joking or not. I'm going to assume he is.

"That's my *baby*, sister you've got your hands on."

Not joking then.

Jake shakes his head. "It's all good. We'll talk later when it's quieter." His arm around my waist gets tighter as his other arm moves around me and brings me in close, face-to-face. We're side on to Dan and he's watching intently. Jake bends his head and kisses my fore-head, his lips soft. "I've got to get going, got some things to do. Later?"

I nod mutely, too flustered by his moves, in front of my family, to remember we've broken up. Then he's gone.

"We've got to get going too," says Tom.

He and Baz follow Jake out the door and I'm left standing in front of my brother.

Dan reaches out and takes my hand. "Well, I'm glad my coma provided the opportunity for some matchmaking, even if I didn't get to see it happen." He laughs and it turns into a cough.

I squeeze his hand and wait until he gets his breath back, ignoring his comment. Then I move in for my hug. It's awkward with the hospital bed and the tubes but I don't care. Hugging my brother has never felt this good.

And having him hug me back?

Priceless.

"Hey." I'd say more but my throat is tight.

Dan reaches out to lightly touch my bruised cheek, his eyes filled with concern. "What happened to you?"

"It's a long story," I say. "And I'm hoping you can fill in some blanks."

The tears break free and roll down my face. I rub my eyes with the back of my hand, willing them to stop. But it's just too much. Dan is finally awake and I've got to tell him I've lost his business. That his best friend has stabbed him in the back.

"I'm so sorry," I say when my voice works again. Dan hasn't taken his eyes off me. "But it's gone. I tried but I couldn't hang on to it."

"What are you talking about, sis?"

"The bank foreclosed on your business." I take a deep breath before I tell him the rest, how his best mate has backstabbed him. How Jake bought the business out from under him while he was unconscious.

"They found a buyer. It's Jake, Dan. The buyer is Jake."

"Thank fuck," says Dan.

I blink. "What did you say?"

Dan glances over to where Mum stands with Dad and Uncle Bob and Aunty Joy. "Sorry for swearing, Mum."

He looks back at me and pats the bed beside him. "Sit down, Alex. You look like you're about to fall over."

I hoist myself up onto the bed. I'm so close to Dan right now. I lean in further. My voice is low and hostile. "Not the swearing. What did you mean by the thank you?"

Dan grins, oblivious to my tone of voice. "Jake and I have been working on a buyout plan for over six months. It was taking forever to come together. I thought it would have totally stalled while I've been out of action. That's great news! Why didn't Jake tell me?"

"Probably because he thought it wasn't his story to tell," I say through gritted teeth. I flick back through all the conversations I've had with Jake, the half-truths and omissions I sensed. I'm going to kill him, damn it.

But on the plus side, he hasn't betrayed my brother.

And I've been a total idiot. My heart starts to sing and a lightness fills me. I'm going to track that boy down and crash hug him the first chance I get. After I finish kicking his butt for not telling me it was all part of Dan's plan, that is. Then I'm going to kiss the living daylights out of him and never let him go.

Uncle Bob clears his throat. "I'm going to have to ask you some official questions," he says. "We'll need a full statement later but if you can give me something to go on I'd appreciate it."

"We'll just go and grab coffee," Mum says. "Come on Dave, Joy. We'll give them some privacy."

They leave and close the door behind them. Now it's just Uncle Bob, Dan, and me.

"Questions?" Dan looks confused. "What's going on?"

"It's about Lenny White and the cause of the fire. And the money."

"I'd like to know about all that too," I say. "Especially the money. Because I've been busting my butt to turn your business around so the bank didn't sell it. I succeeded, but they sold it anyway. And then I find out you've borrowed a hundred thousand dollars from a loan shark and I've got to pay him back before he kills you."

Dan's face goes white. His hands are shaking and when he speaks it takes him several goes to get the words to come out.

"Alex," he says. He clears his throat and starts again. "Are you okay?"

I nod. "I am, but it was a close call." My hand goes up to my cheek.

"I don't want you mixed up in all that. What the fuck?"

"It's too late, Dan." I sigh. "But he's been arrested after he blackmailed me and then tried to kill me."

"What?" Dan's jaw is clenched.

"Oh, don't worry," I say, waving my hand around airily. "I got away. It's all good. Just a little bruising to show for it. Not all of it mine, actually. I got him a good one, didn't I, Uncle Bob?"

Uncle Bob puts his hand on my shoulder. "That's enough, Alex." He looks at Dan with a piercing glare. "You've got some explaining to do, son. The fire wasn't an accident. We're pretty sure that Lenny White was responsible. He's in the lockup at the moment and the evidence Alex got should be enough to put him away for a long time."

A flurry of emotions flit across Dan's face at Uncle Bob's words.

Worry, anger, relief and hope. I think.

I mean, it's not like I'm in his head or anything.

Dan throws his head back into his pillow and closes his eyes. When he opens them he looks first at Uncle Bob and then at me. His hand goes to my cheek again and then drops back on the blanket. I pick it up and hold it in mine.

"I've made a huge mess of things, haven't I?" he says. "It just spiralled out of control."

"Why don't you start at the beginning? Uncle Bob asks.

Dan takes a deep breath and lets it out slowly, like he's bracing himself.

"You know I set up the business with the money from Nanna?"

We both nod.

"In hindsight I never should have done it. I'm not really cut out to be a business owner." He lets out a small, self-depreciating laugh. "I'm sure you've figured that out by now, sis."

"The paperwork *was* a bit of a mess."

"No matter what I did the business was losing money. I had an overdraft and got a loan to buy the panel beating equipment and put in the paint shop. I thought that would boost business."

"But it was taking too long. When I saw how much money Jake would get selling his car after it was fully restored I thought it was an easy out. Grab a bargain, fix it up, sell at a huge profit and put the money back into the business."

"I've seen your 'bargains'. I'm not sure you're even going to get back what you've paid for them."

"That was a mistake. Especially because I borrowed money from Lenny to buy them. He got me to sign a contract which I didn't even read, I was so desperate. I thought I'd miss out on the deal of a life time if I didn't move fast." He looks down and starts picking at a loose thread on his hospital blanket.

"That's what I don't understand. Why Lenny? How did you even get in touch with him?"

This is the question that causes Dan to break. He covers his eyes with his hands and hunches forward, his body racked with sobs. I rub his back until finally, he regains his self-control.

"I'm so ashamed," he whispers, his eyes red. "Mum will never forgive me."

"Is this about her necklace?" I ask softly.

He nods slowly. "How did you know?"

"Short version? Suze bought it from the second-hand shop and I saw her wearing it. Thought it looked like Mum's. Mum confirmed it when she found the engraving on the back." I shake my head. "Dad bought that for her, Dan. She never took it off except for that one night. She's devastated."

Dan rubs his hands down his face. He's shattered. I feel a moments pity and give him a break.

"Suze gave it back, it's all worked out."

Dan's tears start falling again. He's a broken man and it's hard to watch. Uncle Bob walks over to the window to give him a moment. I just keep hold of his hand, my thumb running over it in circles until he gets himself back under control. It takes a while. My heart goes out to him. I feel so much love for him right now.

"Okay, I'm all right," Dan says, finally. "I can't believe I was so stupid."

"What happened?" My voice is still soft.

"Things just went from bad to worse, but the final straw was the soccer club. They were pestering me for a donation for their big fundraiser night and I had no money. They didn't know that, of course. And what could I do? People are sharks. If anyone knew how bad things were they would have been in for the kill."

I shake my head. "I don't think so. I think you'd be surprised how supportive people have been since you've been in here."

Dan looks surprised. "Really? At the time it felt like I had no choice."

"You could have just said no." I think of Cindy the soccer mum. She's pretty scary. I'd probably have a hard time saying no to her too.

"How would that look? Big successful businessman won't help out the kids in his local community. That's what I thought anyway. I had a reputation to uphold and the only way to do that was to donate something big. So I borrowed Mum's necklace, cashed it in with Lenny, and ordered a signed soccer ball online." His eyes flick to the charred soccer ball on the bedside table. "It was the one thing I pulled out of the fire."

"I was going to get the necklace back from the pawnbroker before the time was up. But I didn't make it. I was in here unconscious when the deadline passed. Obviously they put it out in the store and sold it."

Something about his story isn't adding up. "How long do you get to come up with the money to get it back?"

"A week, sometimes two." Uncle Bob moves back over from the window.

"So the necklace isn't the first time you've hocked something." It couldn't be. The pawnbroker might be how he met Lenny, but it wasn't because of the necklace. The timing is off.

"No, it wasn't," Dan agrees. "I can't even remember the first time, I was selling stuff I didn't need to top up the business bank account for months."

Which explains the deposits on the bank statement which didn't seem to belong.

"But it *was* the first time I hocked something that wasn't mine." Dan looks me in the eye but he can't hold my gaze. He starts rubbing at his eyes with his clenched fists. He's moments away from a complete break down.

"You're just lucky it was Suze who bought it."

"Do you think Mum will ever forgive me?" His voice is shaky.

"You'll have to talk to Mum about that." I take pity on him and try to lighten the mood. "But you did save Dad from the fire. I think you've got a bit of leeway. I wouldn't leave it too long though."

I get off the bed and walk to the window and back. "I've still got questions, Dan."

"Fire away." He pulls at the thread again, staring down at his hand.

"So, Jake? What was the plan there?"

"Jake came to me about six months ago. He could see the business was struggling and he wanted to buy in, become a partner. The cash injection would pay for the paint and panel shop and bring in new business.

"It was a no-brainer. I was hoping to sell him the whole business and go back to being an employee."

"I'm not cut out for it, sis." He shakes his head. "Jake's been running the workshop, planning the jobs, rostering the staff, ordering parts, all that. The only thing I had to do was look after the paperwork. But I couldn't even do that. I did my job, the mechanic part, but everything else was too hard.

He scoffs at himself. "Except when I was grasping at straws, buying old cars to restore."

"I've made a huge mess of things. I owe more money than I can ever pay back. I've stolen from my own mother. It would have been better if I never woke up." He buries his face in his hands and his shoulders start shaking, wracked with sobs. He's a broken man.

"Don't say that. Everything can be fixed." I lean into his space and force another hug on him. "I love you, Dan. We all do. I can't imagine life without you here and awake." I rub his back, holding him close, and keep talking. "Your friends have missed you, you know. All

I've heard is what a great guy you are. Even if you do play soccer instead of footy."

Finally, his sobs ease and he wipes at his eyes with the back of his hands. His eyes are red but he won't look at me. I pour a glass of water from the water jug and hand it to him.

"For what it's worth," Uncle Bob says. "You've made some mistakes. No question there. But everyone's entitled to a second chance. It's what you decide to do next that will show people what sort of a man you are."

Dan sits up straighter, his hand clenched around the plastic tumbler. He takes a deep breath, getting himself under control. "You're right. I've got a long way to go to make it up to Mum, and it's going to take years to pay back all the money. But I'll do it. If it's the last thing I do, I'll do it. I'll prove to everyone that I'm not a scumbag, low life, rat bastard."

"And what about afterwards?" I smile at him. "You're allowed to have a dream too, right?"

Dan looks me in the eye. "I was always a bit jealous of you, sis. You got to leave this town and travel the world. Go wherever you wanted, free as a bird. I've always felt trapped here. Like I had to stay and do what was expected."

"So what do you want to do, if you could do anything?" I tilt my head to one side. I never wanted to leave but always felt I had to. I ran from my parents' expectations.

"Travel. I want to see the world."

"Then that's what you should do."

All I want to do is move back home for good. To settle in, get married, raise a family. Hell, I could even open my tea shop.

"I hate to interrupt all the warm and fuzzies, but we've still got to sort out this mess." Uncle Bob, ever the pragmatist. Then he surprises me by reaching out to clasp Dan's shoulder. "I've got faith in you, son. It's all going to work out, and you'll get to do your thing. The hard part's over."

49 FREEDOM

I'VE BEEN AT THE POLICE STATION FOR MOST OF THE DAY WITH Uncle Bob. When Mum, Dad and Aunty Joy came back I decided to give them some space. Dan was going to come clean about everything and I'd had my quota of emotional scenes for the day. Uncle Bob shared my sentiment so he took me down town to make my statement about everything that happened with Lenny White. They're keen to nail down his boss as well and are hoping Lenny will talk.

By the time I was done Suze had knocked off work so she gave me a lift back to the hospital to see Dan.

He was looking a lot better tonight, laughing and joking around. More like the big brother I remember. Mum and Dad had gone home, so I'll have to wait to talk to Mum to see how forgiving she's feeling now that she knows the truth about Dan.

The doctors are going to keep him in for another couple of days while they do more tests, but it looks like he's going to be fine.

Suze intercepted when Tom offered to give me a ride back to the apartment. She said she wanted to. I went along with it, assuming she wanted to talk about Dan but I am so over not having my own car and having to rely on other people.

"How are you doing?" Suze glances across at me while we wait at the traffic lights. "It's been a big day."

"It's been swirling around in my brain since this morning. I think I've made a huge mistake by breaking up with Jake."

"You think?" Suze sounds amused.

I remember the way Jake kept me close to his side after the rescue. "After Lenny attacked me he was there for me, but I'm pretty sure it was the heat of the moment, thinking I'd got hurt."

"You did get hurt," Suze snaps.

I touch my cheek. "Well, yeah, but it was just his protective instinct coming out."

"Why do you think he's got that protective instinct? I mean, if it was me he'd be there to help, sure. But he couldn't stop touching you."

"Tom told you about that?"

Suze nods. "Yep."

I sigh. "I've really messed things up with him."

"Don't take this the wrong way, but I'd like to know what your intentions are. Are you planning to stick around? Because that man is head over heels for you. I've never seen him like this. If you make up with him and then decide to leave town..." She breaks off and sighs big. "He's my friend, Alex. You're my friend too, and I'd like nothing better than the two of you to get your happy ever after. But I won't help if you're going to be a bitch and break his heart."

I sit up straight in surprise and turn to glare at her. "What did you say?"

How dare she!

"Not judging, calling it like I see it." Suze waves her hand in the air in a dismissive gesture.

"Oh." I deflate. From where Suze sits I look like a total bitch.

"All right, honesty time." I'm going to lay all my cards on the table. "I've been in denial. But when I thought Jake betrayed Dan it felt like he ripped my heart out. I was ready to tell him I loved him. It hurt so much.

I fold my arms across my chest, sinking into myself. I look over at Suze. She keeps her eyes on the road but her grip on the steering wheel tightens. I push on.

"I felt like a fool, falling for him, when he was just using me to get the business in shape so he could swoop in and buy it. He didn't just betray Dan, he betrayed me too." I shake my head, the hurt still raw. "Before Dan woke up I was planning to run. Far, far away."

"I knew it," Suze mutters.

"But Dan told me it was part of their plan. He wanted Jake to buy his business. Dan doesn't want to do it anymore. It turns out, Jake was keeping Dan's confidence by not telling me." I glance at Suze. "Apparently you were too. Although a heads up would be appreciated next time."

Suze shakes her head. "I can't breach confidentiality, Alex. I said as much as I could."

"Sorry, I shouldn't have asked." My hands twist in my lap.

"So what's next for you?" Suze glances over at me, then back at the road. "You've got a big stack of cash to spend, once the police are finished with it anyway. Are you going to buy another property? Something to live in? Or you could travel, as long as you come back. You don't have to pay the bank or Lenny anymore, so you've got options."

"I feel free." I smile. The weight on my chest has been steadily lifting all day, ever since Lenny got arrested. "You know what I really want?"

"What?" Suze puts her indicator on to go back down town, instead of to the apartments. She must be planning on picking up some takeaway.

"I want to stay here, in Tempest Beach. And I want to open my tea shop." I sigh, picturing it. The picture extends and I share further. "Then I want to settle down, marry Jake, and eventually, have his babies. I know that sounds a bit lame when I could do anything. I mean, I could go and see the world, or do another degree, or move to

Hawaii. But I don't want to. Freedom means being able to make the choices I want, and that means staying here."

"Not sure where Hawaii came from." Suze lets out a small hmph. "You do realise that Tempest Beach is paradise, don't you?"

"I do. I think I did all along, deep down, even when I first left. I just didn't realise." I smile. "It's good to be home."

"I'm so glad you're going to stay." Suze shoots me a look, her grin lighting up her face.

"Now I've just got to find Jake and apologise to him. And convince him that we belong together." My tummy somersaults. What if he won't listen? "Any ideas where he might be?"

"As a matter of fact I do," Suze says. "And seeing as you're not planning on breaking his heart, I'll even take you there."

50 MAD HATTERS

Suze comes to a halt outside Frankie's dress shop. The front has been repaired and a new sign hangs over the front door. 'Mad Hatters.' The newspaper is still over the windows so we can't see in, but light glows around the edges and from under the door. The owners must be working late on the renovation. Nothing else shows any signs of life this time at night. It's nearly nine o'clock on a Thursday night and late night shopping is well and truly finished.

"Why are we stopping here?" I ask.

"Out you get," Suze says. "You've got an appointment."

"What? I thought you were taking me to Jake." I take another look up and down the street, thinking I must have missed something. Maybe he's over the road on the beach.

"In there, girlfriend." Suze nods her head towards Frankie's, now Mad Hatters. "Off you go."

I shake my head but there's something about Suze's smile. I realise she was heading towards this place even before she agreed to help me find Jake. Something's going on.

"All right. But if I end up dead or missing it's on you." I glare, but Suze ignores me.

"Call me if you want me to come and get you. But somehow I don't think I'll be needed." Suze waves her hands at me. "Now shoo."

I take a deep breath and hop out of the car. I walk slowly to the door of the shop, my stomach in knots. I'm pretty sure I'm going to find Jake inside. The only question is, why?

THE DOOR OPENS IMMEDIATELY after I knock revealing Jake, smiling. He knew I was coming. I remember the text message Suze got just before we left the hospital and how she insisted on being my ride, despite Tom offering.

"Hi," says Jake. He grabs my hand, pulling me gently inside and locking the door behind us.

I take two steps and stop dead. It's a large space and it used to have some sort of carpet on the floor. That's all gone. The floor is now a beautiful hardwood timber, polished until it gleams. It matches the wood on the window frames and the wood between the six glass panels of each window. In the front door are glass panels separated by the beautiful timber. Newspaper has been cut to size and taped to each glass panel, protecting it from the timber stain. A hint of paint lingers in the air and the walls are a fresh pale cream that accentuates the floor perfectly. The light bulbs are bare, waiting for covers. Something chandeliery would go well. I can picture it. With round wooden tables stained the same rich mahogany and matching chairs, some tables seating two, some four and some six or eight, it would be perfect for my tea shop.

There is one such table placed in the perfect centre of the room. It has two chairs placed opposite each other and two place settings, silver cutlery and blue and white willow pattern plates. A candelabra sits in the middle of the table holding two candles, already alight. The overhead lights suddenly flick off and our only illumination is now from the candles. It makes the already spectacular room, amazing.

"You like?" Jake asks, voice low in my ear, his hand touching the small of my back.

"It's perfect." I spin around to face him and his hands move up, linking around behind my neck.

"What's going on?" I push at his chest to give myself some space but he isn't having it.

His head dips, and he kisses me.

I pull back, not ready to go there with him just yet, but then his tongue hits my mouth and I'm gone. My lips part and his tongue touches mine.

I'm kissing him back, my arms taking on a life of their own and seeking maximum contact. His hands move from my neck, one tangling in my hair and the other around my waist pulling me closer. We kiss and it's everything I ever wanted and didn't know I could have. It's the only thing I need to survive. If I stop kissing this man the world could very well end. And I know. This kiss? It's the beginning of a whole new world. It's everything.

Jake breaks the kiss, panting hard, resting his forehead on mine. I trace my fingers along his jaw, the stubble rough on my skin. Gorgeous.

"I thought I'd lost you," Jake says, his voice husky. He's silent for a moment while he catches his breath and I wait for him to continue.

"I've never been so conflicted in my life. On the one hand, Dan is my best mate and I had to keep his secrets. On the other hand there was you, and I wanted to tell you everything. No matter what I did, someone was going to get hurt. Then Damien turned up and the decision was taken out of my hands. Bloody Damien."

"Bloody Damien," I agree. I close my eyes. "I'm so sorry Jake. I jumped to conclusions and was too quick to judge. It wasn't until Dan explained everything that I understood what was going on, and why you did what you did."

Jake lifts his head, his eyes on mine and his face serious. His hands rest on my hips and he makes no move to step away.

"I hate to think what would have happened if he didn't wake up." I shiver.

"You were going to run, weren't you?" Jake asks.

"Probably." I shake my head, thinking about all the decisions I've just made. Would I have still made them if Dan hadn't woken up? I'd like to think that I would. "Maybe not."

"I would have come after you. I thought long and hard about what happened and I'd come to the conclusion that Dan would be okay with me sharing his plans about the business. This was before he woke up, before you faced down the loan shark." His hands tighten on my hips and anger flares in his eyes. "I'm not happy about that, either. Tom didn't tell me until the last minute or I would have stopped you."

"It wouldn't have worked if you had been there," I say.

Jake nods, but he's still not happy. "I know. That's the only reason I'm still talking to Tom." He gives his head a little shake as if to clear it. "Anyway, Dan said I should have told you when we spoke earlier. After he got up me for hitting on his little sister."

That doesn't surprise me. Dan has always been overprotective.

Jake grins. "He wasn't too happy about that. I had some explaining to do. About how good we are together, that I love you, but then there was bloody Damien and now I've got to win you back."

His face goes serious. "So are you still running? I understand if you still want to leave town, but I want you to listen to me before you do." He takes a deep breath and exhales as he lifts his hand to cup my jaw. "I've got a lot to say."

"You love me?" Nice speech, but I'm focused on those three little words. I whack him on the shoulder. "And you told Dan before you told me?"

He grins. "Got that backwards, didn't I?"

"Well?" I fold my arms over my chest and tap my foot. "I'm waiting."

"Jeez, Blondie. No pressure." Jake takes my hand and leads me over to the table. "Take a seat. I've got this all worked out in my head and I'm sticking to the plan."

I sit, feeling the butterflies rising in anticipation. I can hardly he said it to Dan. Did he mean it? I hope he means it so badly my heart feels like it's about to explode.

Jake sits across from me and reaches out to take my hand. He grimaces as he bumps the candelabra, knocking it sideways. He catches it before it falls but it's too late for one of the candles. It teeters, then tumbles to the floor and sputters out. The candelabra won't balance with only one candle in it.

Jake stands, frustration etched on his face, the candelabra clenched in his fist. "Didn't think that through, did I?" he mutters.

I giggle and move to stand so I can turn on the light.

"No, I've got this." Jake looks at the candle on the floor. "Here, hold this." He thrusts the candelabra at me and disappears through a door at the back of the room. A light goes on, and then he returns with a second small table and a box of matches. He sets the table down next to us and grabs the fallen candle off the floor, jamming it back into the candelabra, before sitting it on the extra table and lighting it.

"Right, where were we?" Jake resumes his seat and reaches out to grab my hand again. "This is a lot easier without a whopping big candelabra in the middle of the table."

"You love me?" I ask. My face hurts from smiling so much but it's a good hurt.

"Yes. Alex, I love you." His voice is low but his expression takes my breath away. So much love there. "Can you forgive me? Will you stay here and try to make a home with me?" His thumb brushes over my knuckles. The way he's looking at me completely undoes me. Like I'm precious. Like I'm the most precious thing in the world. My eyes fill with tears and my throat goes tight.

"Hey, don't cry." Jake is suddenly right there, kneeling beside my seat, his arms wrapped around me. He smooths my hair gently.

"I, I, I..." but I can't talk. The tears are coming and I can't help it. I burrow into Jakes neck, hands pressed tight against his chest.

Several minutes pass before I regain control. I take a deep, hiccupping breath and lift my head to look at him.

"You okay?" he asks.

I nod. "Happy tears," I say. I draw in more air and touch that rough jaw. "I love you too, Jake."

"Thank fuck." Jake closes his eyes and rests his forehead on mine.

"SORRY THE FOOD ISN'T BETTER," Jake serves the meal much later. It's takeaway Thai from the restaurant down the road. "I was pushing hard to get everything finished and the table set up just right. I kind of forgot about the food."

"It's all right. I love Thai," I say. "This is great."

"So what do you think of the place?" He gestures around the room. "If there's anything you want to change you can. And we can get whatever furniture you want."

"What?" I stare, and then look slowly around the room, hope filling me. "You better explain yourself, Jake Lawson."

"This is my investment property. If you want," he smiles. "And no pressure. But it's yours if you want it to open your tea shop."

"Seriously?" I'm in shock. This place couldn't be more perfect.

"You can change the name. I just thought, you know, Alice in Wonderland and the Mad Hatter's Tea Party." He looks away. "Don't worry, it was a stupid idea."

"No, Jake." I jump to my feet. "I love it! But it would only be short term, I want to buy my own place."

It's a shame because this really is the perfect location.

He smiles. "I'd love to be your landlord, but I know how important it is to you to be independent. So if you want to buy this place off me I'll give you good terms. You can rent for six months and test it out, and if it goes well the rent can go towards the purchase price."

"You'd do that?"

He nods, his eyes never leaving mine.

I tug on his arm to get him to stand. When he does I fling my arms around his neck and jump up and down with excitement.

"Thank you, thank you, thank you. This is absolutely perfect!"

His hands go to my hips and I stop jumping. "You're not just saying that?" he asks. "Because it was just an idea."

"This is seriously the best idea you've ever had," I say. "Thank you Jake. This means the world to me. *You* mean the world to me."

EPILOGUE

ONE WEEK LATER

I pause at the bottom of the stairs from Jake's apartment—

our apartment now—before entering the workshop.

It's seven o'clock Friday morning, exactly four weeks since I arrived back in town, and I'm heading out for my run on the beach. It's going to be another beautiful day in Tempest Beach.

Paradise.

I ran as far from here as I could when I finished high school four years ago and now I'm back and I couldn't be happier.

A strange sound comes from across the space. Stomping, grunting and weird shuffling sounds. Or not so strange, now that I know what it is.

Movement catches my eye. I smile. It's Jake and he's shirtless. His upper body is glistening and I know those muscles aren't just nice to look at.

He's moving through a series of movements, his martial arts form, his body flowing as he kicks, blocks and punches, twists and turns, forward and back, now jumping, now darting forwards or sidestepping. It's beautiful. The sun is streaming through the back window highlighting the curve of his shoulders and biceps and the dips of his six-pack stomach. I stand there as mesmerised like I was that first day I stood at the roller door. I'll never get sick of looking at him.

Abruptly he swings and shoots towards me in a flying side kick move, straight out of the movies. I squeal and take two steps back as he lands mere millimetres from where I had been standing.

I look up at him. His messy, wavy hair falls across his eyes until he flicks it away.

He smiles, his eyes on my mouth. "Morning, Blondie."

I take a step forward and run my fingers lightly along his chest. There's still a spark. I still want nothing more than to rub myself all over him like a giant cat. Except if I do that I'll never get to the beach, and Bri is waiting for me.

I step in closer and stretch up on tippy-toes to kiss him lightly on the lips.

He's having none of it. He wraps his arms around me and kisses me like he means it, long, hard and deep.

How can it be just four weeks ago that I laid eyes, and hands, on this gorgeous man with the brilliant, sky blue eyes, for the first time?

Even our Mad Hatter's date seems so long ago and it was only last week. I went home with Jake that night and his apartment became our apartment, just like that. I guess, really, it was from the moment I walked in.

It's been a long week.

Uncle Bob helped me get the evidence together on Lenny. There was a lot of it. My phone recording from the beach wasn't perfect, but I'd managed to capture Lenny's face in a couple of the frames so there was no doubt it was him doing the talking.

The video footage from the workshop the day he attacked me was from four different cameras. I knew about the one in the office, but there was also one in the kitchen, pointing down the long hall, and another overlooking the entire front workshop area. The final camera, the one with the money shot, was above the door in the paint and panel workshop meaning the entire final battle was captured on camera. And yes, I'm calling it a battle. Even though the guys laughed their arses off when they watched the replay.

"Laughing with you," Baz told me ruffling my hair. "Just make sure you go to class next week so Clance can teach you some more moves."

I rolled my eyes, but I'm definitely continuing my martial arts training. I'm loving it.

The police also had an eyewitness to the attack on Liam, which happened right before Lenny came in to meet me that morning. Lenny had rammed into Liam's car and run him off the road with his stolen monster truck. He didn't stop, so he didn't realise Liam had walked away unharmed.

All in all, they had a watertight case. The officer-in-charge had been investigating Lenny for a long time, so he was pretty happy. They still don't know who Lenny's boss is, but that's a problem for another day.

It turned out the fire wasn't lit by Lenny after all, so Mum and Dad got their insurance payout. A faulty part in the air-conditioner caused it to overheat and catch alight. Dan can take that one off his conscience.

I got my money back straight away. The police decided it wasn't needed as evidence after all. Phew! So I was able to repay the bridging finance immediately. Suze was happy about that. She told me later, at Tempest Serene before class, that the auditors had picked this week to visit and were asking questions about the loan. She could have gotten into big trouble.

The other thing that happened this week was a biggie. I had a visit from Gavin and Valencia. They turned up in town and phoned me to request a meeting. They wanted to take me out to dinner to apologise. I declined, but I did end up meeting them for coffee. Jake came with me and him being there made it less awkward.

Gavin said he couldn't leave things as they were. I was great at my job and had shown a lot of management potential. Valencia apologised for overreacting. I'm not sure how sincere the apology was, but

I know Gavin meant every word even though he was very careful not to overstep any boundaries, making him a stilted version of the man who had been my boss.

So I was gracious and accepted the apology. It took a lot for Valencia to turn up and I got the feeling she didn't have much choice in the matter if she wanted to save her marriage.

"You're one of the good ones, Alex," Gavin said as they were leaving. "There's always a job for you if you want to come back."

Valencia glared at me but kept her mouth shut. It was pretty clear that I wasn't going back.

"You going to pick out the rest of the furniture today?" Jake asks, his hand still wrapped around the back of my head.

"Yep. Do you want to come with?" Mad Hatter's is becoming a reality. I've done my business plan and I think my tea shop is viable. It's happening! I'm so excited and have been getting all the legal stuff sorted. The business name, GST registration and so on. We've drawn up a lease agreement for the premises. I thought about buying the building off Jake but he wouldn't hear of it.

"I'm going to like being your landlord. And you can invest your money into something else. You'll need working capital anyway, while you get started."

He's right so I didn't argue.

Now I'm up to the fun part.

"I'll have to pass. I've got job interviews today." Jake is hiring an admin person to keep on top of the paperwork which frees me up to do my own thing. I could have stayed at the workshop but it's time for me to follow my own dream. "Don't forget, dinner with the guys tonight."

"I know. Dan's coming too," I say. We're heading to the pub for Friday night drinks and then dinner. "I'm looking forward to seeing him with everyone."

Dan is staying in Tom's apartment while he reassesses his life and makes plans for the future. He's still got a way to go before things are right with Mum and Dad, but moving out is the first step.

With Jake buying the business from the bank, that debt's all sorted.

Uncle Bob is looking into the legality of the loan from Lenny. There was a signed agreement so it's looking legit. The original loan was fifty thousand, and with twenty percent interest the most he'll have to repay is sixty grand. Which is a lot, but better than one hundred. Not really sure how Lenny came up with that figure.

Jake helped him find a buyer for the two bomb cars and he was able to get enough to repay the sixty thousand plus a little left over to travel, which is all he ever really wanted to do.

I think he realises what a lucky escape he's had.

I TAKE A DEEP, contented breath and let it out. Jake's hand comes to my jaw.

"What's that for?" His eyes are soft and melty.

"Just happy," I say. I wrap my arms around his waist and burrow my head into his chest. He holds me tight, his heartbeat strong in my ear. "Just happy to be home."

WANT MORE OF TEMPEST BEACH?

SUZE'S STORY, SING, IS COMING SOON.

SING

Her perfect man is safe, settled, and stable...
...everything he's not.
The fact that he's her younger brothers best friend makes him totally
off limits.
There's no way she's falling for him.
Is there?

Want to know when it's being released?
Sign up to Tracy's 'Let Me Know' list - http://bit.ly/2pZqqpl

Here's a sneak peak...

SNEAK PEEK OF SING

(TEMPEST BEACH BOOK TWO)

THE CHEMISTRY IS OFF THE CHARTS WHEN A FORMER ARMY officer helps his best mates older sister when she's dragged into Tempest Beach's shady underworld.

SUZE HAS THE PERFECT LIFE. A great house with a view, a loving family, and she's on the fast track career-wise. The only thing missing is the perfect relationship and a family of her own.

And seeing as she's fast approaching a milestone birthday she needs someone with long term potential. Definitely not her brothers best friend. Her *younger* brothers best friend.

Even if their chemistry is off the charts.

EX-MILITARY OFFICER SAM has just gotten out of a hard situation and is in recovery mode. He's taking things slow, reconnecting with his music, and trying to work out what comes next in his life.

He's not relationship material, and even if he was, he'd never go there with his best mates sister.

Not even if his heart is telling him she's *the one*.

WHEN SUZE IS DRAGGED into Tempest Beach's shady underworld, Sam is the only one she can turn to. But will it all blow up in their faces?

WITH A KICK-ASS CREW of sexy martial artists and a gorgeous beachside location, *Sing* is a delicious mix of adventure, mystery and mayhem, complete with a love at first sight affair.

Tempest Beach Book Two

ALSO BY TRACY BRENTON

Sing - coming soon

Her perfect man is safe, settled, and stable...

...everything he's not.

The fact that he's her younger brothers best friend makes him totally off limits.

There's no way she's falling for him.

Is there?

Tempest Beach Book Two

High Tide

Lilly has one wish for her sixteenth birthday – for Liam to see her as more than just a friend. But when a beach adventure goes horribly wrong, her priorities change from romance to survival. Will she get her heart's desire?

A Tempest Beach Short Story

https://books2read.com/HighTide

Out With A Bang

Uni student and new Zombie, Luke, had one goal for the year – ask Liv out. But now he's evolving into a Vampire and the clock is counting down to midnight. All he has to do is work 'I wanna suck your blood' into the conversation while he saves her from the horde. Who said romance was dead?

http://a.co/bF2e0EL

ACKNOWLEDGMENTS

With thanks to my fabulous fellow writers of the Romance Writers of Australia and the ladies from Kissing Books 101 and the Word Count Warriors who inspire me to keep writing every day.

Editing credit goes to Annie Seaton who has taught me so much, thank you.

To my beta readers, Louise, Laila, and Claire, my proof reader Gabi, and all my supportive friends and family, many, many thanks.

And to my husband and sons, a huge thank you and big hugs for supporting me when I disappear into book world. I'll always come back, promise!

A special mention to my mum, who will probably read this despite my warning about those 'steamy' bits! Love you Mum x.

Last but not least, to my readers, ***thank you*** from the bottom of my heart for taking a chance on a new author.

Until the next book, happy reading,

Tracy x

ABOUT THE AUTHOR

Hi there! I'm Tracy Brenton.

My favourite books to read are "kissing books" (full credit to 'The Princess Bride') and if there isn't at least a little bit of romance in a story then I'll probably lose interest. So it won't come as a surprise to learn that all of the stories I write have a romance at their core. Even the zombie ones!

I love all things creative and take way too many pictures of sunsets and all the pretty flowers around my home on the Mid North Coast of NSW. I'm currently working hard on developing a taste for coffee and writing the next book in the Tempest Beach series.

Want to know when it's being released?

Subscribe to my 'Let Me Know' list - http://bit.ly/2pZqqpl

and you'll be kept in the loop.

Tracy x

You can find me online
www.authortracybrenton.com

facebook.com/AuthorTracyBrenton

twitter.com/AuthorTracyB

instagram.com/AuthorTracyBrenton